THE
CHILD
ACROSS THE
STREET

BOOKS BY KERRY WILKINSON

Standalone Novels

Ten Birthdays
Two Sisters
The Girl Who Came Back
Last Night
The Death and Life of Eleanor Parker
The Wife's Secret
A Face in the Crowd
Close to You

The Jessica Daniel series

The Killer Inside (also published as *Locked In*)
Vigilante
The Woman in Black
Think of the Children
Playing with Fire
The Missing Dead (also published as *Thicker than Water*)
Behind Closed Doors
Crossing the Line
Scarred for Life
For Richer, For Poorer
Nothing But Trouble
Eye for an Eye
Silent Suspect
The Unlucky Ones
A Cry in the Night

The Jessica Daniel Short Stories

January
February
March
April

Silver Blackthorn

Reckoning
Renegade
Resurgence

The Andrew Hunter series

Something Wicked
Something Hidden
Something Buried

Other

Down Among the Dead Men
No Place Like Home
Watched

THE
CHILD
ACROSS THE
STREET

KERRY WILKINSON

Bookouture

Published by Bookouture in 2020

An imprint of Storyfire Ltd.
Carmelite House
50 Victoria Embankment
London EC4Y 0DZ

www.bookouture.com

ISBN: 978-1-83888-749-0
eBook ISBN: 978-1-83888-748-3

ONE

I was reading an article the other day that listed the most British things. It contained the usual items, like black cabs and red phone boxes. There was the Royal Family, Big Ben, roast dinners, rain, sarcasm, the BBC, Churchill, cricket, fish and chips, flat beer, country pubs, and a whole bunch of other things. What articles like that always miss, however, is something with which almost any Brit can identify. The thing that every single living person born on these Isles knows only too well. It's ingrained into our souls from birth. As much a part of our day-to-day lives as pounds and pence, or wondering how Piers Morgan has a career.

What that article missed was the sheer, unrelenting hell we go through when using public transport to travel a relatively short distance.

Today, for instance, my first train was late. According to the shifty-sounding station announcer, heat had made the rails buckle. From there, I missed my connection onto a second train and had to get the later one. By that point, the bus I was supposed to be catching at the other end had already gone. The next bus was cancelled for an unspecified reason, so I had to take two more buses to finally finish on another bus, operated by a different company, with separate pricing, and which only takes cash and, naturally, offers no change. After almost losing the will to live on at least three occasions, here I am, a little over one hundred miles from where I started, eight-and-a-bit hours later.

Home.

Well, sort of home.

As the final bus pulls away with a guff of noxious exhaust fumes, I glance up to where the clock atop the building reads 4.05 p.m. The sandblasted building was a library when I was a kid – but now there are wooden boards across the windows and a large sign that says something about a planning application.

There are stars in my eyes as I blink away from the blue sky and take a moment to figure out where I am. This whole area is familiar and yet… not. It's all that little bit tattier than when I was last here. Everything from the pavement to the road to the surrounding houses seems to be covered in a grainy dusting of sand or dirt. The hedge a little up the road is so overgrown that it's enveloped more than half the path. The pub on the other side of the street was once teeming with people, a hub for old men, with spiralling smoke pouring from the door each time it opened. As with the library, the windows are now boarded up, each of them tagged with spray-painted, joined-up scrawl.

The wheels on my suitcase catch in the cracked pavement tile. As I wrestle it free, I narrowly avoid bumbling into a patch of nettles that have swarmed over and around a nearby wall.

It's home but it's not. It's like I'm in an alternate universe; this one grimmer and grimier.

It's only now I'm finally off the succession of buses that I realise how hot it is out of the shade. In my mind, when I was growing up, Elwood had long summers of endless sun. My friends and I were rarely inside during the holidays and I'm back there again now, with the heat prickling my arms and legs.

I pluck the bottle from my bag and have a sip as I take in the poster stuck to a lamp post that's advertising the Elwood Summer Fete on Saturday. It's all standard stuff – I guess bouncy castles and face-painting never go out of fashion – and yet there's a sense that these sorts of thing were once so personal to me. An inflated moment of ego in which I'm surprised this could continue while I was away.

After the drink, I continue along the street, avoiding the bloated hedge, and then cross the road before I find myself close to George Park. It was long after I'd left Elwood that I realised the park had been named after the King, and not some random local named George. I'm almost past that when the back of my hand starts to itch. I'm already scratching when I realise it's because I'm so close to the house in which I grew up. This route was on my walk home from school and the corner at the edge of the park was where my friends would go one way and I'd go another.

There are children playing on the far side of the park, dots in the distance, though their excited shouts carry on the breeze.

I shouldn't have come.

I thought I would be fine, but this place is too much.

A glance back to the stop only reveals what I already knew – that the bus has gone. It's almost two hours until the next one, if it even arrives, so what am I to do? I could stay. Maybe I *should* stay. I have things to do.

I'm brought back to the present as there's a squeal of tyres from beyond the hedge that rings this edge of the park. It's only a few steps to the corner and I turn to see cars parked along both sides of the road. That's another thing that's changed. Not everyone had a car back then, let alone two or three to a house. I could cross this road at any point, but now the only gap appears to be here on the corner.

I almost look away.

Almost.

In between the parked vehicles, stopped in the centre of the road at the turn into Beverly Close, is a car. It's frozen in time and then, in the moment it takes me to blink, there's another squeal and it surges away, disappearing around the corner and out of sight.

The thought that 'everyone's always in a rush nowadays' has already gone through me when I realise how old it makes me feel. *Nowadays*. As if there was a time when people were happily late and nobody ever hurried.

I almost reach for my bottle again, but then I start to walk towards the junction instead. The wheels of my case click-clack across the pavement tiles and it feels like I'm being drawn there. As if a secret part of my brain knows something, even though the rest of me hasn't caught up.

When I get to the junction, I realise the cars aren't parked as tightly as it appeared. Faded double-yellow lines are painted at the intersection and there's a large gap in between the park itself and the Beverly Close sign. There's a verge separating the two, clumped with overgrown grass and mangled plants and bushes that have grown into one another. The area is littered with crisp packets and chocolate wrappers, as well as something that's definitely out of place.

I see the wheel first.

It's almost swallowed by the crown of swaying grass, but light catches one of the bent spokes and, as I take a few steps closer, I realise the wheel is attached to an upturned bicycle. The rear wheel is crumpled in on itself, almost folded in half. The entire back half of the bike has creased in two and the front wheel is detached, embedded in the encompassing branches of a bush.

It's past the bike, at the bottom of the gully, where the horror lies. I want to look away but can't stop staring at the contorted shape of the boy. One of his shoes has somehow flown off and is upside down in a nettle patch. I find myself focusing on that because everything else is too awful to comprehend.

It's hard not to gag at the unnatural kink in the boy's shattered arm – and then, underneath, the grass is no longer the same shade as the surrounding green. Instead, it's drenched a crimson red as, from somewhere in the distance, the drifting sound of playing children continues to hang in the air.

TWO

I don't actually remember calling 999. There's a blank, as if I'm working on some sort of autopilot. The next thing I know, there are sirens in the distance. I'm at the bottom of the ditch, standing over the boy, phone in my hand, though there's a gap in me getting here.

'Is he…?'

There's a woman at the top of the verge, with an apron tied around her waist. I turn between her and the boy, unsure what to do. I did a first-aid course for my job years ago, but my head is empty. I don't want to make things worse by moving him, or doing something else damaging.

'He's breathing,' I reply, though that's more or less all I can say. I look back to the boy where his chest is rising ever so slowly. There are smudges of dirt and blood across his face and his T-shirt is ripped across the middle.

More people appear at the crest of the gully, presumably coming out of the local houses. They all stare down to the boy and then me, as if I either know what to do, or had something to do with this. The sirens are deafening now and it's only a moment until I'm drenched with a strobing blue. Minutes must have passed.

It feels like I'm watching everything happen instead of being a part of it. A woman in a uniform guides me back up to the street and then leads me off towards a police car. A pair of paramedics pass us, heading towards the boy. An ambulance has blocked off the street on one side, with a couple of police vehicles on the other. Their sirens have silenced, but more wail in the distance.

'I'm Tina,' the officer says.

'Hi,' I reply, blankly.

'What's your name?'

'Abigail.' A pause and then: 'Abi, really. Abi Coyle.'

'Did you see what happened?'

I take in the officer for the first time. I turn forty next year and she's perhaps a decade younger than me, with a smattering of freckles across her nose and cheeks.

'I don't, um…' I'm trying to speak, but the words aren't there.

In the meantime, Tina half turns to one of her colleagues and nods towards the road behind us. I'd not noticed before, but there's a wide skid mark that intersects the junction with Beverly Close. The black of the rubber arcs like a crescent across the grey tarmac.

'There was a squeal,' I say. 'Like a car skidding.'

The second officer has taken the hint and is shooing people away from the street, back towards their houses. As he does that, another ambulance pulls in and two paramedics clamber down and hurry across to the ditch.

Tina asks something else, but I don't catch it. I stare past her instead, watching as the new set of paramedics disappear over the bank to join the original pair.

'We can do this later,' Tina adds.

'There was a car,' I say.

'Do you know what colour it was?'

'Dark… I think. Maybe black, or…' I find myself stumbling and then tailing off before I add: 'I don't know.'

I try to remember – but the clarity is not there. There's the shape of a car in the road, but it's like the memory is monochrome. There's no colour; no depth. It's like I saw a photo, rather than actually experienced it.

People are still outside their houses, but everyone has been moved away from the road itself. I open my mouth, but, before I can say anything, a figure darts across the intersection. She weaves around an officer whose arm is outstretched in a weak attempt to stop her. He catches her as she reaches the ditch, holding her back as she stares at the scene below.

They are too far away for me to hear what the officer says to her but, as he tries to move her away, the woman turns back to him and shouts: 'He's my son.'

I'm not sure when I start moving but before I know what I'm doing I'm most of the way across to her. I feel Tina trailing, though she's made no effort to stop me. When I lock eyes with the woman, there's a moment in which it feels as if I've tumbled through time. She doesn't see it – but it's no surprise, she has other things on her mind.

'His name's Ethan,' she tells me. There's a tremble to her voice, though there's a firm undercurrent, as if she knows she has to hold it together. It was always her way.

'There was a car,' I tell her.

The male officer and Tina hover, though neither of them say anything. Down below, three paramedics are crowded over the top of the boy, as a fourth stands a little further back. His arms are behind his back, his face stony and giving nothing away.

'You found him?' she asks, turning between me and her son.

A nod.

She turns back to the boy, though we can see little other than the hunched paramedics. There's probably noise; the chatter of voices, cars on surrounding roads, or those kids on the far side of the park. It feels silent, though. As if the world has stopped spinning. Then she twists back to me and squints slightly. The face of a woman who can't quite believe what she's seeing.

'Abi…?' she asks, doubting herself.

Another nod.

She gulps and turns back to her son. 'It's Jo,' she says.

I have no idea what to say. There's only one thing that matters in the moment and it isn't me. I reply in the only way I can, offering a solemn, and unreturned, 'I know.'

THREE

It's a blur as the paramedics eventually bring Ethan up the bank on a stretcher and put him into the back of an ambulance. Jo follows and then, as they head off to hospital, it's left to Tina and the rest of the police to figure out what's next.

A police officer is already taking photographs of the skid mark, while more uniformed officers have appeared to talk to residents. Tina asks me a few more questions, though I'm not sure how much help I am. I stumble over answers until she takes my phone number and closes her notebook.

I figure we're done but, out of nowhere, she places a comforting hand on my arm. It feels motherly, though I'm older than she is.

'You look like you need a good sleep, love,' she says.

I stare at her, but the freckles are now fuzzy and unclear, like she's behind misted glass.

'It's been a long day,' I reply, fighting a yawn.

'You've done great,' Tina adds, although it takes me a second or two to realise she's talking about calling 999.

She moves towards one of her colleagues, who is heading in the direction of one of the patrol cars. The street is now largely empty of onlookers, with only a couple of residents standing at their doors chatting to officers. It's now I realise that I abandoned my suitcase on the corner. It's still there, the handle high and extended, untouched by anyone who was here. In London, it would have been nicked the moment I'd left it – but not Elwood. At least, not the Elwood in which I grew up.

The horror of everything that just happened is impossible to blink away, but I don't know what else to do. I was unsure from the moment I got off the bus, so I retrieve my case and drink from my bottle. The liquid is warm and anything but refreshing, so, after one more glance towards the skid mark on the road, I head off along Beverly Close.

It's only a minute until I reach the junction, barely two minutes' walk from where Ethan was hit.

I stop and stare up at the corner house that was once so familiar. It's on the end of a terrace, the type of two-storey place that sprang up everywhere in the 1950s. There's a small garden at the front and a far larger yard at the back. The house feels recognisable and yet not. The curtains are drawn, which is unsurprising, seeing as there will be nobody inside. There was always a strip of soil dedicated to flowers along the side of the garden but, as I step onto the path, I can see that it's now overgrown with flourishing green weeds. It doesn't look as if anyone's been near it in a fair while.

I reach into the pocket at the front of my case and take out the envelope emblazoned with the purple and orange FedEx logo. The solicitor's return details are printed on the back. I received it four days ago, though it feels longer.

My former boss said I couldn't have the time off to return here, and that was the last time I spoke to him. I've ignored the missed calls and don't know what happens next. Everything I own is in the case.

The tab across the top of the cardboard envelope has already been pulled and I empty the key into my other hand. The letter drops out, too, though I already know what it says, so put it back in the envelope before heading along the path.

It takes little effort for the key to fit the lock, but I have no satisfaction from the fact that, after all the years of unsuccessfully saving for a deposit, I am finally now a homeowner. It just so happens to be the home in which I grew up.

It is unspectacularly ordinary as the door creaks inwards. I haven't been inside since the day I left twenty years ago.

I close the door behind me and then turn to where the light is shining from the landing upstairs, cascading down the stairs and drenching the hallway in searing sun. There's a shelf off to the side that's plastered with the same old trophies that were here decades ago. Dad won them for everything from athletics to football to darts to chess – though they're all older than me. At one time, he'd sit on the stairs and polish them, while telling stories of heroic victories and unfortunate defeats.

That was a long time ago.

Dust now sticks to my finger as I run it around the rim of a trophy that's in the shape of a dartboard. I return the award to the shelf, but it isn't only that which smells of dust. The entire hallway is like the inside of a vacuum cleaner.

I continue into the kitchen, where there is a sinkful of dishes. The big plate at the front is plastered with sticky ketchup and there's a dripped trail of gloopy, dried coffee across the nearby counter. A wire scourer has been abandoned on the windowsill, where there's a plant pot with a dead twig sticking sadly out the top.

There's a moment in which I think about washing up, but it's barely a sprout of an idea before I turn away. I've cleared up too many messes in this house and it's not the time for one more.

I decide not to bother with the living room and am about to head back towards the hall when I spot the note that's stuck to the fridge. It's held in place by a magnet in the shape of the UK. My father once had beautiful, calligrapher's handwriting, something he said was beaten into him at school. This note is in shaky blue scrawl. The curl to the capitalised letter 'A' tells me it's still his writing, though the rest is an interwoven mess, even though I can still make out my name. My phone number is written underneath, something that hasn't changed in a good decade.

I unclip the note from the fridge and run my fingers against the crumpled page, before glancing instinctively to the landline phone that's still pinned to the wall next to the fridge. It's as grubby and dust-coated as everything else, though that doesn't stop those memories of the phone calls my parents would make while leaning on the fridge. I could hear either of them shouting into the receiver, no matter where I was in the house. My mum would be bellowing at her friends as she made plans for whatever they'd be getting up to that night. Dad would be on to the bookie or one of his mates. Neither seemed to realise that phone calls could be made without having to shout.

As for mobiles in more recent times, they are something for the twenty-first century, and I'm not sure Dad was ever fully comfortable with the twentieth.

He certainly didn't much care for phones of any sort. It's hard to remember the last time we spoke. The best I can come up with is new year, which was seven months ago. It wasn't New Year's Day itself, but maybe the second or third of January. He'd have been leaning on the fridge right here while he said something about having to get off because he was on his way to a football game. I think that was his way of ending the call early, even though he was the one who contacted me. His gnarled, hoarse voice was enough to let me know how he'd spent the morning.

It's longer still since we actually saw one another. Perhaps seven or eight Christmases ago, when we were at a grim service station halfway between here and where I lived in London. I had a car then and was probably over the limit. I have no doubt that he was.

I return the note to the fridge and then head back to the hall. It's like opening the door of a hot oven as I carry my case up the stairs. The sunlight burns through the windows above, dousing everything below in ferocious heat. My bare arms tingle as I reach the landing and then stop on a shaded patch of carpet.

I shiver and spin, feeling a whispering breath on my neck, although there's nobody there.

The unsettling feeling cloys at me. I'm not sure what it is at first, but then I realise it's the silence. The soundtrack of this house was never quiet. It wasn't only the shouted phone calls: the living room TV was rarely off, even overnight, and the sport or news would always boom upwards to where I am now. The opposite is true now. There are no phone conversations and no television. I can't even hear anything from the street. The only thing that echoes is the unrelenting, all-consuming silence. It makes my arms itch.

I blink away the unease, or try. There are too many ghosts in this house and I'm not sure the anxiety I feel here will ever leave.

I stand undecided at the top of the stairs. There are four doors from which to choose – the bathroom, Dad's bedroom, my room, and the spare bedroom. I ignore the others and head into the door on the left. The door sticks in the frame, as it always did, but I press it hard until I find myself in my childhood room. My feet are planted in the doorway, not quite able to move any further. It's like there are two versions of me. The one who lived in this room – and the one who disappeared off to London just before the turn of the century. I was in search of something I never found. That's a whole chapter of my life now written off, because here I am, back at the start, with so little to show for the time away.

Aside from the same coating of dust that permeates everything else in the house, my room is eerily close to how I remember it. There is a hi-fi stereo in the corner, complete with double tape deck, with which I would copy music from the Sunday afternoon chart show. I cross the room and run my fingers across the stack of grubby cassettes. It's mainly Britpop. Everything was back then and I was always more of a Blur girl, than Oasis. The originals of *Modern Life Is Rubbish*, *Parklife*, *The Great Escape* and *Blur* itself are all there. I can't remember what album came after that. I used to think I was into them before anyone else, simply because

I'd read copies of *Melody Maker* and *NME* that I'd nicked from local shops.

The evidence of that is the posters taken from the centre of magazines that are on the walls. Yellowed sticky tape is still clinging to the paint, holding up my pictures of Damon Albarn, Jarvis Cocker, the Glastonbury Pyramid stage and, among others, Crispian Mills from Kula Shaker. All the men look so young.

My bed is still made, though, until now, I had forgotten the Garfield duvet cover under which I used to sleep. I'm not sure I was ever into the cartoon and I don't know where it came from.

There's more, too. My old school exercise books are crammed into a box under the bed, there are swimming certificates in the drawer of the bedside table, plus another drawer full of make-up long past its use-by date. It's hard to know why Dad kept everything as it was. Things are dusty, but there isn't twenty years' worth of grime. He must have cleaned periodically, without clearing out any of my things. He can't have believed I was coming home and, even if by some miracle I did, it wouldn't have been the teenage me.

I put my suitcase on the bed and set up my laptop on the desk. I open the curtains fully, then a window, letting the early-evening warmth spill inside. The clammy summer air is still better than the murk of this old room.

Even with that, I can't face too much longer here – not now – so I head back downstairs and check the fridge. There's a packet of ham that's somehow not gone mouldy, plus some stinking old cheese. I'm never sure if the slight bluey mould is a good or bad thing. There are packets of crisps and biscuits in the cupboard, but that's about it. The type of junk a teenager can put away day after day, but not someone of my father's age.

I'm not feeling particularly hungry, anyway.

There isn't much point in putting it off further, so I press into the living room. The curtains are open at the back, though closed at the front, leaving me blinking into a mix of dark and light.

I head to the cabinet in the back corner. It stretches from floor to ceiling and is probably the most expensive item of furniture in the house. Everything else is cheap stuff from catalogues, but this is made of heavy, expensive wood.

Dad's pride and joy.

There's a keyhole on the door, but I don't ever remember it being locked. It's certainly not now as I pull it open to reveal the row of mostly empty vodka and whisky bottles. The only surprise is that there's anything left at all.

I unscrew the top from Lidl's Western Gold, but it might as well be Jim Beam, given the way they've copied the label. I have a sniff, wincing slightly at the acrid smell, and then I take a mouthful anyway. My teeth chatter involuntarily as it burns its way down my throat. Whisky is not my drink.

As I'm returning the bottle to the cabinet, I almost miss the envelope tucked in at the very back. It's brown and crusty, the type that looks like it might have been around longer than two or three generations of kids. It's bulging and, when I untuck the flap, I find a thick wad of ten- and twenty-pound notes. The fact they're plastic, instead of the old-style paper notes, means they have to be relatively recent.

I fan the money onto the table and then count almost six hundred pounds back into the envelope. I almost return it to the cabinet, but then figure Dad won't be needing it any more, so it goes into my bag instead. I do a lap of the rest of the room and it's astounding how little has changed since I left. The sofa and armchairs are the same, although the brown fabric has faded into near grey. The carpet is still the horrid bluey-grey abomination it always was, though it's far patchier now. The tiled floor below is clear in places, though I have no idea why there are tiles in a living room.

My father bought a newspaper every day that I knew him – and there are three stacks in the corner, close to the front window. I finger through the closest pile, trying carefully not to send everything toppling. One of the issues from the middle that's sticking out slightly is from six years ago. There will be a news organisation somewhere going out of business because Dad had spent all these years propping them up.

I leave the papers and turn to the rest of the room. There's a newer flat-screen television, but I don't recognise the make and suspect it was either a cheap supermarket special or that Dad got it from a man who knows a man, and so on. The red standby light glows, so I go to turn it off at the mains. In most places, this would be an easy task, but my father was seemingly trying to break every fire safety rule in the books. There are blocky, plasticky adapters plugged into other adapters that are wedged into an ancient, dusty four-gang. It takes me a couple of minutes to disentangle everything before I can finally turn it all off.

It's when I'm done stopping the house from burning down that I spot the crack in the skirting board, close to one of the armchairs. It stretches from the floor to the top of the wood, maybe five or six centimetres long. When I crouch and look more closely, there's a dot of inky reddy-black embedded in the ridges. It doesn't smudge or disappear when I scratch a finger across it. Before I realise what I'm doing, I am rubbing the spot close to my temple where there's still a raised line of a scar. It's faded over time, no longer a bright white slash, but closer to the colour of my skin. I glance back to the blob of reddy-black and then turn away.

I need to get out of this house.

FOUR

I'm not sure how the passing of time escaped me, but it's almost dark when I leave the house. The warmth of the August day hangs stickily under the blackening skies. The streets are quiet, aside from the vague sound of someone's music in the distance, while the singed smell of barbecue wafts airily on the gentlest of breezes. I have another drink from my bottle and then head along Beverly Close towards the park, where the music is louder. It looks like a bonfire has been lit on the furthest side of the park and someone's having a party.

Things are far more subdued on this side and there's only one other person around. Even if I hadn't seen her earlier, I think I would have recognised Jo's silhouette. She is standing on the spot close to the verge where I found Ethan. She's always had a way of slumping slightly to one side when standing, as if one leg is a little longer than the other.

I sidle in close, saying her name and trying not to startle her. Jo turns and blinks blankly towards me. One half of her face is in shade, the other illuminated by the searing white of the full moon. She was always the one to whom the boys gravitated when we were young. I used to tell myself it was her natural blonde hair and the way her chest exploded when we were only twelve. That was the age when some of the slightly older lads were starting to notice us and we certainly welcomed it. It's hard to remember the time when any of that mattered.

Jo's arms are folded across her front and she turns to stare down at the ditch, where a couple of people have already left bunches of flowers.

'Ethan's in intensive care,' she says quietly. 'The hospital told me to go back in the morning. Said there's nothing I can do. They'll call if anything changes.'

Her phone is in her hand and she holds it up into the light, as if willing it to ring.

There's a bench a few steps away, one of those ones with a small plaque on the backrest, to say who it's in memory of. I touch Jo on the arm and it's enough for her to understand the intention. We end up sitting side by side on the bench, staring across the park towards the fire. It's a while until either of us speak. For me, there's not a lot I can say. My family and, by extension, I, was never the type to offer much in the way of sympathy, let alone meaningless platitudes. I can hardly tell her that everything will work out all right.

Jo's voice is croaky when she speaks. 'I didn't think I'd ever see you again,' she says.

'Dad died.'

'Oh.'

'I'm back for the funeral.'

'Oh.' There's a long pause and then she adds: 'I think I knew that. Holly told me.' Another gap and then: 'I'm sorry.'

'It's fine,' I reply, though probably too quickly.

A firework surges up with a whoosh from the other side of the park. There is a flash of sparks, a fizz, and then a boom as a kaleidoscope of red and green splashes across the sky. It surely can't be long before the police are out again.

'They reckon it was a hit-and-run.' It takes me a moment to realise that Jo means Ethan. I don't know what to add, but she continues anyway. 'Scum. Absolute scum.' She nods towards

Beverly Close and the estate beyond. 'I can't believe someone from here would do that.'

'Do they know it was someone from around here…?'

Jo turns slightly and looks to me. Her eye twitches as her brow rises. 'You've not been gone that long, have you?'

She has a point. Elwood is the end of the line. It's not on the way to anywhere else and provides very little industry for anyone who isn't already local. The people here are those who live or work in the town. Why else would anyone be driving around the park and then turning onto the street where I grew up? The red-brick terraces and rows of battered cars means it's not for the range of scenery or cultural importance. It should have been obvious, but perhaps I *have* been away too long.

Whoever left Ethan in that ditch is someone from around here.

Jo yawns and it quickly turns into a second and third before she settles again. 'He was on his way back from Petey's house,' she says.

'Is Petey one of Ethan's friends?'

A nod. 'He was on his bike. He probably comes down this way three or four times every day. He cycles to school when it's not the holidays.'

'How old is he?'

The reply is a snapped: 'Eight.'

It takes a moment for me to realise why her tone changed so dramatically. She will have been getting those sideways looks ever since Ethan was found. In our day, an eight-year-old walking or cycling to school, or getting around during the holidays, would be no big deal. Everyone did it. Now, in the days of helicopter parenting and Facebook scare stories, I suspect that's not the case.

'I didn't mean it like that,' I say, though she doesn't reply.

I have another sip from my bottle and Jo eyes it before another firework booms. Then, without the hint of a siren, spinning blue lights flare through the trees on the other side of the park. This will probably make the local paper, although I suppose it won't be the front page. Not now, anyway.

'Mum…?'

I jump at the sound of a man's voice. Jo and I turn to see the tall, thin shape of a young man in a large padded coat that's surely too warm for this weather. He glances momentarily to me, then the bunches of flowers in the ditch, and then focuses back on Jo.

'Owen,' Jo says, almost to herself.

'I'll take you home,' he adds.

Jo stands, as if ready to move, but then her body goes rigid. Her tone is harsh as she jabs a finger towards him. 'Where were you earlier?'

Owen stiffens, too, and he takes half a step back: 'When?'

'When I needed you. Where were you? Your brother had been rushed to hospital and you weren't answering your phone.'

'I was with Beth.'

Jo shakes her head in annoyance. 'Ethan was on his way back from there.' She turns to involve me in the conversation. 'Petey and Beth are brother and sister.'

Ethan's journey seems like news to Owen. He shares the same frown as his mother. 'We were out. Beth wanted to—'

'I don't want to hear it.' Jo cuts herself off and then sighs, before throwing up her hands. She takes a step towards her son and then turns back to me. 'Have you got your phone?'

I suppose it's a fair enough assumption that everyone has a phone nowadays. I take mine out and she starts to tell me her number unprompted. She has to say it twice because I wasn't ready.

'Call me now,' she says, making it sound like a command. I do and the phone in her hand lights up. She doesn't answer, though she holds it up. 'I've got your number now,' she says.

'Good.'

It feels like the correct sort of reply.

She takes another step away, Owen at her side, before she turns and holds up the phone again. 'Imagine if we'd had these in our day. Would've saved a lot of hanging around the park, wondering where each other was.'

She laughs humourlessly as I give a slim smile in return. Then she turns and continues along the street with her son, before disappearing into the night.

FIVE

There's a strange moment when I wake up in which I feel like two people. There is the me as I am now, with the neck that aches all too often and the sluggish time it sometimes takes to remember a person's name. Then there's the me that used to awaken underneath these same posters. The me of half a lifetime ago.

I hadn't necessarily begun the day yesterday with the intention of sleeping here, but I suppose my critical thinking wasn't that strong. I was always going to visit this house, but it's not as if the area is blessed with a range of B&Bs or hotels. I certainly hadn't thought this old bedroom would be more or less as I'd left it. There's something both comforting and unsettling about it.

The curtains are pulled shut, with only a dusky murk peeping around the edges. The Garfield duvet cover is on the floor and I move it to the side until I find my bottle buried underneath. I already have the bottle to my lips when I realise it's empty. My throat is dry and lips probably cracked. I can smell my own breath and it's nothing good.

The hallway is similarly dim and I continue past the door to the spare room and Dad's old room, before pushing into the bathroom, washbag in hand. There are no curtains in here, only rippled glass, and the morning sun blasts inside, making me groan and wince at the same time. Last night, with light from the dim bulb overhead, I'd not realised the extent of how grim this bathroom is. The once-white sink is covered in a browning-greeny crust of something that might be limescale.

I cup my hands and drink from the tap, before cleaning my teeth and using the toilet. That done, I have to consider whether to brave the shower. The bath is in an even worse state than the sink and I'm not sure I want to know what the coating truly is. There's no specific shower unit, only a botchy-looking set of tubes connected to the bath taps, with a grimy plastic head that is dangling close to a plughole almost completely clogged with wiry grey hairs.

It's nearly too much, but my own sense of needing a wash overcomes that of the bath's.

After I'm done, I wrap a rough, patchy towel around myself and head back onto the landing. I pause for a moment outside my father's bedroom door. There's so much to do around here, but I feel unable to face much of it quite yet.

When I get downstairs, the accusatory empty vodka bottle sits on the kitchen counter. Another cheap supermarket knock-off brand. I don't think Dad bought anything else because price was always more important than taste or quality.

I'm in the process of burying it at the bottom of the bin when a warbling, tinny version of 'Greensleeves' starts to play. It takes me a moment to realise what's happening. The doorbell on my old flat was a satisfying and traditional ding-dong. This is more of an all-out assault on the ears.

At the front door is someone else who is easy to recognise. Her hair is shorter and greyer, while the wrinkles that were always there have grown into one another, leaving her eyes sunken into her pallid, grey skin.

'Hello, love,' she says, unsurprised at seeing me for the first time in twenty years.

'It's been a while, Helena,' I reply.

'It sure has.'

She smiles, but it doesn't seem to come easily to her. Like a right-hander trying to write with their left. Helena lived next door for the entire time I was growing up. For all I know, she's lived in the house her whole life. She has to be in her seventies now and stands with a slight stoop.

'I wanted to call when I heard about your dad, but I didn't know your number.'

'I heard from the solicitor.'

Helena purses her lips. 'Oh… that's no way for someone to hear about…' She tails off and I offer a slim smile to tell her it's fine. In the end, except for a hospital or the police, it was the most likely way I'd hear about my father's death.

Helena shifts her weight, angling towards her own house before looking back to me.

'Are you back for good?'

I start to reply but stop myself. She ends up apologising.

'It's okay,' I say. 'I don't know how long I'm here for.'

'Is it yours now?'

I don't get what she means straight away and she must see my confusion because she nods towards the house.

'Yes,' I say. 'That's why the solicitor contacted me.'

Helena bites her lip and I suddenly realise we're not having the conversation I thought we were.

'You're not selling, are you…?'

I glance backwards, as if to confirm the house is actually there.

'Your dad was very quiet,' she adds. 'Very security-conscious. Always keeping an eye out. You don't know who might move in…' She lets that hang for a moment.

'Like who?' I ask, innocently enough.

It could be that she doesn't want to live next door to a family that might cause problems, but it doesn't feel like that.

'You know…' she replies, lowering her voice, even though there's nobody to overhear us.

'I don't,' I say.

Helena glances around and then leans in closely, speaking even more quietly. 'Foreigners…'

She angles away a little and then checks behind again. There's still nobody else on the street, though I'm not that surprised she said it out loud. People do in places like this. My dad used to talk about 'brown people' plenty enough, although he'd often use far more offensive terms. It's almost refreshing that people are honest with their reasons, rather than spewing a long list of nonsense that anyone with half a brain knows is being used to cover the truth.

Almost refreshing.

'I've not decided what I'm doing yet,' I reply. 'I only arrived back yesterday.'

Helena nods shortly, unconvinced. I wonder if she might return to her house, but she isn't done yet.

'Did you hear about that poor boy?' she says, indicating around the corner, towards the park. 'Still, I see them all the time on their bikes, weaving in and out. Was always going to happen one of these days, wasn't it? Surprised it didn't happen before.'

I don't reply because I don't want to get into this with an old woman who, presumably, has nothing better to do. She's one step away from telling me how, in her day, she walked to school and back uphill in eight-foot snow. All that *and* she never complained about it. That is except for bringing it up literally every day since. I suspect Helena and my father had far more in common than they would ever admit to one another.

Thankfully, I'm saved by the sound of crunching gravel as a black car reverses onto Helena's drive. We both watch as a man gets out of the driver's seat and squints across towards us – or, more specifically, me.

He scratches his head and then comes closer. He's brawny across his top half, like a wheelie bin on legs. He's bald at the front, with an abandoned island of tufty hair somewhere in the middle.

There's no fence to separate the two properties, so he steps from the gravel of Helena's drive across onto the weed-infested paving slabs on this side.

'Abi…?' he says, unsure of himself.

'Hi, Chris,' I reply.

It's hard to read his face. His arms are crossed and there's a degree of bemusement, even though he has the same suppressed fart of a smile as his mother.

He keeps moving until he's stood next to his mum. 'I didn't think I'd ever see you again,' he adds, turning between me and Helena. There's a moment in which I think he's going to lean in and try to hug me, but, instead, he puts an arm around his mum's shoulders, squeezes her, and then steps away. In the gap between them, I see there's another woman and at least two children in his car. The sun's glare makes it hard to know for sure, or to make out anything other than general shapes.

Perhaps because she noticed me looking, the car door opens and a woman emerges. She takes a tentative step before striding across to join us. Behind her, two girls are pressed against the back window of the car.

'This is Kirsty,' Chris says abruptly, as the woman joins us. 'She was in the year below us at school.'

'I'm his wife,' Kirsty adds, with all the grace of hammering in a nail.

There's an awkward gap and then Chris quickly motions between us. 'This is Abi,' he says.

I give a meek 'hi' but otherwise say nothing. I want to get inside and away from this part of my past.

Kirsty is looking at me in the same way someone on the street looks at the dog mess they just stepped in. She seemingly knows that Chris and I went out with one another at school. He was my first boyfriend during a time when my hormone-ravaged self thought that meant we'd be together forever.

'Sorry to hear about your old man,' Chris says.

'Thanks…'

'Is there a funeral, or, um…?'

'That's what I'm back for.'

'Right.'

The four of us stand awkwardly until there's a bump from the car. The girls scramble back into their seats as Chris, Kirsty and Helena turn to see the source of the sound.

'We've got to get off,' Kirsty says. She reaches into her bag and removes an envelope that she passes to Helena. 'We only came round to drop that off.'

Helena checks the back of the envelope but doesn't open it. She looks up to her son, grabbing his gaze before he can leave.

'Where were you yesterday evening?' she asks. 'I thought you were coming over for tea with the girls, then you weren't answering your phone.'

Chris glances sideways towards his wife, but she's already taken a step towards the car. 'Are you sure we said Tuesday?' he replies.

'I thought so.'

'Maybe we can do something later? I'll text you.'

'You know I don't like those things.'

Chris spins and starts to trail Kirsty back to the car. 'I have to go, Mum.' He scans back to me and risks a 'Nice seeing you' before hurrying into the driver's seat. It's only when the exhaust flares that I realise how battered the car is. There's a long scratch across the back door, one of the hubcaps is missing and there's a grey scuff on the front wing bumper.

Helena has already taken a step back towards her house when my phone starts to ring with an unknown number. I would usually ignore these but press to answer, hoping it will finally give me an excuse to get away from my neighbour.

'Hello?' I say.

'Is that Abi?'

'Right.'

'It's Tina from the police. From yesterday. I was wondering if we could have a word…?'

SIX

Sergeant Davidson is the type of police officer a child might draw. He's tall, broad-chested, and stands rigidly on his heels. It's as if he's desperately holding off on a trip to the toilet. Even when he's sitting, it's as though he's not quite figured out how a chair works. He's kept his straight back but is perched on the front of the seat, not using the rest. It's all a bit odd.

Tina is at his side but has barely spoken since leading me to one of the police interview rooms. She apologised for the formality, got me a bottle of water and a Twix – which I've already eaten – and here we are.

Davidson nods towards Tina. 'When Constable Kennedy spoke to you yesterday, you said you thought it was a dark car that you saw in the middle of the road.'

It's more a statement than a question, though he looks at me as if expecting an answer.

'I wish I'd paid better attention,' I say. 'I heard the squeal and then got to the corner a few seconds afterwards.'

'Can you be any more specific on the colour?'

'It might have been black… maybe grey? I'm not sure. I suppose…'

'What?'

'I'm not sure it was a *dark* car. It was just a car. I didn't think anything of it until I got down to the junction.'

Davidson does a terrible job of suppressing a wince. I know it's not what he wanted to hear.

Tina wouldn't have been able to see his expression from the side, but she must have felt it.

'It's okay,' she says. 'Nobody could have expected to find what you did.'

She gives me a slim smile and there's a moment in which I wonder if we know each other somehow. Whether she has an older sister I know.

Davidson acts as if she hasn't spoken. 'What did you see when you got to the junction?' he asks.

'Nothing at first.'

'Anything on the road?'

'I saw the skid mark later, but that was after you got there. I didn't notice it at first. It was the bike wheel I saw.'

'Where was that?'

'In the verge. I went over to it – and that's when I saw Ethan at the bottom.'

'Do you know Ethan?'

I open my mouth to reply and then stop, realising how odd it is that I used the name of a boy I didn't recognise and have never met.

'No…' I say.

'But you know his mother…?'

Davidson is staring at me with such intensity that it feels like I've done something wrong. The fact I know Ethan's mum – that I know Jo – is hardly a startling revelation, though I'm surprised they know.

'We were friends at school,' I say. 'It was a long time ago.'

'Are you friends now?'

'Yesterday was the first time I've been back to Elwood in twenty-odd years. I'd not been in contact with any of my old friends until I saw Jo yesterday.'

'That's some really bad timing…'

I'm not sure if Davidson means it as a joke, but it doesn't sound like one. I suppose he's right – the timing of my arrival couldn't have been much worse, given what happened.

'My dad died,' I say. 'I'm back to sort out his affairs.'

Davidson squirms ever so slightly, shifting until he is a little further back in his seat. 'I'm sorry to hear that,' he replies, although he doesn't sound it.

Tina picks up on the awkwardness. 'Are you staying in Elwood?' she asks.

'I was living in London until Monday. I let my lease run out and was at my dad's house last night. I'm not sure. I haven't thought that far ahead.'

She nods and makes a note on the pad in front of her, then adds: 'We might have to talk to you again.'

'I don't know if there's much more I can say.'

She smiles again, probably trying to be reassuring. 'You never know. Sometimes things you won't expect can jog a memory.'

I nod along, although I'm not convinced. When I think about what I saw, it feels strange to admit that it was only 'a car'. That the colour and any other features just aren't in my mind.

There are a few seconds of silence, which I find myself breaking: 'Are there cameras anywhere?'

'Elwood's not that sort of place,' Tina replies.

I suppose I've not lived here recently enough to know – but I can't imagine it's like a city, where there are CCTV cameras on every corner, and where every shop has another of their own.

'Is there anything else you might want to add?' Tina asks.

'I don't think so.'

She turns to Sergeant Davidson. 'I think we might be done, then…?'

He eyes me with something that's probably annoyance, before he stands. 'Sounds like it.'

After we've tidied off a couple more formalities, Tina ends up walking me out of the station. She waits until we're standing together outside before saying anything other than the odd word.

'Don't worry about him,' she says, nodding back towards the building we've just left. 'There's already a lot of pressure coming down on us to find the driver.'

'I can't help it if I don't know the colour of the car.'

'I know. *He* knows that, too.'

'I *think* it was a dark car, but it's not clear.' I tap my head, wanting the memory to be there.

'We'd rather you were unsure about something than outright wrong.' She rests a hand on my arm in the same way she did yesterday. 'I'll give you my mobile number. If you think of anything else, call me directly. Also, you don't have to stay in Elwood, in case you had that idea. If you want to leave, you can leave.'

'I might do that…'

We say our goodbyes and then Tina heads inside as I continue along the pavement. I have to check Google Maps to figure out precisely where I am. There was a time in which I knew all of Elwood's cut-throughs, when the town was a playground for me and my friends. I had a mental map of all the hedges that could be pushed through and the fences that weren't completely secure. The ways that five minutes could be shaved off a journey by taking an illicit shortcut along the back of someone's garden.

I think about calling Jo but figure that, even if she isn't at the hospital, she will have more important things to be thinking about. Besides, I've got a funeral director to talk to, but I'm not sure I can face that now, perhaps not even today.

I stick to the main roads as I walk back across Elwood. It was never the most welcoming of places, but, in the time I've been gone, the town centre has transformed from largely independent stores into a grubby row of betting shops and takeaways that haven't yet opened for the day. Aside from a bank or two, there's almost nothing I recognise about the town where I used to spend most of my Saturdays. My friends and I spent so much time in the HMV, browsing through tapes and CDs, that the manager would ask us to leave after we'd not bought anything for an hour. That store has gone now, replaced by one of those smaller Tesco's, which never have the things in stock that people actually want.

There's a new Wetherspoon's at the end of the centre nearest the park and I stop outside the front door, thinking about going inside. It's late on a Wednesday morning and they've probably not long opened their doors. I wonder about the type of people inside, the ones who are banging on the door each morning, wanting their cheap pints and microwaved breakfasts. There was a time, perhaps recently, when my dad might have been among them.

I continue on, even though the bigger part of me wants to stop, moving past the entrance to the park to where there's a large blackened circle of scorch marks close to the fountain. A mound of charcoaled sticks has been abandoned in the middle, with a series of empty firework tubes scattered around the flower beds. I guess the town's Britain In Bloom nomination won't be coming this year.

Instead of following the path, I cut across the grass until I'm on the side closest to my dad's house. To *my* house. I follow the path around the row of trees and hedges until I'm back on the street and, eventually, the intersection with Beverly Close. Word has obviously gone around about what happened because the verge has become a carpet of colour. A rainbow of flowers has been spread up and down the bank where I found Ethan, with four more bunches attached to the nearest lamp post. There are footballs interspersed among the flowers, with a red shirt tied to a tree close to the bench where Jo and I sat last night. I crouch and look at one of the tickets attached to a bunch of flowers.

Love you, little man. X

There's a card that's been made from a folded sheet of printer paper. Someone, presumably a child, has drawn a shaky felt-tip picture on the front of a boy with a football. The card has been tucked in next to a ball.

It's strange, but it's only now that it feels like there's a significant weight to what I saw and what actually went on. That this wasn't just something terrible that happened to one family; it feels like something that happened to the community. Everyone will know that the person who left Ethan in the ditch is one of them.

One of *us*.

It's an awful thought, but there's all this and he's not even dead. I wonder if there is some confusion, which led to this outpouring – or if it's simply because this is such a small community. Or, perhaps, I'm out of the loop and things have taken a turn for the worst without me knowing.

I shiver when I stand, that sixth sense that tells a person they are being watched. It is almost impossible to explain, even though everybody knows what it is.

It's not obvious at first, but, in among the row of parked cars on Beverly Close, there is a vehicle that's idling. The exhaust fumes chunter into the air until, with a start, the car shoots out of the space. There's a long scratch across the back door, a missing hubcap, and the scuff on the front bumper. The distance and glare means I can't see the driver, but I'd be almost certain it was Chris who was watching me.

I don't get a chance to think on it further because someone else has appeared on the path next to the park. A woman reaches into a bag and removes a red and white football scarf, which she ties to the lamp post. She bows her head for a moment and then shoots me a narrow smile before turning to leave. I start to do the same before we stop at the same time and turn to face one another.

'Abi…?' she says.

I don't get a chance to acknowledge this because she's already certain. She hurries across the few steps between us until she's directly in front of me, where she looks me up and down.

'Oh my God, I thought you were abroad, or dead, or something.'

'Bit of a difference between those two.'

She laughs: 'Yeah…'

'I'm not dead.'

'It's Holly,' she adds, needlessly. 'Remember?'

'Of course,' I reply. 'How could I forget my first kiss?'

SEVEN

Holly frowns, her plucked and crafted eyebrows almost meeting in the middle before her cheeks crinkle and she starts to laugh.

'I'd forgotten that,' she says. 'That was your first kiss? How old were we? Thirteen?'

I shrug. 'Something like that. I had no idea what I was doing.'

She nods in slightly perplexed agreement. 'I don't know why someone daring you to do something makes you feel as if you have to do it.'

'Probably the vodka.'

That gets a laugh, but it doesn't last long as the weight of the flowers and footballs draws our attentions back to the verge.

'Did you hear?' Holly asks.

'I found him.'

She turns to look at me and there's another moment in which it's like I've fallen through time. This could have been twenty-five years ago, with us in school uniform, wearing skirts that were too short, as we laughed and joked our way to class.

Holly has aged better than Jo, probably better than me. She's in flattering, expensive-looking yoga gear and could be on the way to the gym. The sort of thing worn by those yummy-mummy types who charge around in 4x4s for no particular reason. The ones who post long online missives about having to love yourself before you can love anyone else.

She weighs me up, wondering if I'm making some sort of weird joke. She shifts awkwardly from one foot to the other before apparently deciding this isn't a prank.

'Did you see the car?' she asks.

'No… not really.' I nod in the direction of Dad's house… *my* house. 'A car disappeared down there, but I didn't notice much about it. I saw Ethan in the ditch and then called the ambulance.'

We both look down towards the ditch, but I can't manage it for too long because it feels like Ethan's still there, his crumpled body lying at my feet. I blink it away and turn towards the bench.

'Are you still friends with Jo?' I ask.

'Of course. We were talking about you the other week, wondering where you were. We'd looked you up on Facebook, but you're not on there…'

She lets it hang, a question that's not a question, before continuing.

'We were talking about the old days. Remember that time when we used to pretend we were All Saints? I was Nicole – but then she got to marry Liam Gallagher and I… didn't.'

We share a smirk, but, regardless of whether this is the time, it's definitely not the place.

I motion towards the flowers, while trying not to look at them directly. 'Have you heard anything?'

'Jo texted me earlier. She's at the hospital, but that's all I know. I asked how Ethan's getting on, but there was no reply. Can't blame her, really.'

There's a long pause. I'm not sure who instigates it, but we start walking side by side, across the road and away from the verge. We're moving in the direction of the bus stop.

'Are you back?' Holly asks, with something of a forced cheeriness.

'I don't know. Dad died and there are things to sort out.'

There's a short pause and I get the sense that she already knew. 'I'm sorry.'

'Don't be. I'm back for now, either way.'

'You should come over to mine for a proper catch-up. We could—'

She stops talking so abruptly that I glance sideways to make sure she's all right. It's like she interrupted herself. She misses half a step and then quickly recovers.

'Sorry,' she adds needlessly. 'Rob's probably home. He's my son and, um…' Another pause. 'No, don't worry about it. Come over now, if you're free. We'll have a brew and a chat. I want to hear what you've been doing all these years.'

That last part sounds about as appealing as an anaesthetic-free tooth extraction, but the alternative is either contacting the funeral director, cleaning up the house, or wasting a day at Wetherspoon's.

'It's not far,' Holly adds. 'We can walk.'

'Okay,' I tell her.

'Brilliant,' she replies.

'I just need to grab something from the house,' I tell her.

'Let's go, then. We've got so much catching up to do.'

That's what worries me, I don't say.

EIGHT

After backtracking to retrieve my bottle from the house, Holly leads me off the estate and into an area that was once a series of fields. There's a sprawling mass of red-brick houses now, although every other place seems to be up for sale. Cars are parked on the road, even though everybody seemingly has a driveway.

'Do you remember when it flooded here?' Holly asks as we walk.

I didn't until she mentioned it, but, now she has, the memory feels unleashed. It was before the houses were built, when heavy rain would make the river swell and burst across the grass. One year, it felt as if the rain would never stop and the water went higher and higher.

'We bobbed around on those rubber rings,' I say.

'You remember! Jo says it never happened, but I knew it did. We got the rings from that car wash place that used to be in town, then we played down here on the field. The boys came over from the big school and we had a water fight.'

'Jo went home,' I say. 'I think one of the lads dunked her and she swallowed a bit of water.'

Holly's pace slows a tiny amount. 'I don't remember that…' She takes a breath and then motions towards the furthest end of the estate. 'Ever since I moved here, I've been trying to figure out where everything used to be. The river's still there, but it's all so different.'

We follow the street, weaving around everyone's wheelie bins that are scattered across the kerb from where the binmen have been. We are almost off the estate when we get to a small rank of houses that are surrounded by a flank of swaying trees. There's the vaguest memory that these houses started being built when I left. That must've been a few years before the rest of the estate was built, but none of it is clear.

Holly takes me along an empty driveway and then unlocks the front door before leading the way inside. Her hall is filled with boxes that take up half the space. I follow as she slides past them sideways without explanation. Opposite the boxes are a series of framed photographs on the wall. It's halfway along the wall that I spot a small, square picture almost hidden among the number of photos taken in front of various landmarks. It's the type of point-and-click shot that everyone took before the days of camera phones. It isn't quite in focus, as if there was Vaseline on the lens. It's still easy enough to make out the three people featured.

Holly's hair is separated into high bunches and she's wearing baggy blue sweatpants with an orange crop top.

'Sporty Spice,' she says, when she notices I've stopped.

Jo has red streaks in her hair and is wearing a short dress with knee boots for Ginger Spice. I am Baby, in a short pink dress that I found in the vintage section of Elwood's Oxfam store.

'Wasn't this someone's birthday?' I ask.

'That Esther girl. Her dad used to work abroad all the time and then he'd bring back expensive things. She got a real Prada bag out of it one time – and that silver dress she wore to town once. Everyone else was in jeans. Remember?'

Memories swirl, of faces and names, but Esther doesn't appear – and neither does her bag or dress. It's strange the way some things stick so firmly in one person's mind but can disappear completely from another's.

'We all got trashed and then the neighbours complained,' Holly continues. 'Esther was grounded for the whole summer.'

'I don't remember,' I say. 'Not that bit, anyway. I know we were the Spice Girls.'

We stop and stare at the photo for a moment and I wonder how many of our teenage escapades begin or end with 'we all got trashed'. That's the thing when you grow up in a place like Elwood, especially in our day. It's not like there were loads of places to go in the evenings. Even as an adult, there were only a handful of pubs from which to choose. One of them might have stayed open late, but that usually ended in a ruck on the pavement. If someone was too young to get in somewhere like that, or, worse, if the guy on the door knew precisely how old we all were, then we'd always end up back in someone's garage, shed or attic with a bottle of cheap cider. If someone's parents were away and there was an entire house empty, we'd go a bit crazy.

Holly slips around another stack of boxes, past a door that's built under the stairs, and into the room at the end of the hall. I follow into a kitchen, where there are more boxes pressed against a side wall. Holly clicks on the kettle and slots into a wooden chair next to a table. I sit opposite her, though it feels like the mounds of clutter between us muddy my thoughts. It's mainly letters, opened and not, but there's also an open cereal packet, three unwashed mugs, an oats-encrusted bowl and a pair of lever-arch files.

Before either of us can say anything, there's a bang from the hall and the sound of a box hitting the ground.

'Rob…?' Holly calls and, a moment later, a gawky young man appears. He's all elbows and knees, and cracks his elbow on the door frame as he comes through.

'Knocked a box over,' he says, rubbing his arm.

'We heard,' Holly replies.

'I picked it up.'

'This is Abi,' Holly says, nodding at me. 'She's an old school friend of mine who's back in town. She found Ethan yesterday.'

He stops rubbing his elbow and stoops a little, looking at me over his glasses. 'Hi,' he says, before turning back to his mum.

'Can we, um…?' He nods away from the kitchen and Holly gets the unsubtle hint.

'I'll be right back,' she says, before following her son out of the kitchen and through to another part of the house.

I stand and take a couple of paces around the small space, though it's hard to resist the urge to open one of the boxes. There are probably thirty or forty through the hall and in the kitchen, each a tidy square, with no labels on the sides. The only markings are various felt-tip letters. 'F', 'K' and 'M' are visible in the kitchen. I pick one up, though the weight gives little away. It's not light, though not overly heavy, either.

The fridge is covered with various notes that say things like 'Thurs, 7, Angie', though there doesn't appear to be much order. It's like someone tore out all the pages of a diary and then guessed the sequence blind.

I find myself looking at a photo pinned to the fridge door with Blu Tack. Holly was bigger then, chubbier in the face, with what looks like a blotchy red rash across one of her cheeks. She's next to Rob, who was even ganglier whenever it was taken. He was probably fourteen or fifteen and, grinning, he's showing off a horror-movie mouthful of wire braces. On the other side is a man I don't know. He's tanned orange, relaxed, with his shirt almost entirely unbuttoned. I look closer, wondering if it's someone with whom we went to school. That's when Holly's voice makes me jump.

'That's Tom,' she says, joining me at the fridge and pressing a finger to the man's face. 'He walked out three years ago. That pic's only there because he's Rob's dad and Rob wanted to keep one on display.'

We stare at it together for a moment, though it's hard to know why Rob might have chosen *this* picture in particular. He doesn't come out of it looking well.

'Was he okay?' I ask, turning back towards the hall as there's a bump from the stairs.

'Rob? Just teenagery stuff. He's eighteen and probably off to uni in September. He's waiting on results and wanted to show me some email he got off UCAS. I don't know why he couldn't do it with you there.'

I think back to when I was a teenager and the way I used to be around my father's friends. Around any adults, really. I certainly wouldn't have been talking about my future in front of them.

'We've already been up to Liverpool for a look around the university,' Holly adds. 'I know he's my son and I would say that – but he's clever. Did way better than any of us. He's predicted As for his exams. If I'm honest, I dunno where he gets it from. It's not his father.' She stops and then adds: 'I've been trying to encourage him to find a university closer to here. Liverpool seems so far away…'

I let the thought sit, though the kettle plips off anyway and Holly asks if I want tea. I don't – but say I do out of politeness. We settle back at the table, though I opt for a drink from my bottle instead of the tea.

'What's with that?' Holly asks, as I place the bottle on the table. She doesn't mention that I specifically went back to the house to retrieve it. It's nothing special; just a clear hard plastic bottle with a spout at the top.

'I got used to carrying it around,' I say. 'Save the oceans and the planet. All that.'

It's half empty and Holly eyes the clear contents knowingly. She points a thumb towards the fridge. 'There's filtered water in there if you want it refilling…?'

There might be the merest hint of a smirk in the corner of her lips, though the more likely explanation is that it's in my imagination.

I almost play the game and tell her that would be great – but I can't quite do it.

'I'm fine for now,' I say instead.

She nods and I look for the smirk that doesn't come. Perhaps it was never there.

'Things are changing here,' Holly says, unprompted.

'Changing how?'

'Hendo's is closing. It was bought out by a company in America. They started cutting jobs straight away – mainly the managers – but it's the shop floor next. Some are saying it'll all be gone in a year.' She sighs a long gasp and then has a drink of her tea.

Hendo's is a shoe manufacturing plant. It has been a part of the town for as long as I've been alive. Longer. It was always there, always offering a profession to the people who didn't want to leave the area. There was security in that more or less anyone could get a job there – but it was an insult, too. Teachers would often tell the boys in our class – always the boys – that if they didn't put more work in, then they'd end up working at Hendo's. Some lads wanted to follow in the same trade as their fathers, others couldn't wait to move far away from its possible grip. In the current age of zero-hour contracts and temporary jobs, it would be one of the few places that could still offer a job for life.

Not any more.

'That's terrible,' I say, meaning it.

Holly sinks lower in her chair.

'Did you work there?' I ask.

A shake of the head. 'Not me. Everyone knows someone who does, though.' She jabs a thumb to the side. 'Ian next door's on the shop floor, then there's a lad over the road who started there eighteen months ago. Can you imagine what it's going to do to Elwood when it goes…?'

I don't reply because there's nothing to say. I might not have lived here in a long while, but anyone could see that the town is going to be pulled apart.

Holly has another sip of her tea. 'It *is* good to see you again,' she says, not looking up from the table. 'You left so quickly. I wish you'd said.'

'I didn't plan it. Not really. I just went.'

She peers up now, catching my eye. 'Because of your dad…?'

I can't hold the stare. 'Right.'

We sit quietly. Holly sips her tea and I have my bottle.

'Have you seen Jo since you got back?' Holly asks.

'At the site. I called 999 after I found Ethan. I didn't know his name, or that he was her son. She turned up, then I saw her again last night. She was at the spot where he was hit and I'd gone out late for a wander.'

'Did you talk much?'

'It wasn't the time.'

Holly nods. 'I guess not. Shame you couldn't have caught up when it was better.'

Something feels different now that we're here, compared to when we met on the street. I don't know what to ask Holly about. She has an adult son, for one, and our lives have forked so far apart that none of the things we once had in common seem to be there any longer.

'It's terrible, isn't it,' she says.

'What?'

'Ethan. I was sick when I heard. Actually sick. Poor Jo.'

'When I saw her last night, Jo said Ethan was in intensive care.'

'They said critical on the radio.'

I don't know the difference between those two things, if there is one. Either way, it doesn't sound good.

'Jo thinks the driver comes from Elwood,' I say.

Holly nods along. 'Makes sense.' She bites her lip and then makes eye contact again. 'Have you met Neil?'

'Who's that.'

'Jo's fella. He, um…' She tails off and turns to the fridge, using her mug of tea to shield her mouth for a moment. Whatever she wants to say isn't coming straight out.

'What is it?' I ask.

'It's just… don't tell Jo I said this, but…'

I wait – and then it comes, all the words pushing into one another.

'He's banned from driving. He built up enough points. I think it was speeding that did him in the end, but he got caught going through a red light at some point, too. It was all in the paper. That was about three months ago, but Rob reckons he saw Neil driving the other week.' A nod towards the hall. 'That's the other thing he told me just now. I guess that's why he didn't want to talk in front of you.'

I take a drink – of tea this time – and then press back into the chair. I have no idea who Neil is, but it doesn't sound good.

'Are you going to tell Jo?' I ask.

Holly shakes her head. 'She wouldn't want to hear it. Once she kicked out Mark, she was infatuated with Neil – even though he doesn't have a job and doesn't do anything.'

'*Mark?*' I query. 'Not Mark Ashworth.'

'Right. They stayed together all the way after school and had Owen and Ethan. Then, at some point, Jo moved on to Neil. She kept the two kids with her.'

More names and faces swirl in my thoughts. Mark and Jo got together at some point around the time when we were doing our GCSEs. The idea of them still being together for long enough to have two kids is both unsurprising and strange. It's hard to imagine the two teenagers I knew having a teenager of their own.

'It probably doesn't mean anything,' Holly adds. 'Rob says he's certain it was Neil driving – but it was a couple of weeks ago. What good would it do to bring it up now?'

She lets it hang, but she must be having the same dark thoughts that have flickered through my mind about what happened to Ethan. They must have occurred to Rob, too, if he shared them with his mother.

'There's no reason to think he was driving yesterday,' Holly says, although it sounds more like she's trying to convince herself than me.

'No,' I reply.

It's the truth, of course. There is no reason to think Neil might have hit his stepson and then disappeared. I've never even met him. And yet, whoever left the scene did stop momentarily. I saw that much. Anyone could have done that – but the fear of driving illegally would be a big reason to disappear.

'Maybe you should try to find out what Neil was up to yesterday?' I say.

'Hard to do that without asking outright.' Holly finishes her tea and then stretches to place the cup in the sink. She turns back with a long gasp and then continues with a cheery-sounding: 'So what about you…?'

'What about me?'

'Are you married, or…?'

'Not quite.'

There's a gap and I wonder if she's going to push.

She waits and it's a stand-off, wondering who's going to break first. Luckily, it is neither of us – because the doorbell sounds.

Holly gets up slowly, as if she's expecting a quick reply from me before she goes. She doesn't get it and I stand, following her into the hallway, ready to make an excuse and head off. I never wanted to talk about myself anyway.

Holly squeezes past the boxes and gets to the door just as it rings a second time. She pulls it open to reveal Jo on the step. There are streaky tear stains down her face and a tissue in her hand.

Jo steps inside. 'It's Ethan,' she says through a sob.

NINE

Holly stands to the side, allowing Jo fully inside. 'He's not…?'

Jo shakes her head. 'He's still in intensive care.'

Holly lets out a long, low sigh of relief. It's not great, but intensive care is better than the alternative.

Jo looks up and notices me. She reels a little with surprise and then turns between Holly and me.

'I guess the Spice Girls are finally back together,' Holly says.

Jo smiles, though it's more of a sob as Holly nods towards me. I was going to leave, but I can hardly do that now. Instead, I lead us back past the boxes into the kitchen. Jo takes the seat where Holly was and, as Holly stands in the small alcove near the back door, I sit in the other chair.

'The hospital staff told me to go home and rest,' Jo says. 'It's not like I can sleep, though. Then the police came along.' She wipes her eyes with the tissue in her hand – but that only smears the streaks wider.

Holly catches my eye and I know she must be thinking about Neil.

'What did the police want?' Holly asks.

'They want me to go on TV,' Jo says. 'Do some sort of appeal to the driver, asking whoever it is to come forward.'

Holly glances towards me again and there's a moment in which it feels like the past twenty years haven't happened. That we've slotted back into these roles as if we never stopped being teenagers. Where the things unsaid are as understood as the things that are.

'When are you going on TV?' I ask.

Jo stares at me wide-eyed, as if I've just asked why she has two heads. 'I'm not doing it,' she says. 'You know what they did to my dad.'

Holly and I are having a silent conversation with only our eyes. She raises a single eyebrow.

'I'm sure they're trying to help,' I say, trying to be tactful.

'It killed him,' Jo says firmly, more angry than upset now. 'That's down to the police. When he got out of prison, he was never the same.'

I don't look up to Holly because I already know how she'll be watching me with scepticism. This happened while we were in our final year at school and there was never any doubt that Jo's father was guilty of stealing the TVs for which he was convicted. He'd been knocking on doors in the local area, offering them for sale, and saying they were in his rented garage. When the police raided the garage, they found eighteen televisions that had been stolen from a delivery lorry a week before. Hardly a master criminal and zero chance he'd been 'stitched up' as Jo insisted. He defended himself in court, pleaded not guilty, and got fifteen years. It was barely a week after he was sent down that we all sat our first GCSE.

'You can't trust 'em,' Jo adds for good measure.

'You might have to,' I say.

'I'm going to find the driver myself.' She speaks with firm determination, as if this is a genuine option.

I continue to avoid Holly's gaze, though I know she's searching for mine.

'I'm serious,' Jo adds, with a gentle thump of the table. She turns between Holly and me. 'Nobody knows the area better than we do. We can find the person. I want to know who left my son to die in a ditch.'

The statement goes down as well as a drum 'n' bass track in an old people's home. Aside from the fact that I *don't* know the area that well any longer, and that I've only been back for less than a day, this is definitely a job for the police. I'm also not sure how this has suddenly become 'we', not the previous 'I'. I've never been one of those people who believe in fate, or destiny – and yet here we are, as if it was always going to come back to this.

'The police will stitch someone up,' Jo adds, surely getting that we're not on board. I'm not sure whether she was expecting our resounding support, but she sounds even harsher than before.

'I don't know what I can do,' Holly says, sounding almost as unsure as I feel.

'Ask around,' Jo replies. 'Someone knows something.'

'The driver might not be someone local,' Holly replies.

'Course it is. Who else drives around here? Someone we know did this. Someone's hiding it.'

There's an uncomfortable pause. I have no idea what to say, but Holly at least has a go: 'Do you think Ethan might need you more at the moment…?'

Jo sits up straighter and it feels dangerous. When she replies, it's not the volcano I expected; instead, she sounds far more measured.

'That's why I need your help.' Jo turns to me. 'You, too. I just want to know what kind of person could leave a child for dead…'

I look up and let Holly have my attention this time. It's like we're psychic, because I know she's questioning whether Jo's partner could be the type of person who'd drive off after hitting someone.

'Will you come over later?'

I glance back to Jo and realise she's talking to me.

'Please say yes,' she adds. 'I'm going back to the hospital, but I'll be home for seven. You can come over then. I'd love to do some catching up. It's been so long.'

'I don't know where you live,' I say.

'I'll text you. It's not far from you, down near the school.'

It doesn't feel like the right time, but I can see Jo scratching a nail across the back of her knuckles, where there is already a deep red mark. It's not as if I could say no, anyway.

'I'll be there,' I say.

TEN

The funeral director's name is Damien, which would be either funny, disturbing, or both, if it wasn't for the circumstances. It does remind me that I was with Jo the first time I ever saw *The Exorcist*. It was one of those dodgy videos that my dad had got from a bloke down the pub. We scared ourselves witless watching it one night when he was out.

This Damien speaks in constant hushed tones, as if there's a militant librarian on our tail. The reception of his office – is it called an office? – is fully carpeted, and decorated with plenty of neutral colours and soft, inoffensive prints on the walls.

'Would you like to view the body?' he asks. He's standing with his arms behind his back and leaning forward at an odd angle to talk.

'How do you mean "view"?' I reply.

'It would take a little time, but you could return tomorrow.'

'I'm still not sure what you mean.'

'I can make your father look as he was for you to, um, view.'

'Why would you do that?'

'Some people find it a peaceful experience. It might be a chance to say goodbye. It's entirely your choice.'

It's only now that I notice the melodic piano music in the background. I guess it's supposed to be calming, but everything is *so* toned down that it's having the opposite effect on me. I have a drink from my bottle while trying not to clench my other fist.

'I don't need to see him,' I say.

'That's absolutely fine. All the funeral arrangements were already taken care of by your father with his will. His only major wish was for no cremation. Your father paid for a spot in the cemetery at the Elwood Anglican, as well as the headstone. The main decision left for you is for what type of service you want.'

I glance towards the door, wanting out. I have to take a breath, but Damien misreads it. He steps across to the counter, grabs a tissue from the box, and passes it over to me.

'We don't have to do this right now,' he adds.

I feel awkward holding the tissue, not knowing what to do with it; it's not as if I was going to cry.

'What are the options?' I ask.

'There might be a waiting list, but there's the church—'

'No.'

Damien takes the rejection in his stride, not missing a beat: 'How many people do you think might wish to pay their respects to your father?'

'Not many.'

'Fewer than fifty?'

I have to stifle a snort. 'Fewer than twenty.'

'For a service that small, we could accommodate those numbers here. Either that, or—'

'Here's fine. Just, maybe… different music.'

I look for a reaction, but there's none. This guy must be one hell of a poker player. What sort of chat might someone have to have with a careers officer at school to end up doing this as a job?

'You can have whatever music you want,' he says, as he reaches for a pad from the counter.

He asks if I mind and then makes a note.

'Would you like to say something at the ceremony?' he asks.

'No.'

'Do you think someone else might like to?'

'I doubt it. Can you do it?'

'Of course.'

He writes something down and it's at the point where I'm wondering how much I could request without him reacting.

'Your father paid for a notice in the paper,' he says. 'I am happy to arrange if—'

'Do that.'

'Is there anything specific you'd like it to say?'

'Whatever you think.'

I wonder if there's a norm for this sort of thing. He must have seen relatives stricken with grief, barely able to make a decision, as well as those who have that sort of stoic control when something bad happens. It feels like I'm being rude for not wanting to engage.

'When's the earliest day you can do it?' I ask.

'The service?'

'Yes.'

For the first time, I sense the merest amount of discomfort. It's only fleeting and then Damien reaches for a ledger on the counter. He flips through the pages and then looks up.

'I suppose the earliest day would be Friday but—'

'Two days?'

'Yes, but—'

'Let's do it.'

'There might not be time for a proper notice in the paper.'

'I wouldn't worry.'

'He did pay for—'

'I'm pretty certain he won't mind any longer…'

Damien clenches his lips together, but then breaks into a kindly smile. 'Of course. I'm thinking of you. Sometimes the florists—'

'Flowers weren't really his thing.'

'No, well… in that case, Friday it is. Shall we say four p.m.?'

'Perfect.'

I take a step towards the door, but Damien continues talking. 'Are you sure you don't want a viewing? It wouldn't be much trouble. Sometimes, people change their minds after a few hours or a day…?'

He's trying to be kind, but I can't match his smile. 'Trust me,' I tell him, 'the last thing I want is to see my father again.'

I'm already striding along the High Street before I realise I'm walking away from Dad's house.

My house.

I wonder if I'll ever think of it as mine before I think of it as Dad's. The thought is lost as someone darts across near me, trying to cross the road. He shoots between two parked cars and almost runs in front of a white van. The driver lays on the horn and the pedestrian jumps, before he sidesteps around a car coming the other way. It all happens in a matter of seconds and, as I exchange a quizzical shrug with the white van driver, I suppose it's a lesson that life continues on. It's barely twenty-four hours ago that a kid was hit by a car and now someone ran into the road without looking. People are still going to work; children are still playing in the park, or inside on their PlayStations and phones; deliveries are still being made to shops; people are still ordering pizzas and complaining about the weather. All the while, Jo's little boy lies in hospital.

I should've at least tried to be more helpful when she asked Holly and me to help her find the driver. If it had happened to someone close to me, I'd want to know.

Not that there's anyone particularly close to me.

I have a sip from my bottle and continue along the street. I've got to be here for two more days in order to get through the funeral and then… I don't know. I'm not even sure why I've decided I definitely have to have anything to do with the funeral. A sense of loyalty, perhaps, however misguided.

It's the flash of movement from over the road that catches my eye, maybe even the reflection of the sun from the top of Chris's head. The neighbour's son clambers out of the same scuffed black car as this morning and then checks something on his phone before heading for the betting shop.

There's a strange moment in which I feel as if I know precisely what I should do. I'm a puppet on someone else's string as I cross the road and then crouch to look at his car. It isn't quite black like I thought, it's a metallic grey that's covered with grime and dust. The scratch along the back door looks like someone's keyed it, rather than anything sinister. It's the mark on the bumper that's harder to figure out. The scrape is deeper and far longer than it first appeared. Someone has used a felt-tip, or something similar, to colour in the lighter parts. There's also the hint of an indent on the part of the wing just above the bumper – as well as a crack in the glass of the headlights.

I've got my phone out of my pocket, ready to take a photo, when the man's voice comes from behind.

'What do you think you're doing?'

ELEVEN

I stand, trying to remain tall and confident, as if this is completely normal.

'Had to tie my shoe,' I say, lifting my leg in case Chris somehow doesn't realise what a foot is.

He stares down to me with his eyebrows raised. Even though he towered over his mum, I'm not sure I realised how tall he was this morning. He's comfortably over six foot and with enough bulk for it to feel like more. We're in the open, but that isn't a guarantee of safety.

Chris puffs out his chest, but then he sinks a little.

'Oh,' he says, holding up the scrap of paper in his hand, which I presume to be a betting slip. 'I had to make a quick stop in town. I'm back off home now.' He looks sideways along the road and, as I take half a step back, he reaches towards me.

I wince and he quickly pulls away.

'Sorry. I was hoping we could talk.' His hand remains in the air – but he slowly puts it down to his side, before nodding to the betting shop again. 'It's part of the ritual,' he says. 'There's a game on later.'

'Who's playing?'

'United are in Mexico for pre-season.'

'Is that a big game?'

He holds up the betting slip, with a sheepish grin. It's only now that he reminds me properly of the lad I once knew. Many things have changed, for both of us, but his smile that slips lower on one side than the other is the same as it always was. I am momentarily that teenager again, feeling smitten and weak at the knees. It only lasts a blink.

'Where've you been?' he asks.

'Since this morning?'

He snorts. 'Since forever. You left and nobody seemed to know where you went. I knocked on your dad's door, but he didn't want to talk about it. I didn't know you'd properly left until about a month after you'd already gone.'

'We weren't together then.'

'No… but it would've still been nice to know.'

It's a fair point.

We stand together for a moment, but it's like being the only two people on the dance floor at a wedding. Too much attention. Too much self-awareness.

'Can we do this somewhere else?' I ask.

Chris turns in a circle, taking in the betting shop, the boarded-up shopfront, the overflowing bin and the row of parked cars.

'Sure.'

I follow as he leads us around the back of the bookies into a car park with a low, crumbling wall running around the edge. It's hardly scenic, but then Elwood isn't famed for its landmarks.

Chris perches on the wall and I settle at his side. There's dust and small chips of cement at our feet.

'You left…' he says, as if I'd forgotten.

'I had to get out of Elwood.'

'Why?'

I almost laugh as I hold up my hands to indicate the decaying car park and the rest of the High Street beyond. 'Because of everything.'

'Your dad…?'

'*Everything.*'

He nods slightly, but I wonder if he really gets it. Some people can stay in the same place their whole existence. That's the life he'll have and there's nothing wrong with that. It didn't take me long to figure out that it wasn't going to be like that for me.

'I thought we were okay together,' he says.

'We were kids.'

'Yeah, but…'

'It's not like we ever had anything in common. We went to school together.'

Chris slumps; his head hanging, his chin almost on his chest.

'I was going to ask you to marry me,' he says, speaking as if he's apologising.

I turn to him properly, wondering if it's some strange sort of joke. When he doesn't look up, it's clear he means it. I still have no idea of where to begin with a reply. I suppose I never realised how wildly different our attitudes were to all this. I don't know whether to go with 'why?' or a clarifying 'what?' Nothing comes and all I manage is a stumbled, sorry-sounding: 'I didn't know that.'

'My grandma was married to my granddad for over fifty years,' he says, still not looking up. 'Their wedding was two days before he went off to war. She didn't know if she'd ever see him again, but he was one of the ones who came back. When she died, I got her wedding ring – and I was going to give it to you.'

He gulps so loudly that I hear it.

'When was this?' I ask.

'I was going to take you out to the lake. The one where we talked properly for the first time. There was some party and your friend, Jo, had gone off with that guy—'

'Mark.'

'Right. You were on your own and we were talking about how we lived next door to each other but had never really had a conversation.'

'When was this?!'

I'm repeating myself and it's hard to hide the frustration, but Chris continues as if I haven't spoken.

'We were together for almost two years, but then you broke up with me,' he says. 'You never really gave a reason. You just said it wasn't working.'

It's hard to ignore the angst, as if this has been weighing on him for a couple of decades, and it's only now he has the chance to get an answer.

'We were never going to end up together,' I say. 'We were kids pairing up in the way kids do. We never even…' I leave it there, hoping he'll get it.

It feels like a different me who embraced the madness of believing we would be together with kids, and a house around the corner from where we grew up. It happens all the time, of course. Teenagers look to one another and say 'that'll do' – and that's the next sixty years seemingly plotted.

The worst thing is that, if Chris had asked me to marry him, there was a time when I know I'd have said yes. It didn't matter that we were teenagers, I'd have trapped myself just to get out of that damned house.

'Did you ever get married?' Chris asks.

'People keep asking that.'

Time passes, maybe a minute, but he continues to wait.

'No,' I say. 'Not that it matters.'

'Have you got kids?'

'Why does *that* matter?'

'Just wondering.'

'*You're* married,' I say. '*You* have kids.'

'Yeah…'

Chris's sigh doesn't make it sound as if he and Kirsty are living in a joyous world of married bliss. It's hard not to feel sorry for his two daughters. I would bet everything I own on the fact that, when someone asked my father about his home life, he'd give this same intake of air, followed by a large, lamenting breath.

'What's with the dent on the front of your car?' I ask.

He stands abruptly, almost tripping backwards over the wall in his haste. I continue sitting as he towers over me. The reminiscing of moments before has gone with a curt: 'What dent?'

'There's a big scratch on the bumper and a crack in the headlight.'

From nowhere, goosebumps appear on my arms. It's a warm day, but it doesn't feel it any longer. I continue watching him and can see it in Chris's face. He's like a child who's been caught opening Christmas presents early.

'Kirsty was trying to park and she hit a pillar.' He forces a laugh. 'How can you not see a post, right?'

'Fair enough.'

He pauses for a moment before stepping backwards. His shadow shifts so the sun falls across me once more, leaving me squinting into the light.

'I've got to go,' he says, jamming his hands into his pockets. 'I'll see you around.'

He heads along the car park towards the path back to the High Street. He turns to look over his shoulder at me but, when he realises I'm still watching, he quickly spins back and hurries away and out of sight.

I have a sip from my bottle and hold the liquid in my mouth, wondering how close I was to having this life for myself. Wondering how close I might still be.

TWELVE

There are three hours to kill before I'm supposed to meet Jo at her house. I should go back to Dad's – back to *my* house, but I can't face it and head to Wetherspoon's instead. It's everything I feared, with the sticky tables, old men, and vast range of microwaved food.

It's also perfect for now.

Time passes, though I'm not sure where it all goes. I sit on my own in a booth near the window and watch as the people of Elwood go about their business. I've lived in a big city for so long that I'm indoctrinated to expect a surge through the doors between five and six. People leaving work will pile inside for a quick pint, or some cheap food. There's none of that, of course. Elwood doesn't have a rush hour and there is no twenty-four-seven lifestyle here.

I get to Jo's house at five past seven. I like being that little bit late. If a person is early or on time, they're working at someone else's pace. Being late means control.

Jo's house is one of the places that was built when we were six or seven years old. When it went up, it was the first time I realised fields could be turned into homes. Before that, I think I'd believed that houses existed in a state of always being there. Jo's is on a small estate that backs onto our old primary school. I'd pictured the houses as brand new, but they're more than thirty years old now and it's starting to show. Weeds sprout from the bottom of the wall that rings Jo's place and her house is covered in the same sort of sooty dust that seems to be everywhere around town.

There's a cream car on the driveway, one of those nippy little things that mobile hairdressers buy. I have a brief look for any sort of marks on the bumper, though there's nothing obvious. I'm not sure why I checked.

I have to knock on the door three times before anyone answers. When it does swing inwards, it is Owen who's there. I only met Jo's eldest son when he came to find his mum at the bench last night – though he recognises me straight away.

'All right,' he mumbles, more a greeting than a question.

The noise hits me like a slap to the face as I get inside. There's music booming down the stairs that's blending with a television from the ground floor. There is clutter everywhere; jackets dumped on the floor next to shoes, as well as errant, dirty socks. A vacuum is leaning against the wall, next to an abandoned office chair.

'Through there,' Owen says, pointing down the hall as he heads for the stairs. I watch him disappear and then a door slams from above, which slightly muffles the music.

I move along the hall, into a kitchen, where Jo is arguing with a woman who's dressed in a smart skirt and suit top. The sound of the television pours through from the adjacent room and they're having to shout to be heard.

'I don't want you lot in my house,' Jo says, with a jab of the finger.

The woman is trapped in the corner, next to the back door, and glances towards me as I enter. Nobody else acknowledges my presence.

There's a man I presume to be Neil standing a little behind Jo, almost as if he's using her as a shield. He's utterly unremarkable, neither short nor tall; fat or thin; attractive or not. If I wasn't looking at him, I'm not sure I'd be able to describe him.

'I'm not a police officer as such,' the woman says. 'I'm a support officer. I'm here to help with anything that needs doing and also to pass along anything the police might need to communicate to you. Basically, I'm a link from you to them. If you've got any questions, I can try to get you an answer.'

'I'd like to know who was driving the car that hit my son.'

'I can assure you that we're trying our hardest to figure that out.'

Jo rolls her eyes. 'What's your name again?'

'Zoe.'

'Listen, "Zoe".' Jo makes bunny ears with her fingers, making it clear she doesn't know what the gesture means. 'I know you're young and I know you mean well, but your lot killed my dad. Do you know that?'

Zoe shifts her weight and glances towards me, as if I can offer any help. 'I'm not sure what to say to that,' she replies with admirable calm. 'I can't change anything that happened in the past, but what I can tell you is that I'm with you for the here and now.'

Jo's arms are folded, her mind made up. 'I'd like you to leave.'

'That's absolutely fine.' Zoe picks up her bag from the table. She's quite the trooper. 'I'll be back in contact if there's any news.'

Zoe takes herself along the hall and lets herself out. It's only as the door closes that I realise the cream car was probably hers.

With the door shut, Jo sinks onto the nearest seat. The table is covered with five stacked pizza boxes and a good half-dozen metal trays. She's still not acknowledging me, as if my witnessing all this was entirely planned.

'I can't handle all this, Neil,' she says, as she puts a hand to her head.

The man slips in behind her and starts giving a shoulder massage while staring at me. It's a good eight out of ten on the creepiness scale.

'Any news?' I ask, being careful to focus on Jo and not Neil.

She opens her mouth and then twists to Neil: 'Can you turn that down?'

He pauses for a moment and then heads past me. Moments later, the sound of the television goes silent and then he returns and starts massaging her shoulders once more.

'Ethan's still in intensive care,' Jo says wearily. 'They said I should come home and get some sleep. I asked if I could sleep in the same room as him, but they said they couldn't do it.'

'I'm sure he's in good hands,' I say.

Neil's fingers stop moving momentarily, but then he continues as if he hadn't stopped.

'I know,' Jo says.

I start to say something else, but Neil gets in there first. 'You should have something to eat,' he says.

Jo's face turns to a scowl as she flicks him away from her shoulders. 'I wouldn't be so tired if I didn't have to drive you everywhere.'

He slinks away, chastened and embarrassed as he shoots me a glance to wonder if I know what she's talking about.

'I need to sit down properly,' Jo says. She stands and beckons me into the living room.

She slumps into a reclining armchair and I'm left with one end of the sofa as Neil takes the other. There's a pile of unopened cards on the living room table, with a couple on the floor.

'For Ethan,' Jo says, answering the question to which I'd already guessed the answer. 'How are things with the funeral?' she asks, changing tack so quickly that, at first, I don't realise she's talking about my dad.

'It's sorted,' I say. 'It's going to be on Friday. Just a small thing. Not many people.'

It doesn't seem as if Jo has listened. She looks across to Neil and then nods at me. 'This is Abi,' she says, holding up her crossed fingers. 'We were like that at school. Best friends.'

I nod as if to confirm it.

'This is Neil,' she says, nodding to the other end of the sofa.

We turn to each other and he squeezes my hand too hard when we shake. The unrelenting eye contact is more unnerving, as if he's trying to read my thoughts.

'I'm going to the garage,' Neil says, talking to me, before turning to Jo. 'Is that okay?'

'You don't need my permission.'

'I just thought—'

'Yeah, well, don't.'

He nods meekly and then disappears out of the room. There's a clunk and the sound of a door closing. Jo waits for a moment, with the only noise coming from the muffled music above.

'He's always tinkering with his car,' Jo says. 'He's banned from driving, but that doesn't stop him messing around.'

I play along. 'Why's he banned?'

'Because he's a dickhead.' Jo spits the word and then rubs her head again. 'Speeding,' she adds, calmer this time. 'Stitch-up job. One of those mobile speed-camera things. All about getting money out of decent folks like you and me.'

'How fast was he going?'

'Forty in a thirty.'

'They banned him for that?'

I know it must only be part of the story. Nobody is banned for a one-time thing unless the speed is *really* excessive.

Jo turns away a little and, for a moment, I think I've asked too much. It's none of my business and hardly the point, considering her son is currently in intensive care. There's a large clunk from the other side of the house and it seems to spur Jo into answering.

'Him and that damned car,' she says. 'He'd been caught speeding twice before. I told him to slow down, but then he went and did it again.' She pauses, then adds, 'Still a stitch-up job, though. Worst thing is he's always home now.'

'Because he can't drive?'

She shakes her head. 'Lost his job at Hendo's before that.'

'Oh… I heard it might be closing…?'

'That's what they say. Got rid of a bunch of managers about four months ago. Neil was the first they let go.'

She says it in a way that makes it sound like I should read something into it. As if there was a reason he went first. It's not something I feel like I can follow up and we're interrupted by another clunk from the direction of the garage anyway.

Moments later, Neil reappears in the doorway. 'Did you do something with my car?' he asks, sounding annoyed.

'Like what? I've been at the hospital. Why would I do something to your car?'

'All the mirrors have been moved around.'

'You can't drive it anyway. What does it matter? I don't know why you spend so much time in there with it.'

Neil hovers in the doorway for a moment, staring at Jo. His fists are clenched and, for a moment, it feels like things are about to launch into a full-blown row. He's on his tiptoes and I wonder if it's my presence that makes him sink down once more. He nods slowly and then apparently decides he has nothing else to say. He spins and disappears back to the garage, leaving us alone.

Jo is scratching her knuckles again, and even from a distance I can see the red sores starting to form.

'How could someone drive off?' she says, more to herself than me. 'Wait till I get my hands on him. They should bring back hanging. I'd do it myself.'

I let her fume, though it's hard not to wonder whether it'd be more productive to focus on her son in the hospital than it is on vengeance. I suppose there is no normal in this. It's not like I have children to know an acceptable way of reacting. Even if I did, everyone is different. It does feel like a big assumption that it's a 'him', though. Perhaps hit-and-run drivers are statistically more likely to be men? I have no idea – but I doubt Jo does either.

'Can I get a drink?' I ask, holding up my near empty bottle.

'There's vodka in the cupboard,' Jo replies quickly, pointing towards a cabinet on the back wall.

'Just water.'

'There's a jug in the fridge… or there should be if Neil remembered to fill it up.'

She speaks with such spitting hostility that I wonder if this is always the nature of their relationship, or if what happened to Ethan has brought it on. Or if it's because Neil lost his job. Anyone would be under stress, but I don't know her well enough to have any certainty.

'Do you want anything?' I ask.

She eyes the cabinet with the vodka but shakes her head.

In the kitchen, I finish the contents of my bottle, rinse it in the sink, and then fill it with water from the fridge. There was a full jug, after all. I can still hear Jo muttering to herself from the other room, though can't make out the exact words.

I rest against the counter and enjoy the cool drink – which is when I notice the child through the window. He's in Jo's back garden, hovering close to the door. He can't be older than ten, wearing a hoody despite the summer weather, and is staring at his phone. When he looks up and sees me, he blinks, shrinks away in the way anyone would if they were caught somewhere they shouldn't, and then tucks himself in behind a wheelie bin.

I continue watching as he peeps around the corner. When he sees I haven't moved, he ducks away once more. He doesn't leave the garden, however.

I call out for Jo.

'You all right in there?' she asks.

'There's a kid in your back garden.'

There's a shuffling from the living room and then Jo hurries into the kitchen. She heads directly for the back door, using the key to unlock it and then standing on the precipice.

'Petey?'

The boy reappears from behind the bin and heads to the back door. Jo says something to him, but I don't catch it because she's lowered her voice. Because of the angle through the window, it's hard to see precisely what's happening – although I definitely see Jo reaching into the pocket of her trousers and then passing him something. It's only when he counts the notes that I realise it's money. He puts it into his hoody pocket and then passes her something back. She says something else to him and then he turns, risks one more glance towards me through the window, and heads for the back gate.

Jo waits out of sight in the alcove by the back door for a moment. It's only when Petey is through the gate that she re-emerges into the main area of the kitchen.

'Find the water all right?' she asks, with a forced breeziness.

I offer up my bottle to show that I found the fridge and Jo nods through to the living room. I take a couple of steps in that direction and then glance over my shoulder in time to spot her slipping something into the bread bin. It's hardly a covert military operation, but I don't think she realises I've seen her.

Back in the living room, we revert to our original seats. Jo obviously realises there are unanswered questions, so she pre-empts them. 'That was Petey,' she says. 'Ethan was on his way back from Petey's house when he got hit. They're friends.' She nods upwards. 'Petey's sister is Owen's girlfriend, Beth. Well, I assume they're going out. He's never said, but they're together all the time.'

It does help some of the pieces slot together. When I saw them by the bench last night, Owen said he'd been with Beth when Jo was trying to get hold of him after Ethan was hit. It still doesn't explain what Petey was doing at the back door, nor why Jo gave him money or what she snuck into her bread bin. It's none of my business, but I'm intrigued.

'I just want Ethan back home,' Jo says out of nothing. 'Where he belongs.'

'I'm sure everyone at the hospital is doing all they can.'

'I know…'

She glances towards the vodka cabinet again but says nothing.

'I'm glad you're back,' she says.

'I, um—'

'It'll be like the old days. Remember what we were all like? We practically ran this town.'

'We were only teenagers.'

'I know but… me and Holly haven't been talking that much recently…'

That's news to me considering I was with Holly earlier – and so was Jo. And because Holly said they were talking about me and the old days 'the other week'.

'What happened?' I ask.

'Things,' Jo replies cryptically as she stares into the distance. 'We were always best friends, though, weren't we? You and me. It wasn't the same with Hols.'

I suppose there's a degree of truth in that Jo and I were friends before we got to know Holly – but it's the childish way Jo says it that leaves me worrying. I've not thought about a 'best friend' since I left school.

There's no chance to follow it up because there's a momentary blast of music and then footsteps on the stairs. Owen soon appears in the doorway, focusing on his mum.

'Where'd the police officer go?' he asks.

'I sent her home.'

Owen opens his mouth but doesn't say anything, not at first. He nods along and then tries again. 'Can I visit Ethan with you in the morning?'

'They said not too many visitors.'

'That's why I'm asking. I want to go.'

'We'll see. I don't want him being crowded.'

Owen nods along glumly.

Holly said her son, Rob, would be off to university soon – and, though Owen must be around the same age, it doesn't feel as if he's anywhere near that point in his life. He seems the sort who could still be living here at thirty.

Owen glances to me but says nothing as he steps back into the hall. He's out of sight when Jo calls after him and he reappears in the doorway.

'Petey says Beth's not taking it well…?' Jo says.

It sounds like a question, though it is hard to know for sure.

Owen purses his lips, considering what's just been said. 'Where'd you see Petey?' he asks.

'Never you mind.'

There's a small moment of stand-off before Owen spins and heads out of the room, without answering his mother's question.

Jo waits until a door closes upstairs. 'Something's going on with him,' she says.

'Like what?'

A pause and then: 'Who knows? Something. I hope he's not got that girl pregnant. That's the last thing I need.'

THIRTEEN

I've decided to stop kidding myself that the house will ever be anything other than Dad's. It certainly doesn't feel like mine, regardless of what it might say on the deed. I wonder if I might have been happier if he'd left it to some charity, like those mad cat women who put their pets in their will. My life was hardly brimming with success away from here – and it isn't like I had to drop much to return – but I never had the sense of being trapped that I do now. I don't want the house, but it's some sort of home when it doesn't feel as if anywhere else will have me.

I press my forehead to the front door and whisper to myself that all I have to do is put the key into the lock. It's something I'd do day after day anywhere else, but, here, it feels like an effort. I tell myself I could get back on the bus and leave. I have some savings and don't desperately need to jump into a job, here or anywhere. Even as the thought appears, I know I won't disappear a second time. Not right now, in any case. Perhaps it's because I'm the one who found Ethan, but I suspect it's more than that. I'm invested and involved again in this place now. Elwood has a way of sinking its claws into the people who come from here, and it doesn't like to let go.

The key slips easily into the lock and I push open the door. I am only half a step inside when I'm frozen by the gentle undercurrent of Old Spice. It must have been there before, but I'd somehow not noticed. Dad washed with it every day of his life, even back in the period when it was a kitsch brand associated with old blokes.

I'm not sure how they managed to repackage it to still be around now, but they did. I can imagine him being delighted when he no longer had to go hunting through pound-shop shelves for end-of-line stock and could instead find it anywhere.

There's an air freshener on the windowsill and I empty a good quarter of the can into the hallway, backing into the kitchen as I do so. Once properly inside, I go for the liquor case at the back of the living room. I grab another bottle of the knock-off cheap vodka and then head upstairs.

The shower is another ordeal of not wanting to touch anything and somehow feeling unclean, even when I'm directly under the water. This whole room needs to be ripped out and replaced with literally anything that isn't this. A leaking pipe would be better than the current state of things.

I stop outside my father's bedroom door again and try to make myself go inside. It'll have to happen sooner or later – although 'later' definitely seems like a better option for the moment. For the 'sooner', that bottle of vodka has my name on it.

Despite the situation, there is something delightfully satisfying about drinking vodka straight from the bottle while sitting in my childhood bed, covered with my childhood Garfield bedding. I don't even bother getting undressed and, before I know it, I'm pressed into the corner giggling to myself.

I own a house outright!

My dad's funeral is in two days!

I'm back home after twenty years!

I've spent much of the day with my old best friends!

It's only when I remember Ethan in that ditch that I stop sniggering to myself.

I have another sip from the bottle as a pipe clangs overhead. When I was a girl, the noisy central heating would wake me up in the night. I was convinced there was a burglar in the attic and would lie awake for hours. Each time I almost fell back to sleep, there would be another clink and I'd end up staring at the ceiling, wondering what might be coming.

Imaginary burglars were the least of my worries, of course.

From nowhere, I start to yawn. One becomes two becomes ten. Yawns are like chocolate Hobnobs: one is never enough. I rest my head on the pillow and close my eyes, listening as the pipes continue to chime a melody that might usually be associated with a hyperactive kid who has a set of saucepans and a wooden spoon. Unlike in those years before, it's calming. Comforting company in a place where nothing and yet everything feels familiar.

When I next check my phone, it's a little after one in the morning. Two hours have passed in a blink. The pipes are silent, but when I close my eyes again, there's something there. A sort of… scratching.

I sit up and open my eyes properly. I've not closed the curtains and, though it's dark outside, the glow of the street lights from the back of the house is sending an orangey haze across the room. When I swing myself out of bed, my foot slips across the empty bottle that's lying on its side. It rolls under the bed and tinkles into something.

The scratching continues… but it might be more of a tapping. Perhaps someone knocking gently on the window next to the front door? There's a gap of a few seconds in between each noise. It's only as I slip into my shoes that it occurs to me it might not be someone *tapping* on the window, it might be someone trying to *open* a window.

I peep through the glass down to the garden below. I've not been out there since returning and it's more of a forest than a yard. The grass is up to around waist height and it's unclear where that ends and the line of hedges at the back begins. There's a path somewhere, but it would barely be visible, even if it wasn't for the murky mix of moon and street light.

The noise is back – definitely a mix of scratching and tapping. It's not coming from the pipes above, it's from below.

I suppose the obvious thing to do is turn on some lights and make a noise, but I'm not sure if I've ever been the obvious type. Instead, I creep onto the landing and start down the stairs. A cricket bat is leaning in the corner of the stairwell, a reminder that Dad did once used to play. Or so he said – he never did so when I was old enough to understand. All his glories were before I came along to ruin everything. I grab the bat and continue down to the ground floor, pausing in the hall and waiting until…

Scritch-scritch-scritch.

It's not coming from the front of the house.

I inch open the kitchen door and creep into the darkness. The blinds are drawn here, though I don't remember closing them. Dim light edges through the slats, leaving a lattice pattern across the tiled floor. The sink is still filled with dishes and, as best I can tell, everything else is as it was.

The door to the living room is open and I duck my head inside, looking from one end to the other, although there's nothing new to see. It's as I move back into the kitchen that something passes across the window. The light that's splayed across the floor is momentarily blacked out by whatever's on the other side of the window.

Scritch-scritch-scritch.

I can't figure out what the noise might be. It's definitely not someone knocking. I can't remember whether the window was closed and don't think I noticed in the first place anyway. The weather has been warm, so there's every chance it's been ajar since before the time I arrived. If it *is* a little open, it could be someone trying to lever it wider.

I move quickly across the floor, not bothering to be quiet now. The key is already in the back door, but I fumble by turning it the wrong way at first, before finally getting the door open. There's a small porch area, which is filled with a stack of buckets, two ladders, a rusted barbecue and all sorts of other clutter. By the time I get past all that, I know it's too late. There's a rustling from the far end of the garden, a flurry of movement among the shadows near the back gate and then a distant scrape of footsteps on crumbling tarmac.

The kitchen window *is* open a crack; though, when I try to pull it open with my fingers, it's locked in place. If someone *was* trying to get in, they would've had to make far more noise than they actually did.

It's only as I reclose the back door that I realise there was something vaguely familiar about the way the shape moved over the gate. The light was poor and I'm tired, but it was the knees-in gait that takes me back to my teenage years of walking to school with my then boyfriend, Chris.

FOURTEEN

It's almost sad to see how Hendo's has become a sorry imitation of itself. When I used to walk past it on my way to school every day, the factory was the thumping, vibrating heartbeat of the community. The three-storey red-brick building soared high above almost every other structure in the town and it was probably the easiest way for anyone to give directions. Before Google Maps, people would arrange to meet outside Hendo's at a set time. Taxi drivers would be told to take a left or right just after Hendo's and then the rest of the instructions would follow. There would be a near constant throng of workers hanging around the back gates, slightly off company property, where they were allowed to take their smoke breaks. It seemed normal then, and I'm sure 'different times' would be the excuse, but some of the men would always want to talk to the schoolgirls who passed. I was as guilty as anyone for stopping to chat and trying to bum cigarettes. It might be called grooming now – but that was how things had been for many years before me and my friends started doing it.

There is no sign of anyone at the back gates now – whether young girl, or old man. It might be a sign that smoking itself has gone out of fashion, but I suspect there's more to it than that. Instead of the thrum that used to be attached to the factory, whatever used to make that noise is silent. The building itself seems largely abandoned, with the car park barely a third full and no sign of anyone in the windows.

I continue walking along the path at the back of the factory and there are no cigarette butts mashed into the gutter, let alone the smell of stale tobacco that used to cling to the gatepost. It's probably better for everyone and yet I feel a surprising sense of melancholy, as if something's been taken from me. I walked this way every day for years and now, without my knowledge, it's changed. When this place closes for good, it will be like the town itself has shut down.

At the end of the path, as I get close to the High Street, there is a new generation of teenagers hanging around on the low wall next to the war memorial. There are five girls, perhaps thirteen or fourteen years old, sitting in a semicircle, all staring at their phones. I struggle to remember what we used to do when we would hang around here. I think it was just sitting around gossiping and joking. Did the generation before us sit here and do something else? In another twenty years, will it be people's virtual holograms in a group? People and trends might change – but places like this never seem to.

I head into the Lidl on the corner, trying to remember what it used to be. I can vaguely picture a building with a large candy-striped awning at the front but have no memory of what it housed. As for the Lidl, there's the usual mass of random items across the centre of the store, as if snorkelling or mountain climbing in Elwood is a regular thing. I buy a basket full of cleaning supplies and basic foodstuffs, add a bottle of their own-brand vodka for good measure, then pay with the cash I found at the house, and leave.

The bags are heavy, but I can't bring myself to go past Hendo's again, even if it is the shortest route back to the house. Instead, I take the path that goes closer to the park, although it isn't long before I have to stop at a bench and give my hands a rest from the way the bag handles are digging in.

It's perhaps a surprise that the newsagent that used to be on the corner is still here – in spirit, if nothing else. When I was a teenager, I would steal those copies of *NME* and *Melody Maker* from here. It was the place that stocked seemingly every magazine, plus the daily newspapers. Apart from cigarettes and chocolate, I don't think it sold anything else.

Even without going in, I can see through the door that it is now one of those local stores that sells a bit of everything. There is a pallet-load of orange squash bottles a little inside the door, with rows of Pot Noodles on the shelf behind.

There are newspaper bins outside, like the ones at petrol stations, and there's a handful of *Elwood Echo* copies remaining with today's date. I never read it when I was younger myself, but Dad did and my school was in there semi-regularly for the various events in which we were involved.

HIT-AND-RUN HUNT
Boy, 8, in intensive care

The front page keeps things straightforward with details of where and when the collision happened, plus a quote from Sergeant Davidson, asking for information about the possible driver. It mentions that the car could be 'black or grey'. I'd love to think someone else gave them this information, but what if this is entirely down to me? What if I'm wrong and people will now be looking for the wrong vehicle? It's not as if it was fun and games before, but my lack of clarity suddenly feels a lot more serious.

Ethan isn't named and I have to go through the article twice to realise that, except for Sergeant Davidson, nobody is identified. Ethan is called either an 'eight-year-old' or 'the victim'.

I put the paper back on the rack and turn to my shopping bags on the ground. I'm about to leave when I have another thought and pick up the paper once more. It's hard to find anything among the pages due to the sheer number of adverts. Entire pages are devoted to pictures of cars and sofas and it's easy to see why publications are going out of business if this is the best they have to offer. I'm near the back when I finally find the announcements section underneath a pair of crosswords. Damien said it might not make it, but, at the bottom, surrounded by a neat box, are the words that somehow make it more real.

NOTICE OF FUNERAL

DENNIS JOHN MICHAEL COYLE passed away on 10 July at his home in Elwood. He was 66 years old and is survived by his daughter, Abigail. Funeral services will be held at Elwood Funeral Services on Friday at 4 p.m. Donations are not expected.

I read the notice three times and then find myself counting the content.

In the end, my father finished as forty-one words at the bottom of a page, underneath a crossword. A tenth of those is simply listing his name. Another tenth is telling anyone interested in going that they shouldn't give any money. He's across from another page, on which a company is selling discount flooring.

I'm not sure what to make of it. I guess we're all reduced to something similar in the end, but, with my father, it couldn't even list any achievements. What would it say?

I put the paper back a second time, then pick up the shopping bags, and continue on towards the house.

I'm at the edge of the park, close to the bus stop where all this started, when I spot the boy standing on the street corner with an older girl. From the way she's arched over him, it looks like she's telling him off, but I don't catch the actual words and, by the time I get to them, she's stopped.

The boy's eyes widen as he recognises me, but I'd already clocked him as Petey, the lad who knocked on Jo's back door. I put down the bags and rub my fingers into my palms, trying to get a bit of life back into them. Petey looks younger up close, definitely no older than ten and probably younger. That would fit in with Ethan only being eight.

'You're Petey, right?' I say to him.

He doesn't reply – but the girl who's with him takes a small but noticeable step to stand in front of him.

'And you're Beth…?' I add.

She frowns, but the way she scrunches up her face doesn't change the fact that she's blonde-haired, brown-eyed and small-town pretty. It's somewhat harsh, but, though she would be anonymous in a city, Beth could unquestionably have her pick of the boys in a place like Elwood.

Jo implied that Owen might have got her pregnant but, if that is the case, it certainly doesn't show. Beth is seventeen or eighteen and has a skinniness that, in my case at least, ebbed away through my twenties and was a long-distant memory by the time thirty rolled around.

'Who are you?' she asks, although there's more in the way of intrigue than there is hostility.

'I'm Abi—' I say, though don't get a chance to expand because Beth cuts in.

'Jo's friend,' she says.

'Right. I used to live here but moved away.'

'You found Ethan.'

'Yes.'

Independently of one another, we each glance down the road towards the blanketed tribute on the verge. Her identity was something of a guess, although Jo told me that Petey's older sister was named Beth. I'm not sure how she knows me, however.

Petey steps out a little, eyeing me around his sister, although he doesn't say anything.

'Have you heard anything?' Beth asks.

'About what?'

'Ethan.'

'Only that he's still in intensive care as of last night. Nothing this morning.'

Beth half-turns to her younger brother. 'Can't believe he was on the way back from ours. I babysit the pair of them sometimes.'

'I'm not a baby!'

Petey sounds indignant at the very idea, though I can tell from the hint of a grin on Beth's face that she used the word on purpose to wind him up.

'Were you looking after them on Tuesday?' I ask.

'God knows what they were doing upstairs, but I suppose so. Mum was still at work, so I was going to do them fish fingers for tea.'

'Ethan doesn't like fish.'

We both look down at Petey, who, unlike the boy in Jo's back garden last night, suddenly seems his age.

'You could've said,' Beth replies.

Petey shrugs it off as Beth grimaces.

'Anyway, Ethan said he was going home and then…' She takes a breath. 'I keep thinking I should've stopped him. If I'd said "wait a minute" or something like that, then the timings would've all been different.'

She glances to Petey and then along the street towards the tributes on the verge once more. There's not much else to say and I'm not sure why I started the conversation anyway. Beth checks her phone and then turns away. It feels like the end of the conversation and she even manages a 'See y'around' as I pick up my shopping bags, ready for the final part of the journey home. That's when I surprise myself.

'Was Owen there?' I ask.

Beth turns back to me: 'Where?'

'At your house when you were looking after the two boys.'

She blinks. It's none of my business, but she answers anyway. 'Owen...? I've not seen him since the weekend.' She pauses and then quickly adds: 'Why?'

'No reason,' I say, unable to come up with something better.

She stares at me for a moment, wondering what she's missed.

I need to say something and manage: 'I was round Jo's house last night and he was talking about you.'

'Was he?'

Petey starts shuffling restlessly, in the way children do.

'I can't remember what he was saying. Nothing bad. I think that he was with you at the weekend, or something. He was talking to Jo.'

Beth shrugs. 'He's got his driving test next week. Can you believe that? He was saying he didn't feel ready and now this happens to his brother. I dunno if he'll go through with it.'

Petey continues fidgeting and Beth spins back to him. 'Will you stand still?' she scolds.

'I'm bored.'

She sighs. 'Fine! We'll head back.'

'I can go by myself.'

'Not now, you can't. You know what Mum said.'

Petey stomps his feet as Beth offers a conciliatory shrug in my direction. 'See ya,' she says.

Petey continues to protest while they head off side by side in the opposite direction to Ethan's tribute.

I watch them for a moment and then continue on towards the house, though the bags feel heavier than before. I stop once more on the bench next to the flowers and footballs. It was here that I first met Owen two nights ago, when he'd come to find his mum. It was here that he said he was with Beth when his mum couldn't get hold of him after Ethan had been hit.

Which means at least one person in this town is lying.

FIFTEEN

When I get to Jo's place a little after midday, there's a man in shorts, T-shirt and a baseball cap carrying cables from a grey van into the house through the wide-open front door. I wait at the entranceway, tapping on the door frame, though nobody answers.

'Hello…?'

My voice echoes along the hall, but there's still no reply, so I edge into the hallway. That's when the man in the cap emerges from the kitchen without the cables he had been holding. He passes me with barely a glance and heads back outside towards his van.

There are voices coming from the living room, so I ease my way inside, saying Jo's name. She's on the sofa when I get in, turned to face another woman who I sort of recognise, although I'm not sure from where. The room has changed completely since I was here yesterday. There's a TV camera on a tripod set up in front of the windows, with the curtains drawn and bright white light spilling from a bulb off to the side. A whitish inverted umbrella is behind the light, reflecting it back into the room.

Neil and Owen are hovering awkwardly in the corner and, aside from brief glances, neither of them acknowledge me.

'…is that clear?' the second woman says.

Her hair is lacquered into a bob that I'm fairly sure wouldn't move in a typhoon. She has teeth so white they could star in their own toothpaste commercial, plus manicured bright red nails that are drumming a steady beat on a yellow US-style legal pad.

Jo looks past the woman towards me. 'This is Abi,' she says. 'One of my best friends.'

The woman turns to take me in. 'Lovely to meet you,' she says, not moving from her spot and then immediately twisting back to Jo.

'I'm going to be on telly,' Jo adds, still talking to me. 'This is Diane Young. Have you seen her show?'

I suppose this is why I recognise Diane without specifically knowing her. I don't think I've seen her show – or even know what it is – but these things tend to sink in through osmosis.

Diane forces a smile in my direction.

'I've seen the show,' I say, though I'd be as certain as can be that Diane sees right through me. She doesn't seem the sort to tolerate arse-lickers or yes-men.

'Great,' she says, although her tone has an incredible way of making it clear she couldn't care less *and* knows that I'm lying.

'Can she stay?' Jo asks.

I don't get a chance to say I only came over to see if there were any updates on Ethan because Diane snips a reluctant 'fine'. She turns to me and nods to an uncomfortable-looking dining chair that's been jammed into the corner. 'You can sit there.'

It's hard to know why I go along with this, other than that Jo's son is in hospital and it's hard to say no to anything she asks. There's also the not small matter that, when Diane says something, it very much feels like that thing should be done immediately.

With me dealt with, Diane turns back to Jo. 'I won't ask anything with which you might be unhappy,' she says. 'I just want to ask you about Ethan and the type of boy he is.'

Jo's nodding along, but there's something off about her eyes. She's staring intently, although, at the same time, doesn't seem focused on anything in particular. She has every reason to be nervous or edgy, of course. Not only as she's seemingly going on television but also because of what's happening with Ethan. It's a lot for anyone to go through in such a short period.

As I watch, I find myself wondering how this all came about, considering Jo was so insistent she wouldn't work with the police in appealing to the driver to come forward.

'Is that all right?' Diane adds.

Jo nods quickly. 'Yes, yes.'

Diane is too smart not to see Jo's jitters – and she takes Jo's hand in hers. 'You're going to do brilliantly,' she says. 'When Ethan's recovered, you'll be able to show him the time you were on TV and he'll be so proud.'

Jo gulps away a sob that's appeared from nowhere and half turns away. 'You reckon?'

'I know it, Jo. I just need you to keep being strong for the next hour or so. Okay?'

'Okay.'

Diane pushes herself up from the sofa and turns to Neil and Owen in the corner. She's shorter than both of them and yet somehow seems taller. When she addresses Owen, the teenager stands up straighter.

'I need you to talk about Ethan as a brother,' she says. 'Perhaps tell a story about something you've done together? Maybe a time when he helped you with something – or you helped him.'

She's barely finished the sentence when Owen starts nodding. If Diane was after world domination instead of daytime television ratings, she'd be dangerous.

'And Neil,' she continues, 'you love Ethan like a son, obviously. If you could perhaps come up with a time you bonded over—'

'Football,' Neil blurts out.

'Football it is,' Diane confirms, unflustered. 'The pair of you will do terrifically. Now, where's Nathan…?'

Diane heads back into the hallway and returns moments later with the guy who was ferrying cables inside. A second man appears and the pair continue setting up the equipment as Diane takes her place in the armchair. The trio of Jo, Neil and Owen are somewhat squashed on the sofa, although Diane manages to make them relax by explaining how everything is to be recorded for tomorrow's show. She then tells a story about how a celebrity even I've heard of locked himself in their studio toilets and fell into the bowl while trying to escape the cubicle. In anyone else's hands, especially considering the circumstances, it could be offensive. In Diane's, she somehow has all three members of the family laughing at the same time.

As they're coming off the back of that, Diane switches gears in a blink, turns to the cameraman, gets a countdown – and then she's off.

It's hard to take my eyes from her as she's such a force of nature. Whatever she said seems to work because Jo is perfect. She doesn't stutter or repeat herself and is calm and measured when talking about the difficulties she had when pregnant with Ethan. She says she was in hospital for thirteen days after complications with the birth. Ethan's *actual* father isn't mentioned, but she talks about her son's love of football and enthusiasm for life in general.

It's only as she continues talking that I begin to wonder whether Jo is enjoying the limelight a little *too* much. At one point, she answers on behalf of Owen – and, in the space of a few minutes, she comes out with more than I've heard her say in two days. As soon as the thought arrives, I push it away. The entire point is that Jo's *supposed* to be talking about Ethan.

After Owen and Neil have had their say, Diane turns to a camera and records a segment she calls 'Diane's thought for the day'. I thought Jo might end up appealing for the driver to come forward, but, instead, Diane does it. There's no rage, or hint at vengeance. She's calm, firm and, if I'm honest, scary as hell.

'I'm talking to you now,' she says. 'The you that was driving that car. I know you're scared and that this was a horrible, horrible mistake. Nobody sets out to do the thing you did. There are many victims in what happened on Tuesday. Three of them are sitting with me today; another – poor Ethan Coyle – is lying in hospital. But there is someone else in all this. You'll have spent a lot of time by yourself in the hours that have passed, hearing the sound it made when your car hit Ethan. You'll be replaying the images over and over in your mind. That will never, *ever* leave you – but what you *can* do is set things straight. You can put your hand up, admit you were driving, and get yourself on the route to getting through this. For Ethan's sake, and your own, it's time to do the right thing.'

It's mesmerising and so sincere that I'm almost out of my seat ready to admit I was driving, even though I wasn't.

Diane pauses for a second, holding the earnest pose and then nods to Jo. She thanks her for her time, and then turns to the man who was bringing in cables and says 'I think we're done.'

As he starts unplugging things, Diane twists back to Jo.

'You were wonderful,' she says. 'Perfect, in fact. Ethan will be so proud when he sees it.'

Jo nods along but doesn't answer.

It's while everyone's finishing off that I realise I can get a few seconds to myself. I push up from the chair and head through the hall into the kitchen on the spur of the moment. I have a quick look over my shoulder, only to see that I haven't been followed. With nobody around, I open the bread bin, where I find…

Bread.

It's nothing special, a supermarket own-brand medium-slicer. I take it out and check behind, but there are only crumbs. Whatever Jo sneaked into her kitchen yesterday has gone.

I return the loaf to where it was and then head into the hall. The two men are carrying equipment back outside, while voices continue to come from the living room. Diane calls something, or somebody, 'wonderful', but I don't catch anything else.

I'm about to go back in the living room when it's like I'm hit with a memory from the past. When we were all teenagers, Holly was once caught hiding booze under her bed. She was grounded for a week and, perhaps worse, her parents confiscated it. After that, we came up with a hiding place that would definitely be present in all our houses and which, through the rest of our times together, was never discovered.

There are still voices coming from the living room, so I creep upstairs and try each door until I find the bathroom. It's nowhere near as dirty as in Dad's house, but the bath and sink are both stained with browny-grey watermarks close to the rim. I ignore them and move to the toilet, feeling around the back of the cistern and then lifting off the lid. It's far heavier than I thought and I almost drop it as I turn and lower it onto the wet towel that's been left on the floor next to the bath.

There's almost relief that, as much as things have changed, with this, they're still the same.

That's all the relief there is, however.

It's not booze that Jo's hidden in the cistern; it's a small, sealed Tupperware tub of orange pills. I pull out the tub and pat it dry on a towel that's hanging from the shower rail. The tablets inside are small and round, with no identifying marks. I slide them around, though they're all the same and there are around twenty in total.

I take out my phone to take a photo, wondering if I'll be able to identify them from that alone. That's when there's a creak from outside and the handle on the bathroom door starts to turn.

SIXTEEN

I freeze, the tub of pills in my hand and the lid to the toilet cistern still on the floor. The handle turns and then the door sticks in place. In my haste to get inside, I thought I'd left it unlocked – but I suppose some habits are more automatic and ingrained than others.

'Anyone in there?'

It's Jo's voice, slightly muffled through the door.

'I am,' I say. 'It's Abi. I need a minute.'

'Okay.'

I push the lid back onto the tub, making sure it's sealed, and then drop it into the cistern. I set the toilet flushing to mask the grunts of effort I need to pick the lid back up and get it into place. When that's done, I wash my hands – habit again – and then unlock the door.

Jo is waiting on the landing, leaning against the wall and thumbing her phone. She looks up and smiles weakly.

'How was it?' she asks.

'The toilet?'

She smiles: 'Downstairs – with Diane.'

'It was perfect,' I say. 'She's amazing. You were great, too.'

Jo nods along, but she's distant, not quite here. Hard to blame her for that.

'How is Ethan?' I ask. 'I was going to say something before, but it didn't seem the right time.'

'Nothing's changed. I was there this morning and am going back in a bit.'

She's been staring through me to such a degree that I turn and check the wall behind. There's nothing there.

'They called me this morning,' she says.

'Who?'

'Diane's people. I think one of them had read an article online about what happened to Ethan. It's in the paper today.'

'I saw it.'

'They asked if they could come around and film something.'

'I thought you didn't want that…?'

A shake of the head. 'Not the police. It's nothing to do with them. It's all Diane. I said yes and they were here two hours later.'

She steps around me, heading towards the bathroom. I almost stop her and ask about the pills. There was probably a time when she would've told me what they were and, even now, that might still be the case. The truth is that what she told Diane isn't true. I'm not one of her best friends. I was at one time, but now we're strangers who have somehow fallen back into one another's lives.

'Can I ask you something?' Jo says.

'Of course.'

'Will you come to the hospital with me later?'

I try to think of a reason I could say I can't, but there's no way I can do that if I'm going to spend any amount of time in this town.

'Of course,' I say again.

'You're such a good friend.'

Jo gives another watery smile and then heads into the bathroom, where the lock clicks closed.

I wait for a moment, listening for the sound of the cistern lid and wondering if she's actually come upstairs to take whatever's in that Tupperware tub. Did it really come from Petey? Is that eight-year-old kid I saw fidgeting next to his older sister some sort of drug dealer? If so, does that mean anything in regards to what happened to Ethan?

When the taps start running, I figure I'm wasting my time – and sticking my nose into somewhere it's likely not wanted – so I go downstairs.

In what I thought was the short amount of time I was away from the living room, the cleaning fairies have been in and got rid of all the scattered TV equipment. Everything is seemingly back to how it was, there's no sign of Diane, and, aside from the original man carrying a large plastic case outside, it's as if none of the filming ever happened.

Neil is slouched on the sofa using his phone, so I head back into the hall, where Owen is saying goodbye to Diane's assistant. He closes the front door and then jumps as he finds me a little behind him.

'Sorry,' I say.

'I didn't hear you.'

He angles towards the stairs but has to go around me and I don't move.

'I heard you've got your driving test next week…?' I say.

'Who told you that?'

'Probably your mum? I don't remember. How have the lessons been going?'

Owen folds his arms across his front and backs away a little, avoiding eye contact. 'Okay…'

'Is this your first attempt?'

'Yeah.'

He shuffles half a step closer to the stairs and I give him some room. 'I could never get to grips with my instructor's car and ended up taking my test in a friend's. What about you?'

'Um…' Owen looks around, probably hoping someone might interrupt and give him a get-out. 'Instructor's car,' he adds.

'I passed second time around, but the examiner had it in for me the first time. Made me reverse around a corner three times and do two emergency stops. He said I had too many minors. I found it's all in the mind. You know what you're doing when it comes to driving, it's just about showing someone you can do it. If you can try to think of the examiner as just another passenger, then it will probably help you relax more.'

Owen nods along, being the teenager he is. Not wanting to engage.

'When's your final lesson?' I ask.

'Tuesday.'

'I'm sure you'll do fine.'

Owen gasps with relief as there's a bump from the stairs and Jo starts to descend. He mumbles a swift 'bye' and then disappears around me and up past his mum, disappearing through the first door at the top.

Jo watches him go and then turns back to me. Her hair's wet and there's a few droplets of water clinging to her eyebrows. 'I need a brew,' she says, leading me into the kitchen and flicking on the kettle. 'What were you talking about?' she asks, nodding upstairs.

'Driving lessons. It's some bad timing that his test's next week.'

'Is it?' Jo frowns. 'I'd forgotten. He keeps to himself so much. I hardly ever know what's going on with him. If he's not in his room, he's with Beth.'

I let it settle, wondering if she's going to say something, and then dive in. I'm seemingly on a roll with getting people to answer my questions. 'What happened with you and Owen's dad…?'

There's a long, breathy pause as the kettle bubbles and then clicks itself off. Jo dumps a teabag into a mug, slops in some milk, pours on the water, and then goes to town with a teaspoon. Heresy. I figure she isn't going to answer, but then she does.

'Do you remember Mark?'

'Of course. You were seeing him while I was with Chris. Holly was annoyed because she was the only single one of us.'

Jo's misty-eyed slow nod makes it feel like we're travelling back in time together. 'I think we got together too young,' she says slowly.

'By the time we had Owen, we'd already been together for…' she stops to count on her fingers, 'seven years? Maybe eight? We were still only twenty-three, but I felt so much older. Neither of us could afford our own place and we were paying the rent together on a flat, so we were a bit stuck. Then my gran died and left me a bit of money. I could suddenly afford a place for myself and was thinking about ending it. That's when I got pregnant with Ethan.'

She sighs again.

'Is he…?'

Jo nods. 'Mark is Ethan's dad. Owen's too. We'd been together for sixteen, seventeen years by the time I was pregnant with Ethan. We'd been married for about ten. Owen was a bit of a handful when he was that age. I was just so… *tired*.'

'You broke up with Mark when Ethan was born…?'

'About a year after.' Jo has a sip of her tea and glances through towards the hall, making sure it's clear. 'He hit me…'

She catches my eye and holds it. She knows what she's saying and to whom she's saying it.

'He wasn't drunk, or anything,' she adds calmly. 'Just angry. There was this look in his eye that I'd never seen before. His football team had lost and he'd had some sort of disciplinary thing at work. His mum was ill—'

'That's not an excuse.'

'I know. I was looking to get away anyway and I guess that was the final thing. He said sorry and all that. I had Holly over when I told him he had to move out. I thought there might be trouble, but he just accepted it. Packed his stuff that night and that was it. I suppose—' She stops because there's a knock at the front door. There's a pause and then: 'Can you get that?'

I get to my feet and have a quick peep into the living room as I pass, though there's no sign of Neil. When I open the door, I'm met by Petey, who is clinging onto his bike. He goggles at me and then looks sideways at the house, probably wondering if he's somehow got the wrong place.

'Ethan's mum in?'

He speaks with an assured confidence that eight-year-olds don't usually possess. There's certainly no nervousness about talking to an adult. I turn and call for Jo, only now wondering why she wanted me to answer the door. It was always likely to be for her.

Jo hustles along the corridor and stops on the welcome mat, turning between Petey and me. 'Why are you at the front?' she asks.

'Mum sent me,' Petey says. 'She said the police have found the car.'

SEVENTEEN

At times over the past couple of days, it's felt like events are already set and that I've had little control over my own choices. It's almost as if the past two decades haven't happened, that Elwood itself does this to people. I hadn't set out to end up in a car with Jo and yet, somehow, here we are.

Considering what happened to her son, there is some irony in the appalling state of Jo's driving. My fingers clasp the sides of the passenger seat as I hold on tightly and hope she doesn't get us killed. I'm not brave enough to say anything, mind – and neither is Neil in the back seat. Nobody is talking and the only good thing I can say about Jo's driving is that she does at least appear to be watching the road. That doesn't change the fact that she's barrelling along narrow country lanes at twenty over the speed limit and barely slowing down for the hedge-banked corners.

I realise I'm holding my breath as she crosses the faded central line for the fourth or fifth time, before she swerves back onto the proper side of the road. We surge past a rusting sign for a quarry that's covered with graffiti tags and then swing onto a gravelled track. The car jolts up and down, creating a cloud of dust around us that makes it impossible to see through the side windows. Jo seems to know where she's going as she takes a sharp left, continues through a wide gate that's been left open, and rolls to a stop in front of a Portakabin that's stained grey with dust and clamped closed with a series of chunky padlocks.

Jo gets out of the car first and I trail behind as she stands at the front of the car, close to a wire fence. There is a vast quarry ahead that stretches from the edge of the car park far into the distance before being swallowed by green swathes of forest. There are three police cars on the other side of the fence, having presumably used some sort of service road to get closer to the quarry. Towering to the side of them is a large crane that's anchored to the ground with a pair of thick metal supports. The arm is angled over the crater, with the heavy chain stretched out of sight below. There is no other machinery; no sign anyone has worked here in a long time.

It's only as we watch that I realise I've been here before. The memories are fuzzy, like looking through the window on a misty morning. There was music and sunshine; booze, because that's what we did – and then boys jumping off the quarry cliffs into the water below.

It feels like Jo can read my mind as we stand side by side. 'We never jumped,' she says. 'Holly did, but we didn't. It was so high.'

There's a booming metallic groan from the crane and, for a second or two, it feels as if the whole thing could topple sideways into the canyon. It doesn't though. There's a screech and then the winch begins to crank the chain upwards.

Jo doesn't wait as she pushes through a gap in the fence that I'd not noticed. It's not an official door and instead appears to have been snipped apart by someone with bolt cutters.

A uniformed police officer steps out from behind a car, but his outstretched arms do little to prevent Jo stepping around him. The winch has stopped moving now and Jo shouts 'Is that the car?' across his instructions for her to turn around.

I wait a few steps further back and Neil joins me, keeping his arms folded as neither of us say anything.

As she gets no response with which she's happy, Jo shouts louder until a man who was previously hidden by the crane strides around the vehicles towards me. Sergeant Davidson is in a suit, but his shoes and the bottom of his trousers are caked with dust. He's focused on Jo but glances across to Neil and myself on the other side of the fence without acknowledgement. As he gets closer, he offers a small smile and asks Jo how she is.

'Is that the car?' Jo demands once more, nodding towards the main crater, where there isn't even a car in view.

Davidson's gaze darts to Neil and myself once more before he focuses back on Jo. 'Can we have a word in private?' he asks.

'Anything you've got to say, you can say in front of them.'

Davidson is unflustered, though he pauses for a moment, perhaps choosing his words. He doesn't send us away and, as Neil edges through the fence, I follow his lead until the four of us are huddled in a circle. The uniformed officer has disappeared. Davidson opens his mouth but, at that moment, the whine of the crane begins once more. We stop and watch as the cranking mechanism grinds and then a car appears over the precipice of the gully. It would have originally been a dark hatchback, but it's now caked with sand and dust. The windscreen has a large splintering crack in the centre and it doesn't look like there's any glass in the rear window. There isn't a number plate on the back and all four tyres are flat. The crane slowly swings the car around until depositing it with a thump onto a patch of land that's obscured by the main cabin of the crane itself.

'Whose car is it?' Jo asks, trying to peer around Davidson towards the car. 'I want to know who hit my son.'

'There's no specific reason to believe this vehicle belongs to whoever hit your son,' Davidson replies calmly.

'Then why are you here?'

'We received a report overnight that there was a car in the quarry. That's why we're here.'

'But why are *you* here?'

'Because we're not ruling anything out, or in, Mrs Ashworth. We're determined to find whoever it was that was driving the car that hit your son. That means following up any leads – including this one.'

Jo opens her mouth, but then closes it again.

It's Neil who speaks next, seemingly to the surprise of everyone, including me. He's not said anything since Jo specifically told me to 'sit in the front' when we were leaving her house. 'Don't you recognise the car…?' Neil says.

He's watching Jo, but it's Davidson who reacts, turning towards the crane and the hidden vehicle beyond.

'What are you saying?' Davidson asks.

'I know whose car it is.'

Jo stares open-mouthed at him, while Davidson has the fixed frown of a man who doesn't like to be a step behind.

'It's that guy who lives down the road from Holly,' Neil says. 'He's always revving and racing up and down the street. Stephen-something. I don't know his last name. Didn't Holly complain about him to the police once? He almost hit Petey about a year ago…?'

Nobody speaks as Neil turns between us as if everyone else is somehow stupid for not seeing what he does.

'It's got that thin red racing stripe,' he adds. 'Don't you remember?'

I watch Jo's face as it creases into one of furious recollection. Hell yes, she remembers. She turns and starts off towards the fence.

Davidson is a little slow off the mark, calling 'Mrs Ashworth' after her but being ignored. I tuck in next to Neil as we hurry after Jo, catching her only as she gets to the driver's side of her car.

'Where are we going?' Neil asks.

Jo doesn't reply. She gets into the car and thumps the door closed. As the engine starts, Neil and I bundle in just in time before she slams it into reverse.

'Jo?' Neil tries again.

The car spins in a half circle and then Jo smacks the gearstick into first and, almost instantly, second as we heave away with a spray of gravel.

'Where do you *think* we're going?' she spits.

Neil doesn't respond, but the pair of us both turn in unison, watching through the back window towards Sergeant Davidson. He's standing with his hands on his hips, betraying a barely concealed frustration.

EIGHTEEN

Jo is driving even faster back to Elwood than she did on the way to the quarry. She slaloms across lanes and I only allow myself to breathe once we're back on the correct side. For someone railing against dangerous driving, this is perhaps the worst example.

As we pass the 'Welcome to Elwood, Please Drive Carefully' sign, she does finally ease off the accelerator. I release my desperate grip on the seat and check the back window, half expecting us to be trailed by a police car, though the road is clear.

Jo passes the bus stop and takes the turn onto the street on which Ethan was hit. I keep thinking of the flowers and footballs as a memorial, even though he hasn't died. I wondered if it was there because people thought he *had* died – but it's been growing steadily since Tuesday night. I'm not sure I understand it.

As Jo slows further, we see a woman clambering out of a car with a red and white football scarf in hand. She ties it around the lamp post next to the others, and then pauses for a moment to take in the rest of what's been left.

Jo stops the car, too, taking it out of gear and idling in the middle of the road on the spot that must be almost exactly where I saw the vehicle stop after hitting Ethan. Jo strains against her seat belt, looking sideways through the window towards the tributes for her son. As well as what was there previously, a giant soft bear has appeared, decked out in more red and white.

In the park beyond, a group of people are in the process of setting up a large marquee somewhere near to the scorch marks from the impromptu bonfire. I wonder what's going on, but then remember the poster I saw for Saturday's Elwood Summer Fete. It's two days away and it feels strange that life will be continuing as normal at a time when it feels anything but.

Jo starts the car again and eases away, heading past Dad's house and continuing on to the newer, more expensive part of town. I recognise the turn onto the road on which Holly lives, but Jo pulls in before then.

'Which house?' she asks, twisting against the seat belt to look at Neil in the back seat.

'I'm not sure if this is a good idea,' he replies – the first thing he's said since we left the quarry.

'I didn't ask if you thought it was a good idea,' Jo says, barely concealing a fury that's been bubbling. 'Which house?'

'I don't know.'

Jo stares back, as if daring him to admit it's a lie. When he doesn't, she gets out of the car, slams the door and then starts off along the street at a sprinter's pace. The only reason I catch up with her is because Holly takes her time in answering the front door.

When Holly appears, she's barefooted in lounge pants and a vest. She looks between Jo and me, bemused by our presence.

'What's—' she starts, but Jo talks over her.

'Where does Stephen live?' she demands.

'Who?'

'The guy who almost ran over Petey last year.'

Holly quickly glances to me, but there's little I can add. 'Number seven,' she says.

Jo doesn't wait for any more information, spinning and setting off on a charge back the way we came, to where Neil is leaning against the car. She storms past him, leaving Neil, Holly and myself all trailing as Jo homes in on the front door of number seven and then thumps it with her fist.

There's a nervy moment as we catch up with her and the four of us wait on the doorstep. I find myself looking along the street, hoping Sergeant Davidson or someone else from the police will be arriving to stop whatever's about to happen. If not that, then it would be great if number seven is empty. Nothing good is going to happen here.

A bang comes from inside the house and, just as Jo is about to knock a second time, the door swings open to reveal a bemused-looking young woman who turns between us.

'Hello...?' she says.

'Where's Stephen?' Jo demands.

The woman takes a step inside, slightly closing the door as she turns backwards. 'It's for you!'

The door closes until it's a crack. Jo angles forward and, for a moment, I think she's about to kick the door open and barge inside. Holly tenses next to me and she must feel it, too.

The man who appears in the door is not what I'd expected. I'd been thinking a young boy racer; the sort whose awful dance music booms through a neighbourhood every time he turns the ignition in his souped-up dickheadmobile. I thought the woman who answered the door would be a girlfriend, but it's far more likely to be Stephen's daughter. He has grey hair and is something of a silver fox with brooding dark eyes.

'Can I help you?' he asks politely.

'I should've known it was you,' Jo says.

'What was me?'

She points a finger towards his chest. 'What kind of man runs over a child and drives off?'

Stephen purses his lips. He squints, blinks and then puffs out his cheeks. 'I am so sorry to hear what happened to your son,' he says, with a measured calm. 'But you have the wrong person.'

Jo continues as if he hasn't replied. 'Oh, I know your sort. Nothing's ever your fault, is it? Did you enjoy the sound it made when he bounced off the car? Or when—'

'My car was stolen last week.'

Stephen motions to the empty road in front of the house, where a vehicle might usually be parked.

Jo turns to the spot and then quickly spins back to Stephen. 'Isn't that convenient?' she continues.

'Not particularly,' Stephen replies. 'I've been relying on my daughter to take me to work. Someone had parked outside my house, so I had to leave mine by the old post office. I went the next morning and it was gone. I reported the car stolen a week ago. You can check with the police or anyone else you want.'

He's unruffled and I have no question he's telling the truth.

'You're lying,' Jo says, although, for the first time, she sounds unsure of herself.

'I'm not. I hope you find out what happened to your son – but it's nothing to do with me.'

Jo starts to say something else, but Neil grips her shoulder and gently tugs her backwards. 'Let's go home,' he says, coolly. 'We've got to go to the hospital in a bit anyway.'

'I just—'

'It's not him,' Neil adds, although there doesn't seem to be much contrition that it was his declaration that set us off on a rush back here.

He guides Jo slowly away from the doorstep and she edges between Holly and me, heading for the car.

'They found your car,' Neil says, turning backwards to talk over his shoulder. 'The police have just dragged it out of the quarry.'

For the first time since he came to the door, Stephen seems surprised. 'Oh,' he says, his long eyelashes fluttering. 'Nobody's said anything.'

'It only happened half an hour ago.'

Stephen checks his watch and starts to nod. 'Right…'

He waits in the door as Holly and myself turn and trail Neil and Jo along the street. I still can't picture Stephen as a boy racer, but I suppose it takes all sorts.

We all stop again at the car, with Jo leaning against the passenger side door and massaging her temples.

'I just want my boy back,' she says quietly.

Nobody seems to know how to reply, but she already has the door open, before turning to Neil, who is at the driver's side. They lock eyes and then Neil angles his head almost imperceptibly towards me. If I'd not been looking directly at him, I wouldn't have caught it. Neither of them speak, but the look leaves the hairs standing on my arms.

'I'll drive,' Jo says, before heading around the car.

'I'll see you at the hospital later,' I say.

Jo stops on the other side of the car, though her eyes are lifeless. She slumps, using the roof to hold herself up.

'Okay,' she replies – and then she gets inside.

NINETEEN

Jo drives off with Neil still in the back seat like he's some dopey politician getting ferried around. It's only as she takes the corner that I realise how many people are on the street. There are at least five residents standing in front doors watching everything that's just happened, with more faces at windows. Stephen is still in his doorway, peering along the road to where Holly and I are now standing awkwardly.

'Do you want to come in for a bit?' Holly asks.

She starts walking towards her house without waiting for a reply. I quick-step to catch up, mutter a 'yes', and then we hurry away from the street and through her unlocked front door. When it's closed behind us, Holly shuffles around the boxes that still litter the hallway and leads me into the kitchen once more.

'That's going to be all over Facebook within five minutes,' she says. 'If it's not already.'

'Is there a lot of that around here?' I ask.

'It was bad enough when we were kids – but at least it was face-to-face gossip then. I suppose it felt more honest. Everything's over messages, or Facebook now. Someone probably filmed it from across the street…'

Holly takes out her phone, taps something into it and then puts it away again. She slumps into the same seat she was in the last time we were in her kitchen and I take the one next to her. I eye the pile of boxes off to the side, wondering if they've multiplied. Wondering what could possibly be in them. Holly needs a large garage, or a storage unit.

'Why did Jo think it was Stephen?' Holly asks.

I flicker back to her. 'We'd gone off to the quarry because Jo heard they'd found a car. She put two and two together and figured it was the one that hit Ethan. Then Neil recognised the car and…' I shrug, but Holly gets it. Madness breeds madness.

'It's not the first time,' she says.

'What isn't?'

'Jo's always had her moments when she's gone a bit hyper. Remember that school trip when we were fourteen or fifteen and she was freaking out at that guy for speaking Spanish? She was telling him to "talk English" – and we were left there watching, not knowing what to say.'

The memory drifts through the curtain of my mind. Some bloke with a dodgy 'tache who didn't deserve to be shouted at. Different times, as people say now. 'That was a long time ago,' I say.

'It's not only that. Her and Neil are as bad as each other. There's always some sort of drama or falling-out. Did you see Neil go to get in the driver's seat before remembering we were there?'

I try to replay the moment, wondering if that *is* what I saw. There was certainly something, but the look Neil gave Jo might have been a silent reminder that she had to drive. That he knew he was banned but was too embarrassed to say it in front of other people. I'm not sure what it was, not with any certainty. It felt wrong, whatever it was.

'I saw something,' I reply, trying to remain neutral.

Holly doesn't respond to that, instead glancing towards the kettle. 'Brew?'

'Not for me.'

She glances to the bottle next to me on the table but doesn't say anything about it as she clicks the kettle on anyway.

With us in the same slots around her table as we were yesterday, it's more evidence that I've somehow ended up back in this Elwood groove. I wonder what I might have been doing had I not found

Ethan on Tuesday night. Could I have gone to Dad's house and started clearing it without running into any of my old friends? I might've been done by now and then made a few decisions about what to do next. I came to Elwood without much of a plan and it's hard to admit that this could be what I wanted all along… except for the hit-and-run, of course.

'It's not true,' Holly says out of nothing.

'What isn't?'

'I didn't see it, but, from what I heard, Stephen didn't almost hit Petey last year.' She motions towards the street at the front of the house. 'Petey was doing wheelies in the middle of the road and Stephen was trying to park. Petey overbalanced and fell off. He grazed his knee and chin. There was a bit of blood, but nothing serious.'

'Neil and Jo said you complained to the police about Stephen…?'

Holly shakes her head: 'That didn't happen. Jo wanted me to after Petey's wheelie thing. She kept saying it could have been Ethan – but I didn't even see it. None of us did. We were all in here and one of the neighbours knocked on the door. Stephen does rev his car a bit much – and I've seen him driving really quickly off the estate – but he's not the only one.'

Holly pushes her hair away from her face and scratches at a small flake near her ear. It curls away and lands on the table between us and she brushes it onto the floor.

'We're redecorating upstairs,' she says as an explanation. 'I must have been walking around like this for hours.' She bats away a yawn and then pours herself a mug of instant coffee. 'Not sleeping well,' she adds, without prompting.

'Since Ethan?'

'I suppose. It's Jo, as well. I keep thinking something bad is going to happen with her.'

'Like what?'

'Like today, where she overreacts to something.' There's the briefest of pauses and then: 'She should try some of my oils. I've got some great stuff for helping people to stay calm. I keep talking to her about it, but she's not interested.'

Holly opens the nearest box and pulls out a small vial of dark yellow liquid that has more than a passing resemblance to urine.

'Do you want a sample?' she asks. 'They're good for all sorts of thing. There's an essence of orange that I use on my skin every day, then I use lavender at night to help with sleep.'

I wonder if she's going to acknowledge the fact that she just told me she wasn't sleeping well – but it seemingly passes her by.

She starts unpacking the nearest box, placing vial after vial on the table and listing various benefits that sound suspiciously cultish. I only realise I've stumbled into a sales pitch when she's laid out half a dozen small bottles. 'I could do this lot at cost,' she says. 'I know you'll love them and then we could talk about a bigger order. Perhaps you've got some friends back where you've been staying who'll be interested…?'

It takes me a few seconds to stumble over a sentence. 'I didn't realise you sold this stuff,' I manage, trying to put her off while I come up with a diplomatic way of telling her I'm not interested.

'I run my own business,' Holly replies. 'Most of it's on Facebook, but I host some parties now and then. I got a stall at the craft market in the community centre last month, though it's a bunch of cheapskates round there. Nobody has any money in this place.' She doesn't bother to hide her contempt. 'If you want to start selling things yourself, I can set you up as a distributor. It's guaranteed money. I'm making thousands.' She pauses and, when I don't give an instant reply, adds: 'It's not a scam.'

I resist the urge to point out that most businesses don't need to pitch themselves as 'not a scam'. I glance back towards the hallway and the columns of boxes, plus the ones in here. There has to be thousands of pounds' worth of stock cluttering up the house. Despite her claims, I wonder how much debt she's in through all of this. It's unquestionably some sort of dodgy scheme. Someone would have promised her untold riches while being able to set her own hours. The products change – oils, cosmetics, underwear, protein shakes, or who knows what else – but the methods remain the same. The only people who make any amount of money are those who recruit a lot of people to sell underneath them.

My only surprise is that she didn't start trying to sell me this stuff when I was first here.

'I've got a lot on at the moment,' I say. 'With my dad and everything. I'm not looking to take on anything until I've figured out what I'm going to do with the house. I don't even know where I might end up living. It's the funeral tomorrow.'

'Oh…' Holly puts a couple of the vials back into the box at her side. 'I didn't realise it would be so soon.'

'There was an opening, so I booked it.'

She continues packing the bottles away with a steadily increasing vigour until she slaps the box flaps closed.

'Let me know if you change your mind,' she says, without looking up.

'I will.'

We sit in the awkward silence and it's starting to feel as if we're two people who have nothing in common.

I ask where her toilet is, more to get a break than anything else. She tells me it's the final door on the left upstairs, but, when I get up there, I check each of the other rooms anyway. Call it curiosity, or – perhaps – outright nosiness.

The first door opens into what I assume is Holly's own room. There's a lot of pink, with heart-shaped pillows on the bed. The room next door smells of men's deodorant, though the lights are off and the curtains pulled. It's dark and I don't bother to venture any further inside. The next room has a single bed set up in the middle, though it is largely empty other than that. There's certainly nothing out of the ordinary.

When I get into the bathroom, I sit on the edge of the bath and close my eyes.

I could just leave. Not only get away from Holly's but also the town. Every hour I'm here makes it feel like I'm being drawn back into the drama that comes with living in a place like Elwood. It's not the extremes of a hit-and-run, it's the little things. There are the arguments over wild rumours – like with Jo at Stephen's door – or the witless moneymaking schemes. Those are the sorts of things with which I grew up. The sorts of things that made me want to get the hell out of here. It might not have been essential oils, but my father was a man who was always involved in some sort of plan with a bloke down the pub, designed to get them rich. It wasn't only them. Jo's dad went to prison for a similar sort of plot, albeit one that was appallingly executed. I suppose I kept telling myself that was the way things were in the past – but I now see how little has changed. Some of that's evident in the sheer number of people home during a weekday, or the emptiness of Hendo's car park. Elwood feels like a place that's dying – and it's going to take down every last person here.

I drink from my bottle and then have a cupful of water from the tap. In case anyone's listening, I flush the toilet, let the taps run properly, and then head back downstairs. Holly is still in the kitchen and it doesn't look like she's moved. She's checking something on her phone but puts it on the table when I come in.

'Have the police spoken to you about Ethan again?' she asks.

'There's not a lot more I can say. The main guy, Davidson, was at the quarry today. He said they were determined to find whoever was driving the car.'

'Do they think it was the person that stole Stephen's car?'

'I have no idea… I'm not sure they do, either.'

Holly nods along.

'It's been two days,' she says after a while. 'They'd have something, wouldn't they? If there was a camera on a shop somewhere, or if there was a better witness—' She stops herself. 'I didn't mean it like that. Not that you're a bad witness, just that—'

'I get it.'

There's a pause and then she adds: 'I hope he's okay.'

It does feel as if Ethan has been lost in so much of what's happened since I found him in that gutter. Does finding the person who committed a crime trump the need to care for the victim?

In everything that's happened today, the dent on the front of Chris's car has largely slipped my mind.

'Sorry to change the subject,' I say. 'But can I ask you something about Chris?'

Holly has her mug of coffee in her hand, but she stops with it part way to her mouth. 'You're not still…?'

'No,' I reply quickly. 'Not that. His mum still lives next door and I saw him the other day. I wondered what he's been up to all these years.'

That seems to satisfy Holly's curiosity. She has a sip of her coffee and then returns the mug to the table. 'He's got a wife and kids, all that,' she says.

Despite the years that have passed, there's a part of myself and Chris that will always be linked. First boyfriends and girlfriends always mean something.

'I met his wife, Kirsty. He said she was in the year below us at school. She didn't seem too happy to see me.'

Holly suppresses a smile and then picks up her mug again, partly hiding behind it. 'I heard he's into some dodgy stuff,' she says.

The day suddenly feels colder, like her kitchen has been doused in shadow.

'Like what?' I ask.

Holly takes her time. She drinks more of her coffee and then puts down the mug once more.

'It's only rumours,' she says.

'What rumours?'

'He was selling dodgy satellite boxes round the estate. Those ones that get all the channels. It was one of those open secrets, so

I don't know how he got away without the police investigating. Then he was in a fight last year. He had too much to drink and kicked off with some bloke after a football game. It sounds like he picked the wrong guy – because he got a right kicking. Everyone I know who was there reckoned he deserved it.'

She pauses for breath and then says: 'He was working at a building supply place a few years ago – but got sacked for stealing. I can't remember everything that happened, but it was something like he was doing deals for his mates.' She scratches her head, then adds: 'There's probably more. You know what it's like round here.'

None of those things sound good, but that doesn't necessarily mean the dent in his bumper is anything other than his wife driving into a pillar, like he claimed.

'Have you talked to him since you got back?' Holly asks.

'A bit.'

She waits, wanting more.

'He told me that, back when we were going out, he was going to ask me to marry him.'

From nowhere, Holly becomes as animated as I've seen her. She bashes the table and almost knocks over her mug. She's a mix of surprised and amused. 'What? When?'

'He talked about taking me to this lake where we first had a good talk. I broke up with him not long after I turned eighteen, so I suppose it was sometime around then?'

'You were only kids.'

'I know.'

'I don't get why—'

Holly is interrupted by her phone dinging. She glances down to the screen and then picks it up off the table and frowns at it.

'It's a customer,' she says. 'I need to make a call. I won't be long.'

She hurries from the kitchen, closing the door behind her, and then disappears.

I stay put for a moment and then act on the urge I ignored the other day. I already know Holly has various oils in the box stacked on top, so I lift that off and then open the flaps of the box below.

More oils.

The box under that contains the same.

Holly's hoarding so much stock, it's no wonder she was trying to fob some off onto me.

I go to the fridge next, where new calendar notes have been added to the old ones. I'm busy examining the photo of Holly with her ex, Tom, and Rob, when the kitchen door goes. I turn, expecting to see Holly – but it's her son instead. I didn't know he was in. He didn't seem to be upstairs when I had a nosy around the rooms.

Rob lets out an 'oh' before turning back towards the hall.

'Your mum's on the phone somewhere,' I tell him.

'Oh, um…'

He turns back to me and bobs from foot to foot, which is when I figure out he already knows this. I've seen plenty of teenage boys nervous about talking to girls – and realise he has come into the kitchen for another reason.

'Can I help?' I ask.

'Yeah, um…'

'Do you want to ask me something? It's okay if you do.'

He takes a breath and sets himself. He looks towards me, though not directly at me. Perhaps to the wall *near* me. 'What's it like out there?' he asks.

For a moment, I think he means outside the front door, in the sun. I'm not sure what to say – but then he clarifies.

'Away from Elwood,' he adds. 'The rest of the world.'

'That's a big question. I heard you might be off to Liverpool.'

'Hopefully.'

Rob bites his lip and it's his little glance back towards the hall that makes me realise he doesn't want his mum to know he's asking.

'You should go,' I tell him. 'Not just for uni, but for life in general. If you get a chance to travel, then take it.'

He half turns once more.

'Your life is your own,' I say. 'Some people are born in one place and never leave. It's fine, but there are people, places and things you'll never experience in Elwood. You see the world in a different way when you get out.'

'What if someone relies on you?'

'I suppose that depends on who it is and why. If you're talking about your mum, I think she'll probably be okay. Liverpool isn't the other side of the planet. It's only a few hours away. Besides, she told me you were the smart one. She seemed proud of you.'

He nods and stands a little taller. I suspect this might be the thing he's been waiting to hear. 'Where have you lived?'

'Mainly London. I've been around, though. I spent a summer working in Spain and a festival season in Edinburgh.'

'Why did you leave Elwood?'

It's my turn to feel awkward – but I'm too far down this hole now.

'A few reasons. Mainly that I wasn't getting on with my dad. I figured there wasn't much for me here.'

He spins a little on the spot, seemingly unsure if he should say what he's thinking. Then, he simply comes out with it: 'Sometimes I feel stuck.'

'Isn't that what going to university is all about? You can't do that here, even if you wanted to.'

'I just—'

'Go. Don't just go to uni and then come back in three years to work around here. You're better than that. Go and never look back.'

He's nodding more vigorously now. 'Can I ask you something else?'

'Sure.'

'If that's the case, why are you back?'

My throat is suddenly dry and it's like my tongue is too big to fit in my mouth. 'I'm not sure I know the answer to that,' I say.

TWENTY

As I walk towards Dad's house, the sun is as hot as I can remember. The way the heat tickles my arms leaves me reliving those summer holidays where Holly, Jo and I would sleep until lunchtime and then meet in the park. There were no mobile phones to make plans then – but we all knew where to be.

There must have been rainy days during the summer holidays – but the only times I recall are those when it felt like the sun shone from first thing to last. The three of us would waste day after day sitting around talking about who knows what. If not that, we'd watch the boys play football or cricket. In the evenings, we'd sit under the trees as the sun went down, drinking whatever illicit booze we'd been able to get. They were the best of times – and yet they really weren't.

I change my mind and start to take the long route around, putting off the return to the house. The sooner I sort out the house, the sooner I can move on; literally and figuratively. That's what I think I want and yet there's an irony that I can't do that while I'm going out of my way to spend as little time as possible there.

I'm drawn to the High Street and the first thing I spot is Chris's car parked outside the bookies again. I figure he's in the betting shop – but then I see a shadowed head bob back and forward and realise Chris is in the driver's seat. I'm on the other side of the road and am almost past when I clock a familiar bike leaning against the lamp post closest to the car. There's a collision of unanswered questions from the past couple of days as Petey clambers out of the passenger seat. He leans into the car and says something to Chris before stepping back and slinging a backpack over his scrawny shoulder. With that, he retrieves his bike and pedals off along the pavement, weaving between a pair of pedestrians as he rounds the corner.

I've been watching Petey but, as I blink back towards this end of the High Street, I realise that the driver's side window is now down on Chris's car and he's resting an elbow on the frame, watching me. I feel frozen for a second as he touches his index finger to his temple and gives a salute. I don't know how to acknowledge this, whether to know if it was friendly. I don't get a chance anyway because he turns back to the front, starts the car, and then pulls out into the street, heading in the opposite direction to Petey.

It's Elwood in a nutshell, I suppose. Everything is connected. Every*one* is connected. I can't escape the feeling that, somehow, it all leads back to Ethan and what happened to him. Perhaps that's why I'm still here, even though all my instincts tell me to go?

I walk more quickly now and soon find myself back on the edge of the park. I take the turn into Beverly Close and start to fumble through my bag, hunting for the key. I'm already on the path when I realise there's someone sitting on the doorstep directly in front of me.

She pushes herself up and brushes the hair from her face as she takes a breath.

'Hello, Abigail,' she says.

It takes a second to see past the new wrinkles and the long grey hair – but the recognition is still there, despite all the years.

'Mum...?'

TWENTY-ONE

'You're so grown up, Abigail.'

It jars to hear my full name. Whenever anyone phones and asks for that name, I know it's a marketing company. Anybody who knows me calls me 'Abi'. Abigail feels like someone else.

'People tend to grow up when you don't see them for more than twenty years.'

Mum bows her head slightly to acknowledge the point. 'I gather you left not long after I did…?'

I gulp back the angry response I want to give and half turn, determined not to let any emotion show. This is so sudden, so unexpected, that it feels like I've been hit in the chest. I'm short of breath, struggling not only for words but also to breathe properly.

'You left *me*, Mum. It wasn't just Dad. You walked out on *me* and never made contact.'

'Did you want me to stay there for longer with your father? You were eighteen. I got you through to being an adult. What more is a mother supposed to do?'

'How about *act* like a mother?'

It's unsettling to see her after so long but what's more unnerving is how much we look alike. It could be a false memory, but, when I was young, I don't remember there being much of a resemblance. People used to say I looked like my dad, but never Mum. It's different now, as if I've become a younger version of her without noticing. Our hair is the same length and, though mine isn't as grey as hers, it's on the way. There are crescent wrinkles around the corners of her eyes, the type of which I've been noticing on myself recently.

She moves to the side, letting me get to the door. I unlock it and then wait in the frame, facing inside, away from my mother. I almost close the door behind me but can't bring myself to do it.

I turn to stare at her and it's like she's a ghost. I can't quite believe she's here.

'Are you coming in?'

I hold the door open and Mum passes me. I close the door behind us and, when I turn, she's at the bottom of the stairs, turning to take in the hall. I leave her to it and slip around her, into the kitchen. I'm filling a mug with water when she follows me in.

We stand on opposite sides of the kitchen; her examining the fridge, me drinking next to the sink. The note with my phone number is still on the fridge and there's a part of me that wants to rip it away before she has a chance to either take it or memorise it.

She turns and watches me drink. I stop almost instantly, those stirrings of self-consciousness making me feel like a teenager again.

Mum holds out a hand, indicating the house. 'I'm guessing this is all yours now…?'

'Are we really going to argue about this?'

'I lived here once.' She states this as a fact, not necessarily to pick a fight.

'You left,' I say.

'So did you.'

We stare towards one another and I wish we weren't so similar. We're even leaning in the same way, with one leg bent at the knee.

'Is that why you're here?' I ask. 'Because you didn't get anything in the will. You walked out more than twenty years ago and never tried to contact me. I tell people you're dead. I kinda thought you were.'

I wait for her to say something, but she remains silent.

'Did you try to contact Dad?' I ask.

'What do you think? I left for a reason.'

'What was the reason for leaving me?'

She doesn't answer and, as I clasp the mug tighter, I think about throwing it. She's close enough that I couldn't miss. It would smash her on the side of the head and shatter. There would be blood.

'I thought about trying to contact you,' she says.

'I guess that makes everything all right, then. I think about doing lots of things, but it's actions that matter.'

I grip the mug even harder. Actions *do* matter.

Mum nods towards it and there's a moment in which I wonder if she's somehow read my mind. 'Are you going to offer me a tea?'

'You can make your own.'

I watch as she does precisely that. She shunts the unwashed dishes to one side, fills the kettle, and then returns it to the base and turns it on. After that, she goes through the cupboard until she finds the teabags I bought this morning. At the time, I wasn't sure why I'd bought them. I rarely have hot drinks when I'm by myself.

Mum opens the box, puts a teabag in a mug and then waits next to the kettle. The only sound is the bubbling of the water. Time passes until there's a click and fizz as steam pours from the top of the kettle. It feels surreal to watch her like this, as if we haven't been apart for so long. Like I didn't wake up one morning to find she was no longer in my life. No note, no conversation; just my father to tell me that she'd gone and wasn't coming back. I consider throwing her out now and completing the job that she started all those years ago.

Mum tips the water into the mug and waits. It's only after another couple of minutes that she removes the bag, gets the milk from the fridge and pours a splash on top. She dumps the teabag in the bin and then stoops over it, peering at the bottles in the bottom. When she looks to me, there's definite disapproval.

'Don't you dare say anything,' I spit.

She doesn't. Not about that, anyway.

'Have you got any sugar?' she asks instead.

'No.'

Her top lip curls and she looks towards the cupboards as if I might be lying. She sips the drink anyway, and mutters 'hot' – as if it would be anything else. She then puts the mug down on the counter.

'Would you like me to wash up?' she asks as she looks across to the sinkful of dishes.

'Do you want us to call it quits after that?'

She doesn't respond and I get the sense that I could poke and poke but I'm not going to get anything meaningful.

'Where've you been all this time?' I ask.

'Did you really think I was dead?' It's matter-of-fact again. All business.

'You might as well have been.'

'I was around. I always kept half an eye on everything.'

I stare at her, fighting back the anger. What a stupid reply.

'What does that mean?'

It's becoming impossible to keep the fury from my tone. It's bubbling and ready to explode.

'I grew up in Elwood, Abigail. I know people.'

'Stop calling me Abigail.'

'I named you.'

'I have a few names for you, too.'

She goes to reply but bites her lip instead. It's only that which stops me from going off the deep end. She sips her drink and I wonder if, behind that, there's the slightest hint of a concessionary smile.

'If you know people around here,' I add, 'why did none of them tell me where you'd gone?'

Mum doesn't answer. Again. I suppose there isn't a reply that could ever satisfy me and I already know the truth anyway. Nobody told me where she'd gone because she didn't want me to know.

'I heard you moved to London,' she says.

'You heard correctly.'

She turns to look around the kitchen again, focusing on my phone number that's still pinned to the fridge.

'I didn't leave because of you, Abigail.'

'I know why you left. For the same reason I did.'

We have that in common, too.

We stand in silence for a while longer. It feels like this could go on forever.

'Did you know I was back in Elwood?' I ask.

She nods.

'Why are you here?'

'I figured it was time.'

She waits, but I don't think I have anything to say.

'Did you ever marry?' she asks.

I wait, staring towards her until she turns back to me. 'Everyone keeps asking that,' I say, not disguising the contempt. 'Is that all I am? Defined by whether or not I'm married?'

'It's only a question.'

There's another stand-off, with us glaring at one another. Or, to be fair, I suppose I'm the only one actually glaring.

'I was engaged,' I say. 'We were going to be married next month, but it turned out he and one of my friends had other ideas. Not that it's any of your business.'

It feels like I'm telling this to a stranger, which makes it easier in many ways. Less judgement. Fewer feelings to care about.

'Are you back for good?'

'I don't know.' A breath. It's not true. I do know. If I didn't before, then I certainly do now. 'No,' I add. 'And, before you get to it, you're not a grandmother, if that's what you were really asking.'

Her nose twitches in annoyance and, although we've not been in contact in a long time, I know that's not what she was asking at all.

'What about you?' I ask, surprising myself. 'Did you remarry? Dad said you were divorced through abandonment.'

She shifts her position against the counter. 'Can we sit somewhere more comfortable? I'm too old to stand up this long.'

This is something with which I can't argue; I'm not comfortable either.

We head through to the living room, but Mum doesn't sit straight away. She does a small lap, taking in everything that's barely changed. I suspect she's as shocked by it as I was. She misses half a pace in front of the liquor cabinet, but then continues as if it hasn't happened. It was the thing that drove us all apart, after all.

She eventually stops at the sofa, and sits perched on the edge with her knees crossed, in the way she always did.

'The funeral's tomorrow,' I say.

'Is it?' She might still know people in the area, but the widening of her eyes tells me this is something of which she wasn't aware.

'It's at the funeral directors' at the end of the High Street, as if you're heading out of town. Four p.m.'

'Are you going?'

'I think I'm the only one – unless Helena from next door shows up.'

'Not a surprise, is it? He drove away everyone in the end.'

There's sadness to her tone that I wouldn't have expected and, in that moment, as I look around the room, my stomach lurches at the loss of a life I could've had. *We* could've had.

Mum sees it, too. We lock eyes, but I have to turn away because tears feel too close.

I stare at the stack of newspapers instead. Something irrational and ridiculous that barely feels real.

'Shame about that boy…'

It takes me a little while to realise that Mum means Ethan. I was lost in the past, but she's back in the present.

'I saw it,' I say.

'Saw what?'

'I was there when it happened. I saw him in the gutter.'

'That poor boy…'

It's probably the sincerity with which she says it, the concern for someone else. The fact that she isn't a monster, after all. That's what breaks me. It feels like I'm going to be sick, but, instead, it's a guttural sob. From there, the accompanying tears arrive and I'm left crying into my hands.

'Why didn't you take me with you?' I manage.

Mum passes me a tissue from her bag and I blow my nose long and loud. She doesn't reply. Not for a long time anyway. When she does, she speaks with an exhausted sigh.

'Because, Abigail, I'd already given you eighteen years of my life.'

'What does that mean?'

She waits until I'm looking directly at her. 'It means that I didn't want to.'

It feels like she's slammed a knife into my middle. I try, but I can't speak. The words are stuck somewhere around my chest and all that comes out is a short series of asthmatic gasps.

When I finally get the words out, they're an anticlimax. I should've held onto my fury and not let it be replaced by this. 'I think you should leave.'

Mum nods and then stands. 'If that's what you want.' She crosses the room and then waits in the doorway to the kitchen. 'I—'

'What?'

She stares at me, her mouth open, as if about to say something. Then she changes her mind and turns. The next thing I hear is the front door closing – and then it's only me and my tears.

TWENTY-TWO

Jo, Neil and Owen are already in the hospital waiting room when I arrive. None of them are talking to one another and, if I didn't know better, I'd be sure they were three strangers on adjacent seats.

The room is largely full, with most people either looking at their phones or flipping through magazines. As I say hello to Jo, what becomes immediately apparent is that she's getting sideways glances from all directions. Everyone knows who she is – and why she's here.

There is no place to sit next to Jo and I'm about to take a seat on the next row when a man in a suit enters and says her name. She, Neil and Owen all stand and, as they head off towards the nearest corridor, she waves me across to join them.

The man leads the four of us through a bewildering labyrinth until we reach a separate and exclusive waiting area. He eyes me suspiciously until Jo offers a quick 'she's with us'. It's hard not to see that she's noticeably calmer now compared to earlier, almost to the point of indifference.

The man tells us to wait for a moment and we all hang around in silence as he disappears into the adjoining room. A moment later and he's back, telling us we can head in now.

I've only ever seen it on television before, but it's a shock to see a machine breathing for a person. Ethan is in a room of his own, with tubes attached to his chest, and a mask over his mouth. The machine at his side makes a steady, rhythmical thump. A doom-laden drumbeat. More shocking than that are the bruises across his top half. Both his eyes are black, with spiralling purple and yellow marks stretching across much of his face. He seems so small; so broken.

The room is tiny and it feels cramped, especially with the mass of balloons and cards on the table in the corner.

Jo sits on the only seat at Ethan's side and takes his hand. I'm left not knowing what to say or, perhaps, why Jo wanted me here, as I watch on along with Neil and Owen.

'I want you to come home,' Jo says, talking to Ethan. 'We'll get you a new bike. Whichever one you want. We can go to that warehouse place out on the trading estate. Something better.'

Ethan doesn't respond as the metronomic thump continues. It doesn't feel as if this is a moment I should be sharing.

'We'll find out who did this,' she adds, before repeating herself.

I watch Neil, remembering the way he moved to the driver's door and wondering if it could be true that he's been driving illegally. Whether it could have been him who drove off. If he is hiding something, then he doesn't flinch. He continues to stare towards the bed, his arms behind his back, saying nothing.

Jo shifts slightly and then adds: 'Your brother wants to say something to you.'

She turns and looks up to Owen, who gulps and clears his throat.

'United are in for a striker,' he says. 'That Brazilian guy. I can't remember his name. He had a good World Cup. They had a bid accepted this morning.'

He lets that hang and, as a room, it's hard to ignore how dysfunctional everything is. There's Neil, the banned driver who might be driving. There's Owen, who claims he was in one place when his brother was hit – even though it's almost certainly a lie. Then there's Jo, with the tub of pills in her toilet cistern.

And me, of course. The person whose mother walked out on her because she didn't want any part of her life.

Jo continues talking to Ethan, but she goes in circles. After a few minutes, she peters off to silence. I'd wondered why she hadn't been spending more time at the hospital, but this is the answer. What is there to do? To say? It takes a lot out of a person to sit next to someone who's critically injured and cannot reply. She has no ability to influence anything here.

After a while, there's a knock on the door and the man in the suit reappears. He doesn't say anything, but the slim smile is enough.

Jo squeezes Ethan's hand once more and then stands.

'I'll see you soon,' she says.

I'm not sure what to make of it. She's emotional and yet… *not*. It feels as if there's a distance. Like a person being told a stranger had cancer. There might be a natural human compassion and yet it would be hard to muster a genuine outpouring of grief because there's no direct connection. It feels strange and yet everybody reacts to hardship in different ways. This might be the only way she can cope.

Neil leads the way out of the hospital, with the rest of us following. I've not spoken since arriving and can't figure out why Jo wanted me here. If it was for support, then she had Neil and Owen.

We pass through the sliding doors at the front and, without checking anyone's still behind him, Neil follows the path around to the side and then starts to cross the car park. I'm already halfway across before I realise I have no reason to be following. Jo is in front of me and, I suppose, at the very least, I need to say goodbye. I keep trailing until we're at the back end of the car park, in the shadows of the nearby trees. I spot Jo's car and then realise there's a man perching on the bonnet, looking at his phone. He peers up when we near, squinting quizzically towards me as I reach the others, before settling on Jo.

The man seems familiar, like when a character turns up on television: the actor is recognisable, but it's not clear on which other show they appeared. It feels like I know him.

'How is he?' the man asks.

Jo takes a small step forward, so that she's ahead of the rest of us. 'I don't want any trouble,' she says.

'I'm his dad. All I'm doing is asking how he is. They won't let me in to see him.'

There's a moment's impasse and I realise this is Mark. When I knew him at school, he was a bigger kid, but it's like he never grew any further. In the here and now, he looks the type who'd be well at home with a protein shake. A personal trainer, perhaps. He's certainly aged better than Jo.

It's Neil who answers. 'We can probably get them to let you in,' he says.

Mark clenches his teeth and turns to the other man. 'Oh, you can, can you?'

The contempt is impossible to miss and Neil takes a small step to the side, using Jo as a human shield.

'Leave it, Dad,' Owen says to Mark.

Mark looks between the four of us, focusing on me for a fraction too long before settling back on Jo. 'Didn't anybody think to call me?' he says. 'I was working on a site over the border and found out what happened to Ethan from a Facebook message.'

'We had other things on our minds,' Jo retorts. 'It's not all about you. Besides, Ethan told you months ago that he didn't want to see you. You know that.'

Mark balls his fists and straightens. 'You've been poisoning him against me.'

'No. You've done that by standing him up so often. Don't you remember promising to take him to the football in February and not showing up? How long do you think it's fair to keep doing that? It wasn't the first time.'

They stand, staring fire at one another, and I can barely remember them as the couple they were. It's hard to fathom that they had two children after that. From there to here, I guess.

Neil clears his throat with a definite air of drama. 'Maybe we should go?' he says.

Mark moves to the side, angling his neck to see around Jo. 'You'd love that, wouldn't you?'

'Love what?'

'I'm onto you, *mate*. I know all about you and your driving ban. Kept that quiet, didn't you? I know people who've seen you out and about anyway.'

There's a tremor in his voice as Neil replies. 'Who told you that?'

'Never you mind.' Mark nods sneeringly at Jo. 'Do you know he's driving while banned?'

Jo doesn't answer, but Owen's head shoots from side to side, between his actual father and his live-in dad.

With the silence acting as apparent confirmation, Mark is on a roll. 'Where were you when my boy got hit?'

Jo stretches and pushes him away. 'He was with me,' she says, although it's as convincing as if she was trying to say the sky is pink.

Mark resists the push, refusing to step away from the car. His eyes are fixed on Neil, his lips curled to a sneer. 'Not at work, then?'

Neil moves faster than I would've given him credit for. In a blink, he's shifted out from behind Jo and is squaring up chest to chest with Mark. It feels like Neil is one moment away from getting battered when, before Mark can react, Owen has shoved his way in between the two men.

'Stop!' he shouts.

The two men step away, but any tension has gone as quickly as it arrived.

Mark flicks out a slap around his son, towards Neil, but he's nowhere near close enough to connect. 'If I find out you had anything to do with what happened to Ethan, you better hope the police get to you first.'

Neil doesn't reply, but he does take a couple of steps backwards, away from the conflict.

'You keep walking away,' Mark says with a grin.

'Please go,' Owen says.

'He's not your dad,' Mark replies, nodding past his son towards Neil.

'I know,' Owen replies. 'But please go.'

Mark dances a shuffle on the spot, then feigns a punch.

'I'm watching you,' he says, still looking at Neil. 'I know what you did.'

TWENTY-THREE

The house is achingly quiet when I get home. There's a little part of me that wishes my mother was still here, if only for there to be something other than this encapsulating nothingness. The downstairs curtains are open, but the only thing seeping through is the numbing blankness of night.

I drift through to the living room and examine my father's dwindling booze supply. As inheritances go, there isn't much of a lasting appeal. I grab the final haul of vodka and empty it into my bottle and then dump the glass itself into the kitchen bin. Everything feels strange. I should go to bed but can't face sleeping by myself. I want to leave this house, but I want to be here, too. I never want to see my mother again, but, if she knocked on the door right now, I'd let her in. I'm not sure I ever want to hear Jo's name again, she isn't my friend, and yet, if I'm not looking out for Ethan, then I have a horrible feeling nobody is.

When I sit on the sofa, my head starts to swirl. I close my eyes but, when I open them, the room is still spinning. Dad's newspaper stacks zoom towards me and so I clamp my eyes shut once more. I squeeze the bridge of my nose and lean back into the headrest, forcing myself to take long, deep breaths. It would usually help but not now. All I can smell is that musty reek of Old Spice. Of Dad. I have to sit up again and gulp down the air, willing the sensation to pass.

'Please,' I whisper. '*Please.*'

When I next open my eyes, I've slipped onto the floor without noticing. My back is against the side of the sofa and the walls have stopped blurring into fuzzy circles.

When I look ahead, I'm staring at the crack in the skirting board again. The small crimson dots are clearer now, though when I run my finger across them, there are no raised pimples. I blink, but they're still there. It feels closer than before and I wince as I feel my father's steel-capped work boots first crushing my ribs and then slamming towards my face.

I close my eyes to blank it out again, the same as I did then. I'm tense, waiting for the blows that never come.

This house, *my* house, is my prison, but I know that, until someone finds out what really happened to Ethan, I will not be able to leave.

TWENTY-FOUR

I wake up on the living room floor. Light gushes through the open curtains, sending squares of heat onto the carpet. The ceiling swirls and then starts charging towards me. I close my eyes, but it does nothing to stop the fuzziness.

I know what's coming and heave myself up using the arm of the sofa, then rush into the kitchen. My stomach retches and my throat burns as I empty my guts into the sink, somehow having the awareness to avoid the dirty dishes.

Not that it would matter.

I groan and use the counter to hold myself into something close to a vertical position. I cup my hands and scoop water into my mouth, partly trying to get rid of the acrid taste and partly trying to soothe my grated throat.

The water has the opposite effect and another retch screams through me as it feels like I'm turning myself inside out. As I'm doubled over the sink, there's a moment in which it feels like my mother is standing behind me, one hand on my shoulder, the other holding my hair behind me in a ponytail. I'd forgotten until now, but it happened before, when I was fourteen or fifteen. I was in the bathroom upstairs then, on my knees with my head in the toilet bowl. It felt like I was dying, but she was there with me, making gentle cooing noises and telling me I'd be okay.

I would do anything to have that now.

My stomach erupts once more and I find myself on tiptoes while I retch into the sink. I'm old enough to know I'm not dying now – but it sure feels like it. Everything hurts.

I remain hunched over the sink with my eyes closed, waiting until my stomach has finished clenching and crunching. There's such relief when it's finally over. It's been a long time since I've thrown up this much. It's like when an athlete is training for a marathon. At one point, running ten miles feels like it's much too far and will never happen. Then, after months of building up to it, and when twenty-six miles is within sight, a ten-mile run is barely a morning jog. For me, carrying around my bottle every day is that training.

My stomach gurgles, but there's nothing left in it. I fill my bottle with water and slather three slices of bread with Marmite, before taking it all into the living room. I slump into the armchair – the one that least smells of Dad – and then switch on the television at the mains. The blackness flickers to light and I think I'm hallucinating for a moment as Jo's face swirls into view.

It takes me a moment to realise that she actually *is* on the screen. The shots alternate between Diane Young and Jo – and, as I realise what's happening, I'm amazed at how professional it seems. I can still picture the pair of them as they were yesterday, but something about the lights and quality of camera makes everything seem so much more slick than it did when I was watching in person.

My head is still fuzzy, my thoughts clouded, but that doesn't stop me from seeing what's happening on screen. I missed it yesterday, but the interspersed shots of the town, combined with lines like 'the Elwood underclass', along with 'a close-knit community bonded together by a steady decline in living standards', makes it clear that we are something to be gawked at. That only someone from a place like this could plough into a child and then drive off. Nobody in a respectable community would dream of doing such a thing. God forbid those yummy mummies in their borderline tanks could ever do wrong.

It's only as my anger builds that I realise how defensive I'm feeling over this stupid place. That, deep down, in a way that will never leave me, Elwood still feels like *my* town and that its residents are *my* people.

The interview continues to roll as Diane builds to the thought for the day. As she starts with her 'I'm talking to you now' line, much of the impact I felt from yesterday has gone. It feels rehearsed now and far less sincere. Without waiting for her to finish, I turn off the television with the remote and then down more water from my bottle while still nibbling at the bread.

With the TV silenced, I feel my attention drawn back to the skirting board again. The top-to-bottom crack is still there, but when I look closer, those little pinprick dots of blackened red are gone. I crouch onto my hands and knees and am so close that my forehead touches the wall. Still nothing. Not on the skirting board anyway. The scar close to my temple still has the pimply marks that have been there since the night after my mother left.

I hurry into the kitchen, then out through the back door into the porch to where there's a rusting toolbox with a creaky lid. The crunching hinge makes it feel as if it hasn't been opened in years. There is a hotchpotch of tools inside. When he was younger, my father was handy with this type of thing. He could do a limited amount of rewiring and he redecorated all the rooms upstairs. He built the liquor cabinet with that expensive wood that he sourced himself – although there's an irony in that the contents are what ultimately robbed him of the drive and ability to make similar things.

There is a heavy hammer that I drop on the floor, along with grime-coated screwdrivers, a penknife and a wrench, until I get to the crowbar underneath. Back in the living room, I squeeze the flat end onto the top of the skirting and then slide it down until it wedges itself between the wood and the wall. It only takes a sharp levering and there's a crunch as the board flips away from the wall, leaving four or five layers of crusty wallpaper hanging loose.

I grab the splintered wood and burst through the house until I'm on the front drive. There's a large wheelie bin in the corner, with Dad's house number sloppily painted onto the side. It's full and it stinks of something rotten – but I dump the plank onto the top and then shove everything down before slamming the lid.

It doesn't matter any longer whether there are spots of my blood on there.

When I turn back to go in, I realise Chris's car is parked on the drive at the front of his mum's house. I stare, knowing something's different – something's wrong – though I don't spot it at first.

It takes a few seconds for me to clock that the front bumper has been replaced. Instead of the scuff that was there days ago, the entire unit has been switched with something so untouched that it's completely at odds with the rest of the vehicle.

I goggle for a moment, not quite sure what to do. It feels like I shouldn't ignore it, but what else can I do? Tell Tina from the police that my next-door neighbour's son, my long-ago ex-boyfriend, has replaced his bumper? Or Sergeant Davidson? Is it important?

I'm heading for Dad's front door when next door's pops open and Helena emerges. She calls across to me before I can get away and then hobbles over to catch me on the doorstep.

'I saw it in the paper,' she says. 'I didn't expect the funeral to be so soon.'

It takes me a moment to realise she's talking about my dad. 'I meant to come and knock to tell you, but things got away from me,' I say. 'There was an opening at the funeral directors', so I took it.'

'I'll be there, dear. How many are you expecting?'

'I have no idea. There's me and you – so that's two.'

I force a smile, but Helena doesn't reciprocate.

Before either of us can say anything else, Chris appears from her front door. His brow creases as he turns to take us in, but then he strolls across and rests a hand on his mother's shoulder.

'I've gotta head off, Mum,' he says.

'Are you coming over tomorrow night?'

'Maybe. I'll let you know.'

He kisses her on the top of the head, nods at me and then heads to his car. The engine snarls and then he's off around the corner with a splutter of the exhaust.

When it's quiet again, Helena turns back to me and pats my arm. 'I'll see you at four then,' she says. 'Be nice for your dad to have a proper send-off.'

I'm not sure how I feel about her being at Dad's funeral. There would be a certain degree of justice if it was only me who turned up. I can hardly tell her not to come.

'See you at four,' I reply.

She rubs her arms as if cold, nods, and then heads back to her house.

I'm about to go inside myself when I notice the flicker of movement from the corner of the hedge that borders Helena's house on the far side. I stand and watch as a flash of blonde hair appears.

'Beth…?'

The teenager steps out from behind the hedge and straightens her top. I wonder how long she's been there, apparently waiting for me to be alone.

'Are you okay?' I ask.

Beth nods as she approaches the house. She glances over her shoulder nervously, although there's nobody there.

'I came to say I was wrong,' she says.

'About what?'

'When I said I was home when Ethan left on the day he got hit. I was actually with Owen. I mixed up the times.'

She scuffs a foot along the gravel of the drive and checks over her shoulder once more.

'Was Owen at your house?' I ask.

She shakes her head quickly. 'No. We were both out together.'

Beth twists on the spot, peeping over her shoulder again.

'Are you waiting for someone?' I ask.

'No.'

She tries to smile, but it's forced and nervy.

'You were so specific,' I say. 'You were babysitting and thinking about doing fish fingers for tea.'

Beth bites her lip. 'Yeah, um… I mixed up the days. That was another time. Owen and I were together on Tuesday afternoon. We've been friends for ages.'

The lie is so bad, so transparent, that I don't know how to react. She might as well be telling me she's next in line to the throne. I don't know her well enough to call her out.

'You didn't have to find me to tell me this,' I say.

'I know. I've been thinking about it, that's all. After I talked to you when Petey was there, I was walking home wondering if I'd mixed up the days. I didn't want you getting the wrong idea.'

'About what?'

She squeezes her knees together, as if she needs a wee. 'I, um… well, y'know…' She holds up her phone. 'I've got to get going.'

Beth takes a couple of steps away before I say her name. When she turns back to me, I can see in her eyes that she knows she's failed in whatever this was.

'It's not me you have to convince,' I say.

She doesn't reply, though her arms slump to her sides.

'Have the police talked to you?' I add.

'No.'

'Getting details wrong with me is one thing – but getting them wrong with the police is something else entirely.'

She stares at the ground and then takes another small step back towards the direction from which she came.

'Is there something you want to talk about?' I ask.

Beth pauses and, for a moment, it feels as if she might let me know what's really going on.

'I got confused,' she says. 'That's all.'

She gives a small wave, checks over her shoulder once more – and then she's gone.

TWENTY-FIVE

When I pass Hendo's, there's a man with a long-lens camera taking photos across the car park. I'm past him before I decide to go back. He's older and grey, with a gnarly beard and the expression of a man with permanently rolled eyes.

'What's going on?' I ask.

He eyes me up and down and then unscrews a lens and returns it to the bag on the floor.

'What's it to you?' he replies, though it doesn't feel particularly unkind.

'Just nosy, I guess.'

That gets the slimmest of grins. 'Least yer honest.' He nods at the building. 'Industrial property space, innit?'

'What does that mean?'

'It means it's going up for sale.'

'When?'

A shrug. 'I just take the pictures, love.'

He clips another lens onto his camera and shifts around me, ending the conversation.

I watch as he moves onto the car park and starts taking photos of the wide-open space on which there would once have been long rows of cars.

I leave him to it and continue through the streets until I get to the bit-of-everything shop from yesterday. Inside, and the Pot Noodles on offer have gone, though much of the pallet of orange squash remains. Today's special is Heinz Tomato Soup, with a small mountain of cans loaded into an alcove close to the window.

There's a new *Elwood Echo* on the shelf at the front.

POLICE CHASE LEADS IN HIT-AND-RUN CASE
Boy, 8, remains in intensive care

I scan the story, but there is very little new information. Sergeant Davidson insists they are following 'several leads'. The main note of interest is that 'a car extracted from a nearby quarry yesterday morning has been ruled out of the enquiry'. I suppose that means Stephen's story of having his car stolen checks out.

This time, Ethan has been named. I suppose it was inevitable after the TV company got hold of Jo. There are photos of her with the family, and more still of Ethan as a young boy. The more I read, the more I see the frustration of nothing happening. It almost feels like whoever wrote the story wants a death, because at least something will have occurred. Death by dangerous driving has to sound a lot better than leaving the scene of an accident.

'You gonna buy that?'

I twist to see the shop owner standing with his arms folded.

'I, um—'

'This ain't a library.'

'I was—'

'I know what you were doing.'

I feel like a chastened child. At least this guy wasn't around twenty years ago to catch me nicking music magazines by slipping them into my school bag.

'I'm looking for vodka,' I say, as I return the paper to the pile with the rest of them.

The man nods me across to the counter, where there is a rack of cigarettes and alcohol behind the till. He has Smirnoff and some other brand, where none of the label is in English.

'Which one's cheaper?' I ask.

He offers the bottle with the foreign label and I pay him with a twenty-pound note from Dad's stash, thinking my father would certainly approve of the purchase. The man puts the bottle in a carrier bag and I'm about to turn to go when he coughs to clear his throat.

'Terrible, isn't it?' he says.

'What?'

He nods across to the papers. 'That someone could do that and drive away.'

I nod along, not knowing what he wants me to say. I'm hardly going to disagree.

'Everyone knows who did it anyway,' he adds.

I've already taken a step away when I angle back to him.

'Sorry…?'

'They pulled his car out of the quarry yesterday.'

'I read the police had ruled him out.'

The man shakes his head. 'Not what I heard. Have you seen what they did to his house?'

'No.'

He shrugs. 'You need ta get on the internet, love. Get on Google.'

Back on the street and it feels a few degrees warmer than when I entered the shop. In previous days, I felt comfortable but, after last night and this morning's repercussions in the sink, my stomach is gurgling. I head into the alley at the side of the store, have a gulp of the water from my bottle and then dump the rest down the drain, before replacing it with what I've just bought. My fingers are trembling as I swig down the mouthfuls that won't fit in my bottle, and then I dump the glass into the large metal bin near the shop's back door. I press myself into the shadows and take a few breaths. There is a little over two hours until Dad's funeral and then that part of my life will be done.

When my shaking hand has settled, I return the way I came. By the time I get to Hendo's, the photographer has gone. It's such an enormous site that the idea of it being anything other than what it is now seems incomprehensible. Blackpool has the Tower, London has the Eye and we have Hendo's. I stop and stare for a little while. It feels impossible that it could be something that isn't a sprawling factory.

I blink away the wistful thoughts, telling myself it's the booze. Then, instead of returning to Dad's, I take the turn for Holly's and follow the route towards her house. As soon as I get onto her street, I see what the man in the shop was talking about. It was only yesterday that Jo was standing outside Stephen's house shouting at him about being the one who hit Ethan. Whether it was that, or the news of his car showing up in the quarry, someone has made some serious assumptions.

The word 'murderor' has been spray-painted across his front door, and, in place of the glass in the window at the side, a wooden board is pinned into the frame.

Before I can move, the front door opens and Stephen emerges. He spots me straight away on the other side of the road and I'm frozen.

'Happy now?' he calls.

I only have two options – disappear or cross the road and talk to him. I'm certainly not having a shouted conversation, so opt for the latter and shimmy between a pair of cars to join him outside his house.

'I'm really sorry,' I say.

'Bit late now,' he replies – though he doesn't sound as angry as I expected.

'Did the police—?'

'Already been.' He talks over me. 'I'm not expecting much. None of the neighbours have been round, so it won't be a surprise when none of them have seen or heard anything.' He looks up to the houses around and shouts, 'Yeah, I'm talking about you lot.' He lowers his voice when he focuses back on me. 'Cowards waited until we'd gone out. Weren't brave enough to try it while I was in.' He sighs and looks back to the house. 'Sorry for shouting. I know it wasn't your fault. You tell your friend I know it's not her, either. She's got enough going on with her kid in hospital and everything.'

We turn at the sound of footsteps. Holly has appeared and stands awkwardly, looking between us. She must have been watching from her window and focuses on the graffiti.

Her arms are folded, but she uncrosses them slowly and focuses on Stephen. 'I can send Rob over if you need a hand getting rid of that,' she says.

Stephen lets out a surprised-sounding 'oh', before he straightens himself. 'I'm sure he doesn't want to spend his summer holiday scrubbing my front door. I've got a company who specialises in this coming over anyway. Should be here in an hour or so.' He pauses and then adds: 'I don't suppose you heard anything, did you? It happened last night.'

Holly shakes her head. 'Sorry.'

Stephen glimpses sideways towards me, offering a momentary and silent *told you so*.

'No matter,' he says. 'No real harm done.'

It's quite the change from a few minutes before when it felt like he was ready for a fight, or certainly in the mood to shout at someone. I think he might've simply wanted someone to listen to him.

Holly turns to me. 'Are you coming in?'

'I haven't got long,' I reply. 'I've got a funeral to get to.'

TWENTY-SIX

Damien, the funeral director, welcomes me into the reception with a solemn bow. He's in a suit that's even smarter than the other day, with a dark tie and glimmering black shoes. I don't blame him as he looks me up and down, taking in my loose, cream trousers and vest with a dark cardigan. Covering up this much on a hot day is enough of a sacrifice.

Despite the look, he says nothing about my outfit.

'Everything's ready at the back,' he says.

He starts to lead me through the carpeted area but then stops.

'I know you mentioned changing the music. I hope this is acceptable. There are other options, or you could choose something yourself. I have Spotify.'

I'd not even noticed the music, but, rather than the suicide-inducing piano melody from before, it's some sort of Boyzoney, Westlifey nonsense that is not only hated by me but would have been utterly detested by my father.

'It's perfect,' I say.

I make a move towards the room at the back, but Damien touches me on the shoulder gently. 'There's a couple more things,' he says. 'I know you said flowers weren't really his thing, but I have a friend at the florist and she had a wreath that had been paid for and not picked up. It was going to go to waste. It's in there at the moment, but I can get rid of it if you prefer…?'

'I genuinely do not care what you do with it.'

There's a part of me determined to break him and get even a small reaction – but he's stoic.

'I think I'll leave it in there,' Damien says. 'The next thing is the coffin and whether you'd like it open or closed. I know you weren't keen on a viewing the other day, but this will be the last opportunity.'

'You can padlock the lid closed if you want.'

'You'd prefer it shut?'

'I'd prefer it in the ground.'

Another short nod, but there's still nothing approaching anything other than a professional response.

'The final thing is whether you'd like to speak. I know that you previously said—'

'You can do the talking.'

'Not a problem.' He straightens his suit and then steps to the side. 'I'll go and sort out closing the casket. If you wait here, I'll be back in a few minutes.'

When he leaves, I take a seat in the arc of chairs that is near the entranceway. I swig from my bottle and enjoy the gentle burn of the liquid. I'm under the air-conditioning vent and the chilled breeze leaves me shivering. Another drink sees to that.

I look up when the door goes and Helena shuffles in. She's dressed in a black skirt-suit that I suspect has been making too many appearances in recent times. I expect her to close the door, but she holds it open and Chris and then Kirsty appear, each wearing black. There was no indication they'd be here when I saw Chris earlier and it's hard to hide my surprise.

When they're all inside, Helena comes across to me and clenches my hands in between her own. 'I thought I'd get some support down here for you, love.'

I peer up to Chris, who's shifting uncomfortably in his suit. Kirsty is silently fuming, like she accidentally shredded a winning lottery ticket.

'Thanks,' I say as she releases my hands. 'I wasn't expecting you all.'

'I lived next door to Dennis for all these years. Wouldn't be right if I let him pass without paying my respects.'

Damien chooses that moment to reappear from the back room. 'Everything's ready,' he says, with a thin smile.

I glance up to the clock above him, which reads ten minutes to four.

'You go in,' I say, talking to Helena. 'I'm going to wait out here for a little longer. I'll be in at four.'

Helena doesn't see anything wrong with this and shuffles across the reception, disappearing into the back room with her son and daughter-in-law steps behind. Chris stops in the doorway for a moment, turning and narrowing his eyes slightly as he takes me in. I suspect it's not only my outfit he's querying.

Damien stands close with his hands behind his back. 'I'll wait in the back for you,' he says. 'Give you a few minutes here to compose yourself.'

'Thank you.'

He disappears and I continue sitting and waiting, counting down the seconds.

At four minutes to the hour, the door sounds again and four men shuffle in. They are all in suits but have maintained an air of scruffiness with varying degrees of untucked shirts, trousers that are too short, and small holes in the suits themselves.

All four are still better dressed than me, of course.

They turn, looking where to go, before one of them says, 'Are you sure it's here?'

Another pulls a newspaper cutting from his pocket and scans it. 'That's what it says.'

'Through there,' I say, pointing towards the back room.

The group look down towards me and move collectively in the direction I indicated, before one of them stops and turns. He's likely in his late-sixties, unshaven, with a blotchy red nose and cheeks.

'You're not little Abigail, are you?'

'Not so little any more.'

He looks me up and down, silently querying my outfit. I have no idea who he is, though assume he's some sort of drinking buddy.

'Yer dad didn't think you'd come,' he says.

'I guess he bet his house on it.'

The man narrows his eyes slightly, not getting it. 'He missed yer.'

'I bet he did.'

'Talked about yer loads.'

'What did he say?'

'That you'd gone to London and were doing well for yerself. He was right proud.'

He stands, waiting for a response – but I don't know what to say. The truth is that Dad had little idea how I was getting on away from here. We spoke with enormous infrequency and met even less often. I suspect his pride was closer to guilt.

'Thanks for coming,' I say, though I still have no idea who the men are.

They seem to accept this and head through to the back room.

Three minutes to four.

Two minutes.

The Boyzone or Westlife track changes to something equally offensive, which I take as a cue to push myself up. When I get into the back room, heads turn – though it's only Helena, Chris, Kirsty, the four men, and Damien.

The casket is on a plinth towards the back of the room. It's light brown, with brass handles. Probably expensive, though I suppose it was my father's final expense. I wonder if he knew that, were it left to anyone else – especially me – he'd have been in a cardboard box.

The wreath is resting on top of the coffin, while the rest of the room is decorated with neutral colours and low-lighting. The dreadful music continues to play as I take the seat at the back, closest to the exit.

Damien moves across until he's standing on a step, close to the coffin. He glances up towards the clock and then thanks everyone for coming.

The next few minutes are a blur. Damien bangs on about the circle of life and a whole bunch of other stuff that probably doesn't come from *The Lion King*. I tune out more or less immediately. There's a Bible reading and it's as he finishes that I pull myself to my feet.

'I do want to say something.'

Damien was mid-sentence, but he stops himself and nods in my direction.

'Of course,' he says. 'For anyone who doesn't know, this is Dennis's daughter, Abi Coyle.'

I head to the step at the front, tightly clutching my bottle. As I turn to take in the room, the door opens and a young woman pokes her head inside. I figure she's in the wrong place but, after a brief look inside, she continues into the room and sets herself down in the seat where I'd been sitting previously. The unexpected presence throws me temporarily because she's so young. At a guess, she's fifteen or sixteen, with chestnut hair tied into a ponytail, plus a black dress and thick glasses. It looks as if she's come for a funeral – though I can't imagine any way in which she knew my father.

After she's settled, I realise everyone is understandably looking to me. I clear my throat and then wonder why I stood in the first place.

'Dad was many things,' I start, although, even part way through the sentence, I'm not sure where it's going. 'Many things to many people. He liked drinking and football and racing. He was an Elwood man in every sense of what that means.'

I risk a glance towards the small number of people in the room and see that everyone's eyes are on me. I have no idea what I'm doing or why I'm doing it.

'He was always there for his neighbours,' I say. 'A constant. An acceptable face in an acceptable area. He played football when he was younger. He ran. He liked Springsteen and Elvis and Pink Floyd. His favourite film was *A Clockwork Orange*… or it was the last time I ever really knew him.'

The girl I don't know is watching me eagerly, hanging on the words. I want to ask who she is.

'We weren't close,' I say. 'I've not seen him in eight years. The last time was at a service station. It was Christmas and it was raining. He told me he'd lost his coat and he was shivering underneath four jumpers. We had a Burger King… well, he did. I bought it. I nicked a couple of his chips and then we went in opposite directions. He was drunk but had driven down the motorway anyway.'

I stop and take a breath, then have a drink from my bottle. The foreign vodka is as harsh as an Arctic winter and I can't stop myself from coughing down the final drops. I ignore the guests and continue.

'There's only one time I ever remember him having something to say that was worthwhile. He came home drunk one night, like every night, I suppose. My mum had walked out a day before and I didn't know if she was coming back. He didn't know either – but he punched me to the floor and then kicked me in the face.'

I push my hair to the side, running a finger along the scar.

'He did this – and then he broke my jaw for good measure. I woke up in the bathroom. I was cradling the bowl, like a mother with a newborn. There was blood and vomit on the floor and this smell like nothing I'd ever known before. The worst of everything. Literal hell. It was maybe three or four in the morning and the sun was starting to come up. He'd sobered up a little and he started to cry when he saw me. He told me to leave the house, to get the hell out of Elwood because, if I stayed, he'd never be able to stop. And then, in that instance at least – and perhaps for the first time ever – I did exactly what I was told.'

I have another drink from my bottle and then use it to salute the few people in attendance, as if offering a toast.

'This one's for you, Dad. I'm off to the pub.'

TWENTY-SEVEN

I skip the Wetherspoon's and head for the grotty old man's pub on one of the back streets away from the High Street. This is definitely more Dad's scene, with the faded sports photographs on the wall, the blackened ceiling and the flat, warm ale being served in dimpled glasses with handles.

I'm the only woman here. There are a handful of old men scattered around the various seats, plus two lads on the fruit machines, who either look very young for their age or are getting away with something they shouldn't.

I order a vodka and Coke from the barman.

'You can't have outside drinks in here,' he says, nodding at the bottle in my hand. I'm so used to carrying it that I'd forgotten it was with me.

'It's water,' I say, holding it up.

He gives me a crooked, knowing look but doesn't add anything. He's around my age and I wonder if I know him from school.

I settle myself in a corner alcove, close to a quiz machine. Nobody from the funeral followed me here, not that I particularly expected them to. It wasn't about them. There are TVs on the walls around the room showing cricket, although the sound is muted and nobody seems to be watching.

The first drink is gone in one and then I press back into the booth so the barman can't see as I sip from my bottle. The sun shines through the grimy window and I start to feel sleepy. If it wasn't the fact I'd likely be thrown out, I could nap here.

I thought getting the funeral out of the way would lift some sort of burden. I'd end up feeling freer and happier but, in truth, I don't think anything has changed. Dad was dead before and he's dead now. My tantrum next to his coffin made no impact on that, or him.

I head to the bar and order another drink, then ask the barman to switch a twenty into pound coins. Back in my corner, I feed the first coin into the quiz machine, although I quickly realise I don't know as much as I thought.

As I'm losing my money, a pair of men slot into the booth closest to mine, each nestling a pint of amber.

'I'm not sure about this,' the first man says. He's probably in his fifties and, judging by his accent, local.

'I don't have to use your name,' the other says. 'It would be up to you.'

'Bit late with us sitting in a pub, isn't it? Anyone can see us.'

'True – but perhaps it's best if we do use your name? People who read the piece will understand what you're going through. There'll be employers who might be able to help.'

I sneak a sideways glance and realise I know one of the men. The guy with a local accent is Kevin, a lad with whom I went to school. We were never friends, but it's not like we were enemies. He was one of those kids who actually seemed to enjoy learning, which instantly set him apart from most of the rest of our year. I don't recognise the other guy – but he pushes his phone towards the centre of the table, face up.

'I'm going to record this, if it's all right,' he says.

Kevin shrugs and slumps into his seat, looking defeated. 'Fine.'

'How long have you been at Hendo's?'

'Twenty-one years.'

'And you found out three months ago that you're going to be made redundant?'

'Exactly. My boss didn't know – or that's what he said. I got a letter in the post, saying I was being given three months' notice but that I could leave right away with pay.' Kevin sighs. 'I have no idea what I'm going to do now. There aren't those types of jobs around here. What is there to do? Go and work at the McDonald's on the ring road? Or the KFC?'

'How far would you have to travel to find similar work to what you do now?'

'Maybe an hour – but that would be assuming I could get a similar job anyway. Factories aren't hiring any more. I've been applying, but nobody gets back to you. The job centre wants to send me off to pound shops to stack shelves. I'd be going backwards. You spend your time gaining all these skills, working your way up, and then it's gone. You're back to earning minimum wage and you've wasted twenty years of your life.'

I take my seat again and listen in as Kevin pours his heart out to the guy I assume to be a reporter. When he talks, it doesn't only feel like something happening to him, but something happening to everyone who lives here.

After a while, the reporter stops reporting and asks Kevin what he wants to drink, before heading off to the bar. I've not touched my second drink. I'm considering downing it and leaving when Holly appears in front of me, as if she's materialised from nowhere.

'I was going to go to the funeral,' she says, somewhat breathlessly. 'But I figured it might not be what you wanted, after everything.'

'You figured right.'

Holly sits on the stool across the table from me. 'I heard you'd gone to the pub afterwards. I checked three others before I found you here.'

'News travels fast in Elwood.'

'Always has – and that was before mobile phones.'

'True. Unless there's a kid in a coma – then nobody knows anything about who put him there.'

Holly doesn't take the bait.

'Do you want a drink?' I ask. 'On Dad.'

I'm already reaching into my bag for more cash when Holly waves it away. She's drumming her fingers on the table and fidgeting her legs.

'Did you see Jo on TV this morning?' she asks.

'No,' I say, not wanting to talk about it.

'It was weird. Like watching another person. I've known her all these years but never seen her so… *focused*.'

It's a strange choice of word, probably an odd thing to notice, but I know precisely what Holly's talking about. There was something not quite in character about the way she was in front of the camera, especially given the manic way she'd behaved in accusing Stephen of being the driver not long after.

'Ethan could've died,' I say. 'I guess that gave her strength…?'

Holly doesn't seem convinced.

'Did you talk to Rob yesterday?' she asks.

I'm sitting in the sun that's beaming through the glass behind me. The abrupt change of subject jars and, despite the warmth, a chill flicks along my arms as I realise why she's really come to find me. It's not for a chat about Jo, or the funeral.

Holly's fingers stop drumming on the table and, though I don't look up to her properly, I can feel her staring.

'Yes,' I reply.

'What about?'

'He was asking about uni.'

'Why? You never went.'

Her tone has changed and I can sense that barely concealed fury that I recognise all too well. I know what's coming.

'You'd have to ask him,' I say.

'What did you tell him?'

'I don't remember completely.'

'What *do* you remember?'

'I think I encouraged him to go.'

Holly screws up her face into a snarling picture of indignation. 'That's funny,' she says. 'Because he said you told him to go and never come back.'

I can't meet her gaze. I wish I could disappear under the table and not be seen. 'I, um…'

'You've been sneering since you got back,' Holly says, getting louder.

'That's not true.'

'Just because I don't drive a big car or own a big house, doesn't make you better than me.'

'I don't own *any* car.'

'I run my own business, but when I mentioned that to you, all you could do is turn your nose up.'

I swallow the vodka and Coke, wait a moment, and then finally let her have my gaze. 'It's a pyramid scheme,' I say. 'I wish it wasn't, but you don't own your own business. Nobody gets rich except the people at the top.'

'Oh, and you'd know, would you?'

'Type the name of the product into Google,' I say. 'You don't need me to say anything. I've seen it before.'

'Have you?' She doesn't sound convinced.

'What do you want me to say?'

Holly shuffles backwards on the stool slightly and, as I look past her, I realise everyone is watching us. It's not often this type of free entertainment is on offer on a Friday afternoon. I wonder if, deep down, Holly knows what she's mixed up in. Whether this is why she's angry about Rob and, I suppose, me.

'You should mind your own business,' Holly says.

'I know.'

She pushes herself up until she's standing. 'You're the one who left. It's twenty years on and we're all in the same town. How does that make you better than anyone?'

'I never said it did.'

Holly lunges forward and knocks my bottle onto the floor. The lid wasn't secured fully and the liquid pours onto the sticky wood-grained floor, pooling underneath the seat. 'You're turning into your dad,' she says.

'I'm not.'

She leans in, so that we're almost nose to nose. Her gaze rages. 'You're not better than me, Abigail Coyle.'

There's a moment in which I think she's going to slap me, perhaps a moment in which she thinks that herself. Her hand goes back, but then, before crashing forward, she steps away instead.

'Leave Rob alone,' she says. 'For that matter, leave *me* alone, too.'

'Hol—'

She turns and strides towards the door. I should let her go but try to follow, only succeeding in tripping over her stool and scrambling across the floor. My hands are covered with grit and grime and I get to the front of the pub just as Holly throws herself into her car and drives off. I watch her go, in case she decides to stop for some reason. There's no question I went too far in what I told her son, even if I believe it.

Back in the pub and everyone spins away, almost in unison, pretending they weren't watching.

The barman eyes my grit-flecked hands and arms and nods towards the toilets.

'Are you going to be okay?' he asks.

'I will be after another drink.'

TWENTY-EIGHT

I only realise the day has gone when the sun stops creeping through the window behind. Kevin and the reporter are long gone, as are most of the other people who've drifted in and out of the pub over the course of the evening. There is a haze around the edge of the room and I know I am right at my limit.

The quiz machine makes yet another whooshing series of dings, which it does roughly every minute. I've heard it hundreds of times over the afternoon and evening. It's enough to drive a sane person into an asylum.

The barman stops in front of my table and crouches to pick up my empty glass.

'Can I have another?' I ask.

'We're closing.'

I pluck a twenty-pound note from my bag. 'I can pay.'

'We're still closing.'

'Suit yourself.'

He takes a step away and then turns and perches on the stool where Holly was sitting hours before.

'Do you remember me?' he asks.

I try to take him in, but everything is rough around the edges.

'You seem familiar,' I say, which is the truth. I thought as much when I first saw him.

'Colin,' he replies. 'We were in the same maths class years ago. You sat behind me.'

I rub my eyes, but it doesn't bring him into focus any more clearly.

'I remember,' I say, even though I don't. Nobody wants to be told they're forgotten and forgettable.

'Maybe you should go home,' he replies, kindly.

'My dad's funeral was today.'

'Perhaps that's all the more reason to go home…?'

I shake my head. 'I don't think I have a home.'

Colin stands and disappears to the bar with my glass. He clears a few more from the surrounding tables and then returns to my table with another vodka and Coke.

'On me,' he says, sitting on the stool once more. As best I can tell, it's only us left in here.

I've been around long enough to know what he's thinking as he glances me up and down while trying to pretend he isn't.

'I saw him, y'know…?'

I'm speechless because I was so certain I knew what he was going to say. It was only when he came out with whatever this is that I realise how disappointed I am.

'Saw who?' I ask.

'Ethan. Before he was hit. I was on my way here and he was on his bike. He was riding on the pavement and cut right in front of me. I didn't think anything of it, then I heard a kid had been hit by a car while I was working here. One of the blokes came in and said there were police everywhere. I didn't put it all together until the next morning, when I realised where it happened. I must've seen him about two or three minutes before he was hit.'

My head swirls. I was hoping for… something else – but here we are talking about Ethan instead.

'I saw him, too,' I say.

'When?'

'I was the one who found him in the gutter. His arm was mangled underneath his body. There was blood and dirt and…'

Colin goggles at me and I know I'll be sleeping alone tonight.

'I thought he was dead,' I say.

'Oh… and then you've had your dad's funeral…'

The mention of my father stops me because, despite everything that's happened in the past four days, the two things aren't linked in my mind. What happened to Ethan is appalling. What happened to my father was as inevitable as night following day. The biggest surprise was that it took this long for his liver to bid him cheerio.

Colin nods along, out of his depth. It's not like it's a competition, but I trumped his story of who saw the victim last.

'Did you see a car?' I ask.

'What do you mean?'

'When you saw Ethan. Was there a car nearby?'

He shakes his head. 'I've thought about that every day since – but I can't remember. What about you?'

'I saw the car that hit him, but I don't remember anything about it. I think it was dark, maybe black, but I wouldn't be able to say for sure.'

We sit in silence for a moment and there's still a part of me hoping I didn't misread his thoughts after all.

'Are you going to drink that?' he asks, nodding to the vodka and Coke.

'I've probably had too much.'

'Is that a problem?'

I laugh and then pluck the glass from the table and down the contents. 'Are you trying to get me drunk?' I say, trying to sound alluring, though instantly wondering how hurling a drink down my throat can possibly be seductive.

He glances off to the side. 'I'm married. I'm flattered, but…'

'No, um, that's not what I meant, I…'

Neither of us can look at the other and I'm ready to go. I'm tired of making a fool of myself.

Before I can move, Colin speaks again. 'Do you think it's someone around here? That's what everyone's saying.'

'Ethan's mum thinks it is. Do you know Jo?'

'Not really. I remember her from school. You were friends, weren't you?'

'A long time ago.'

Colin isn't listening. He's already thinking ahead. 'My mum's convinced it's a local. She's been going on about it non-stop, saying it must be someone who lives in the streets around where Ethan was hit.'

I don't reply. The word 'local' sounds creepily ominous.

Colin continues, oblivious. 'She says it's only a matter of time until someone cracks.'

'Why?'

'Mum reckons they're bound to. Nobody can keep a secret like this forever. Whoever hit that kid must've either told someone already or they're going to.'

I wonder if that's true. People live with all sorts of secrets, whether it's cheating on husbands or wives, or any number of awful things. Is this any different?

'What do you think?' I ask.

Colin shrugs. He says, 'One minute,' before disappearing off to the bar.

He returns a few moments later with another vodka and Coke for me and half a pint of lager for himself. He places both drinks on the table, then we pick them up in unison and exchange a 'cheers', before each taking a mouthful.

'I don't think anyone will come forward,' he says.

'No?'

'That's it for them, isn't it? Forget the police, forget any charges. Forget prison. That's almost irrelevant. It's maybe a couple of years in prison? I don't know – but it's over for whoever it is. They can never live here again. It probably *is* someone who lives here – but we both know most of the people who live here have *always* lived here. It's not like there are loads of people moving in and out. Say someone holds their hand up and says they did it – they're done. Not just them, their entire family. They can never live here again – but they've probably been here their entire life, so where are they going to go?'

I picture the graffiti on Stephen's door and his smashed window. That was on the basis of a rumour, let alone anything concrete. Colin is right. If someone ever admits to being the driver of the car that hit Ethan, that person will never again live in Elwood.

Colin is on a roll, getting out the thoughts that have likely been plaguing him ever since he saw Ethan riding his bike. 'In some ways, this is worse than a murder,' he adds. 'At least with that, there would be a motive. Some people would reckon you had a point, or a reason. With this, the driver left a kid to die.' He clicks his fingers. 'A split-second choice to drive away and your life is done. The only way out is saying nothing. That's why I don't reckon the driver will ever be found. Not unless they left some sort of evidence. Who'd admit to doing it? You'd be mad.'

It might be because I'm tipsy but, perhaps for the first time since I found Ethan, it feels as if I understand what's going on in this town. Colin's correct in every way. Of course the driver isn't going to come forward. It's nothing to do with morality and everything to do with practicality. This isn't a big city in which someone can move from one side to the other and lose themselves. Whoever did this had two choices. The first was to get the hell away from the scene and hope life can continue as normal; the second was to lose everything.

Colin sups his pint and then nudges my half-full glass with his. 'I have to clear up,' he says.

I take the hint and finish the drink.

'Do you need a taxi to get home?' he asks.

'I think I'll be all right.'

He stands and takes the glasses. 'Was good catching up. My day off is Sunday, but I'm in every other day if you're in the mood. You should—'

I push myself up and it feels like I'm underwater. There's a glossy mist to the room and, though Colin continues to speak, I can't make out the words. The final two drinks have pushed me over the edge.

'See y'around,' I say, or try to. I think that's what comes out.

I hover for a moment, but Colin is on his feet and starting to collect glasses. When he fails to turn back to me, I head for the door. It feels like my body is a step or two ahead of my thoughts. Or, perhaps it's behind?

It's still warm outside, despite the blackened sky, and I stumble into the wall of the pub as I try to figure out which way will take me back towards Dad's house. The sound of someone's drunken singing clings to the breeze in the distance. The phantom warbler is doing a terrible job of banging out a Meatloaf track.

I walk on autopilot in a way I never did when I lived elsewhere. In a city, there is always another route to get home; always another alley that seems to have appeared from nowhere. Here, even with the new housing estates, it's like I have an implanted homing device to know where I'm going.

As I get to the park, I realise that, while I've spent the day in the pub, other people have been working hard to set up the site for tomorrow's fete. They have finished erecting a huge marquee off to the side, close to the tennis courts; plus there is a long row of stalls along the side, where the bonfire was burning the other night. Red, white and blue bunting is looped around the corner of the park, strung to the lamp posts and trees – and there's a large sign reading 'Welcome to Elwood' that's been hung from the park gates.

The park is seemingly deserted as I drift my way through to the far side, emerging close to where I found Ethan. The flowers and footballs almost seem to be breeding, with the covering now stretching out from the verge and onto the roadside itself. There's a shadow of a figure standing underneath the lamp post, someone lithe and lean, head bowed in a hoody.

I must make a noise because the man turns and looks along the street towards me. We stare at one another and it feels like I've been recognised, even though I have no idea who the figure is.

In a flicker, the man turns and hurries away, hands in pockets, head dipped. It could be one more person wishing Ethan well – and yet it feels like something more. There was something about the way he was hovering that didn't feel right. Something morbid.

Or it could be my muddied mind playing tricks.

As I take the turn for Beverly Close, a shiver creeps across me. I turn and squint into the darkness, though there's nobody there. Nobody I can see, in any case.

I round the corner where Dad's house sits and then hear a scuffed movement from behind. I spin quickly, staring towards the shadows close to the alley that runs along the back of the house.

'Hello?'

Nobody appears. Nobody moves.

'Chris…?'

Helena's drive is clear and Chris's car isn't on the street. I'm not sure why I think it's him, but he's appeared in a lot of places around me since I got back to Elwood.

I look up to the house, but there's a blinking red dot in the corner of my vision and my legs suddenly feel like they can't hold me up any longer. I fumble with the key, scratching around the lock and probably scarring the door itself until I eventually bundle myself into the house. I slam the door and lock it, before rushing through to the kitchen. Sweat is pouring from my head, jabbing into my eyes with stinging tendrils. Trying to rub it away only makes it worse.

It's only as I go to drink from it that I realise my bottle is no longer in my hand. I reach for it on the side, but it isn't there either.

There's nothing quite like that moment of panic when reaching for something like keys or a phone and realising it isn't there. I must have left my bottle in the pub.

I start for the front door again, but then remember the pub was closing as I was leaving. It's only a bottle – and Holly spilled the contents anyway – but it feels like more.

I've closed my eyes at some point and, when I open them again, I see my phone number on the fridge. Perhaps it's that and the thought that my father died here alone, or maybe it's the loss of my bottle. One thing should be more important than the other – but I'm not sure it is. Either way, there are tears rolling down my face and a sinking, longing in my chest that feels like it might never fully be gone.

TWENTY-NINE

I wake in my own bed, though my lower back and neck aches from having contorted myself into some sort of coiled position. I'm way too old for all this. The curtains at the back of the room are open and light bursts across the floor. My mouth is dry, with a bitter, earthy taste lingering. The jingly jangle of 'Greensleeves' sounds from somewhere outside, though it takes me a few seconds to realise it must be coming from an ice cream van.

At some point last night, I took off all my clothes, put myself to bed and plugged in my phone to charge. I remember none of it – but then I'm a good drunk.

My phone says it's Saturday and after midday. It's the day of the fete and town life is continuing without my father and without Ethan.

I head onto the landing, past my father's door, and into the bathroom. I wince every time I see the state of the place, but it's this or nothing. I brush my teeth and shower, then get dressed and head downstairs. The sink filled with dishes is testament to the truth that I'm never going to do anything about cleaning the house. There's a somewhat childish instinct of it not being my mess to begin with – but there's also the fact that I simply don't want to do it. It's one of the great underrated benefits of being an adult that, if you don't want to do something, you can simply say no.

Next to Dad's newspaper stack is a pile of phone books going back at least a decade. I don't touch them, but it does give me the idea to Google local home clearance. I call the first company listed, something called AAA Trash Bang Wallop. It's answered on the second ring by a man who sounds like he's in the middle of doing something else while talking. He introduces himself as Gav.

'Do you clear entire houses?' I ask.

Gav replies with a laugh and 'every day'.

'How much does it cost?'

'Depends on the house. Depends on the contents.'

'My dad died. There's so much he left. If you leave the appliances, you can keep more or less anything you want.'

The sound is muffled for a moment as Gav says something away from the speaker. When he talks again, there's unquestionably more enthusiasm in his tone.

'*Anything?*' he asks.

'I just want it gone.'

'How about Monday?'

'Perfect.'

He takes my address, wishes me a belated sorry for my loss, and then hangs up.

Little things can make such a difference. Nothing has changed, not really, and yet the short conversation makes me feel like I've achieved something. As soon as the clearance guy has been, I'll contact some deep cleaners – and then the house will go up for sale. That's it. The Coyle family – and me especially – will officially be done with Elwood.

I fill a mug with water and drink it down, watching my fingers tremble as I hold the cup. I'm on a second mugful when I realise I'm not missing my bottle. It was almost an extension of me for a while but, now the funeral is done, perhaps it wasn't about me after all.

It feels like a waste to be inside today, so I find my shoes and head out. Upbeat pop music hangs in the air and I follow it around the corner, along Beverly Close, past Ethan's blanket of tributes, and onto the park.

The stalls are all along the far side of the green and, with the big marquee at the High Street end, this side is free for people to claim their patch of England. There's a dad playing cricket with his sons over near the trees. Three short stumps have been jammed into the ground and I watch as he smashes the ball back over one of the children's heads, before setting off to run to another stump and back again. He completes five runs before the boys manage to get the ball back – and then he doubles over, trying to get his breath.

Around the rest of the park, families, couples and groups of young people have laid down blankets, camp chairs or clothes to mark their territory. I weave around six or seven sunbathing teenage girls who've set up their encampment on top of their towels. A similar-sized group of teenage boys are a short distance away, watching the girls, while half-heartedly kicking around a football.

I continue on towards the stalls, stepping around a family of four who have cracked open a picnic basket and are passing around a plastic tub of cocktail sausages. On past them, and I'm two-thirds of the way across the park when everything stops. It's like someone's pressed pause. The trees aren't swaying, people are standing still, the music is mute… except that's not what's happening. Everyone else is continuing to move and it's me who's paralysed.

I've gone back in time as the sickly-sweet smell of candyfloss drifts across from the row of stalls. The memory appears from nowhere of a summer fete here with Mum, Dad and me. The three of us were on a blanket over near the trees, sitting and waiting for the late-night fireworks. Dad bought me candyfloss and we walked across the park together, to get back to where Mum was waiting on the blanket for us.

It must've been thirty years ago. More – but, all of a sudden, it feels like it's now. When I think of family, I never think of happiness. The two things are opposites… and yet I suppose we were happy at one point.

Everything speeds up again and I blink back to the now. There's a big wheel next to the stalls that hasn't stopped turning. A bouncy castle next to that, on which kids continue to bump around. Over near the marquee, someone's lugging a giant marrow or cucumber inside, ready to be judged.

I'm thrown by the memory, wondering whether it's real, or if I've concocted it myself. I turn away from the direction of the candyfloss and start to move towards the man playing cricket with his boys and it's as I'm getting my bearings that I almost walk into Jo.

I don't recognise her at first, mainly because of the large sunglasses that encompass half her face. It's only the people around her that make me notice. There is the same reporter who was talking to Kevin in the pub yesterday, along with a small phalanx of women. There are six people in total, with no sign of Neil or Owen.

'Ethan loved the bouncy castle,' Jo says, speaking with a volume that's above what she would need to be heard by the reporter. He is at her side, holding his phone out towards her. 'I told him I'd get him one for his next birthday party.'

'Do you come to the fete every year?' the reporter asks.

'I've never missed one,' Jo says. 'Even when I was a girl, Mum would never book holidays for this week.'

'And you've lived here your whole life?'

'Yes.'

Jo and her entourage are almost past me when she stops and notices. 'Oh my God!' she exclaims. 'This is my best friend, Abi.'

Before I can move, she has her arms around me. Her skin is clammy and hot and, when she pulls away, her gaze is unfocused. It's the opposite of how she was with Diane.

'He's writing a story about me,' Jo says, turning to the reporter. She sounds so much more excited than she should.

'More about Ethan,' the reporter says.

He narrows his eyes, trying to place me, but not quite able to. The train of women around him who've been following Jo all look at me with suspicion that I might be about to steal their apparent fame. I don't know any of them and I doubt there's a single one who's older than thirty. At least one is young enough to be Jo's daughter.

'Remember when we were kids?' Jo says to me. 'On fete day, there used to be one of those slides with all the bumps on the way down. We'd try to run up it and then slide back down. You, me and Holly.'

The reporter seems uninterested in this, but Jo doesn't realise as she turns to him and points towards the bouncy castle. 'It was right there.'

'I remember,' I say, which isn't true, although there seems no point in getting hung up on it.

Jo isn't listening anyway as she half talks to the reporter – 'It was her dad's funeral yesterday' – then to me: 'How was it?'

The way everyone including the reporter angles away from me makes it clear that it's only Jo who doesn't pick up on my unease.

'It was what it was,' I say.

'Oh, darling…'

She puts her arm around me once more, but she's even hotter now. There is sweat pooling around her hairline and a small damp patch seeping through the navel area of her top.

'How's Ethan?' I ask.

She glances to the reporter and raises her voice slightly. 'I spent three hours with him this morning. I'll be going back after this. I just wanted to come to the fete and see what it was like. For him really. I'll tell him about it later.'

'But how is he?'

She almost shrugs. I see her arms tense, but then she catches herself. 'No change.'

Before I can ask anything else, a young woman appears at my side. She's around twenty, in a short dress – with a boyfriend standing a little further away, watching us awkwardly.

'Excuse me,' the woman says. 'Are you Ethan's mum?'

'Yes,' Jo replies.

The woman giggles nervously and then speaks at a pace that's so quick, it sounds like a foreign language at first. 'I was just saying to my boyfriend that it was you. I saw you on the TV yesterday with Diane Young. She's amazing, isn't she? You were amazing. Gosh, poor Ethan. How is he? How are you? I hope he gets well soon. And that they catch the driver. Have you heard anything? Not that you could tell me if you had, of course. Oh, God, I can't believe it's you.'

It takes a moment for everything to sink in, but, by the time anyone has understood what she's saying, the woman has held up her phone.

'Could I get a pic?'

Jo seems momentarily confused, but then breaks into a smile. 'Sure.'

The women pose together, each giving a thumbs-up for the camera before the picture-taker steps away with another burst of thank yous. If it wasn't for her boyfriend, she'd have almost certainly latched onto the group.

I feel out of breath having only watched the interaction, but Jo is already set to move on.

'I'll show you the big wheel,' she says to the reporter, while needlessly pointing towards it. 'Ethan went on it last year.'

Jo takes a step away and then nods back to me.

'Come on,' she adds, leaving me little option other than to join the ever-growing crowd.

I have no idea from which publication the reporter comes, nor what he's supposed to be writing, but I can tell from the attention he's paying that he hadn't come for a tour of every mundane part of Elwood's Summer Fete.

Jo leads us around the field, pointing out everything from a tree under which she once had a sandwich, to an old toilet block where Ethan is forbidden to go. All the while, people continue to approach, partly to ask after Ethan – but also to have their moment with the woman who was on TV the day before. I wonder what the reporter is making of it. It would be hard to miss that Jo is a person who is enjoying the attention a little *too* much.

After a slow lap of the park, we end up close to the flowers that are marking the spot where I found Ethan. Jo talks and talks, and it's hard not to wince when she says she wishes people had donated money instead of the flowers. The reporter asks what she means and she tries to right the moment by saying Ethan didn't like flowers – though I fear the damage is done. I know what she meant and I suspect the reporter does too. Whether he'll write that is another question.

It's not long before he says he has to go, and Jo replies she needs to get back to the hospital. Over the course of the walk, the group of women have dissipated back to wherever they came – and, at the mention of hospital, the final one drifts back towards the main area of the park as well. As the reporter heads onto the back streets, it leaves just Jo and myself next to the flowers.

'A photographer was round this morning to take pictures,' Jo says. 'He came to the house and then the hospital. I think it's going to be a big piece in the weekend magazine.'

'That's nice,' I say, not knowing how else to reply.

She turns in a circle. 'Can't remember where I parked the car. I've got to get going.'

She eventually decides her car is over towards the bus station and hurries away while looking at her phone. I watch her go and then realise it isn't only me who's keeping an eye on her. Off to the side, half hidden behind a lamp post, is her other son. She walked past him without noticing.

When Owen realises I've clocked him, he turns to walk away, only stopping when I call his name.

'How's your brother?' I ask when I get to him.

Owen's typing something into his phone and takes his time to look up: 'Didn't Mum tell you?'

'She said she'd been at the hospital – but not how Ethan was.' Owen rolls his eyes and I quickly add: 'I think she has a lot on her mind at the moment.'

Owen snorts at this. 'Yeah…' He seems to catch himself and adds: 'Nobody seems to care how Ethan's doing. He's not getting worse, but he's not getting better. They said these things can turn in a second. Like, one minute he's on the machine like he is and then he's fine.' Owen clicks his fingers to make the point.

'Your mum seems…'

'Up and down. I know.'

'What about Neil?'

'What about him?'

I think about playing it straight and asking how he's been coping with Ethan in hospital and Jo's mood swings. Instead, without planning it, I go for broke. 'I heard he might be driving, even though he's banned…?'

Owen doesn't reply at first. He glances down to the phone in his hand again and then looks sideways towards where a couple are heading off into the trees.

'I've never seen that,' he says.

'But you've heard it…?'

There's another gap as Owen sucks on his teeth, weighing up a reply or, perhaps, deciding whether to reply at all.

'Neil didn't hit Ethan,' Owen says.

'How do you know?'

Owen's phone dings and he looks sideways again. This time, instead of the disappearing couple, Beth is standing by herself in a floaty, long green dress with her phone in her hand.

'I have to go,' Owen says.

He doesn't wait for a reply, rushing across to Beth before they both turn to walk away together.

Beth stops for a second to look over her shoulder, perhaps wondering if I'm following. When it's clear I'm not, she turns back and continues at Owen's side. They're not holding hands, or acting like a couple might – but I suppose that doesn't mean much. Some couples can't keep their hands off one another in public; others act as if they're complete strangers.

Moments later, they're swallowed by the crowd and out of sight.

It's only when they're gone that I realise that, while he was talking to me, Owen was texting Beth to come and save him.

The exact reason is unclear – except, of course, that I know both Owen and Beth are lying about where he was at the time Ethan was hit.

THIRTY

I almost forget that I've not really spent any time exploring the fete itself. The tour with Jo and the reporter was more point and look. When I was a child, my least favourite aspect was the food judging that happened in the giant marquee. This was mainly because I couldn't understand why I wasn't allowed to *taste* the food. How was I supposed to know one piece of fruit was better than another if I was unable to try it myself?

It could be proof I've grown up, but I find myself in the tent at the same time as they're announcing the results of this year's 'best carrot'. An older woman whoops and punches the air as they announce she's the champion. She then rushes to the stage to collect a rosette. It's probably the most British thing I've ever seen.

On a loop of the tent, I spot a first-prize rosette on the biggest parsnip I could have imagined, wonder how on earth someone gets interested in growing beetroots and cucumbers, and then park myself close to the cheeses. Carrots are one thing – but cheese is something with which I can get on board.

The serenity of the moment is lost with the sound of shouting from the other side of the display. I follow the voices until I get to a small semicircle of people underneath a large banner that reads 'Sponsored by Hendo's'. There's a mix of people hanging around close to rows of breads off to the side – and I can't figure out what's happening at first. There's a tall man in a suit who stands out simply because he's so overdressed compared to everyone else's summer clothes. He's standing upright, with his arms defensively across his front as Neil squares up to him.

'You're spending money on this?' Neil gives it the full finger point as his words slur drunkenly into one another.

The suited man steps backwards, but Neil continues towards him. 'I, um…'

'You're laying all of us off, while sponsoring *this*?' Neil continues.

'There was already a commitment in place.'

Neil isn't listening: 'You're destroying this town. Hendo's is everything around here. We've given our lives for you.'

The man continues trying to move away as Neil keeps lunging towards him. From nowhere, an older man in an apron jumps between them and starts muttering things like 'I think we should all calm down' and 'Maybe this is a conversation for outside…?' He's looking around for some sort of help, but nobody's going forward, mainly because most of the people in attendance are mild-mannered gardeners, not jack-booted security staff.

'It's from a different budget,' the suited man insists.

'So why not move the money around then? If you can afford this, you can afford to keep on some of the lads.'

The man from Hendo's backs into a table full of Victoria sponges, leaving him nowhere to go. The bloke in the apron has been squeezed out to the side as Neil bears down, fists clenched. That's when the man in the suit does the worst thing he could possibly do by resting a hand on Neil's arm. I'm sure he means it to be some sort of comfort, but it feels as if everyone watching, including me, breathes in at the same time. He knows he's messed up, too, instantly removing his hand and trying to backtrack – even though it's too late.

'I know you're having a hard time,' the man says, 'what with everything that happened to your son.'

'He's not my son,' Neil growls.

'No, well… I mean. It's like… Um…'

'How do you know I'm having a hard time? How much are *you* making a year? A hundred grand? Two hundred? More?'

'It's, erm—'

Neil lashes out with his foot, sending a chair cartwheeling across the grass, where it crashes into a display of turnips. The vegetables cascade out of the containers onto the ground and start to roll towards the door flap. The sound of the collision stops Neil where he's standing and he turns to take in the damage he's caused. It's only a second, but, in that time, the man from Hendo's scoots off to the side and makes a run for the exit.

That does it for Neil. In a flash, he's caught the man and grabbed him by the collar. There's a ripping sound and then the man slips to the floor as Neil stands over him, a scrap of white shirt in his hand.

'Are you even sorry?' Neil shouts.

It's hard to see what happens next because it's all a blur of arms and legs. The man in the suit is trying to get to his feet, while also trying to bat away Neil. The problem comes when he slips. He reaches up, trying to steady himself, and I'm not sure what version is true after that. He either tries – and succeeds – in slapping Neil across the face, or it's an accidental flail of the arm.

Regardless of what's true, the crack echoes around the tent like a backfiring car. Neil staggers and there's a clear 'ooh' from the surrounding crowd.

The suited man is on his feet now.

'Sorry,' he says. 'I didn't mean that, it was—'

Neil launches himself forward and crunches a punch into the other man's jaw. The noise booms louder than the slap as the suited man's head snaps backwards. Crimson spurts from his lip, spraying across the top half of his face and into his eye. He reels away, holding his face and gasping with shock, pain, or both. He then trips over one of the errant turnips and collides with a tent pole.

Nobody has moved – except Neil, who looms over the other man, his fists still balled.

'You think you can do this to me?' he bellows. 'To my family? Then you slap me in the face?'

I'm certain he's about to punch the man on the floor again but, from nowhere, a pair of uniformed police officers dash into the tent with the same sense of timing as a person who's forgotten to put their clocks forward.

The first officer slams a shoulder into Neil, rugby-style, taking them both to the ground. The second then dives in and cuffs Neil's hands behind his back.

They haul him to his feet, but Neil's still shouting 'You don't know what it's like' at the suited man. Cuffs or not, he's trying to get back into the fight – but the police officers are too much for him. They bundle him out of the tent flap, with the suited man just behind them, as everyone else watches on in stunned silence.

Everything's happened so quickly that it takes a moment for anyone to react. In the end, it's the guy in the apron who moves first. He plucks a battered turnip from the ground and holds it up, shaking his head.

'Well,' he says. 'I guess I'm not gonna win this year.'

THIRTY-ONE

When I get out of the marquee, I almost instantly spot Beth, or – more specifically – her long green dress. She's with Owen close to the beer garden, although neither of them are holding drinks. With Jo being at the hospital, someone's going to have to pass on the message that Neil's been arrested, so I figure it might be best coming from Owen.

As if Jo doesn't have enough on her plate, with Ethan in intensive care, now her partner's been nicked.

I set off towards Owen and Beth but as soon as I start walking, they head off in the opposite direction. I figure they're trying to avoid me – but then I realise they've not even seen me.

Beth's brother, Petey, is standing with his bike on the edge of the park, almost hidden by the shadows of the trees. He's by himself, next to a clothes recycling bank – but then Chris steps out from behind the giant metal bin. It's not the first time I've seen them together – but this seems more jarring than when they were on the street. That was in the open, where anyone could see, but there can't be much doubt they've purposefully chosen the darkest spot in the park.

They're talking to one another but are too far in the distance for me to be able to hear anything. Either way, it is odd enough in itself. How many men who are almost forty need to be having regular discussions with eight-year-old kids to whom they're not related?

From the way Beth is marching towards them, I figure she's thinking the same. She's separated from Owen because she's moving so much quicker, while I trail after the pair of them.

I get within earshot a few seconds after Beth has reached the recycling bins. She's pointing an angry finger towards Chris's face.

'Stay away from us,' she says, moving herself between Chris and Petey.

'What?' he replies.

'We're out. I don't want to see you talking to Petey again.' She grabs at her brother's hand, but he pulls away.

Owen's standing off to the side with his arms folded. As best I can tell, nobody's noticed me.

'What's caused all this?' Chris says, sounding surprised and defensive. He nods across to Owen. 'It's not because of your brother, is it?'

Beth replies before Owen can open his mouth: 'I don't care. You're not involving Petey any more. You do your own dirty work.'

Chris folds his arms and starts to shake his head. 'Are you really going to walk away?'

'I'm nothing to do with this' – she turns and points at Petey – 'but he's eight years old and he's not doing jobs for you any longer.'

Petey starts with an 'I—' but Beth cuts him off with a terse: 'Shut up.'

'You can't speak for him,' Chris says.

'Good point,' Beth chirps back. 'I'll get Mum involved, shall I? Let her know what's been going on…?'

Chris shrinks a little. He starts with a more conciliatory 'I think—' but Beth cuts him off before he can finish.

'I don't care,' she says again, talking over him. 'If I see you near Petey again – if I even *hear* you've been on the same street as him – I'll get on to the police and tell them some creepy guy is hanging around with my baby brother.'

Chris eyes her but must know he's beaten. He flicks a glance towards Owen and then storms off towards the stalls. When he's gone, Petey starts to protest again, but Beth is not in the mood.

'Don't you dare,' she says. 'If I see you with him again, I'm going to Mum.'

'I'll tell them what you did.'

There's glee and malice in Petey's little eight-year-old eyes. It's the kind of spite that only children can inflict.

'Do it,' Beth dares him.

Petey instantly looks away and Beth knows this is another battle won.

'That's what I thought,' she says. 'It's time to go anyway.'

She takes a step towards the edge of the park and Owen follows. A beat later and Petey picks up his bike and trails them. It's only watching them leave when I realise I was supposed to be telling Owen that Neil had been arrested.

Beth's marching at a pace that would put parading soldiers to shame and, by the time I've started off towards them, they're well on the way back to the marquee.

I have to jog to close the gap but, as I'm nearing the trio, I spot a man and a woman in suits appearing from behind the fence of the beer garden. I arrive just as the suited pair cut in front of Beth, Owen and Petey.

The man doesn't start with niceties. 'Are you Owen Ashworth?' he asks.

Owen glances to Beth and then the newcomers. 'Yes…' he replies.

I assume they're police officers about to tell him about what's happened with Neil – but it's worse than that.

'I'm arresting you in connection with driving otherwise than in accordance with a licence, and driving without insurance. You do not have to say anything, but it may harm your defence if you do not mention, when questioned, something which you later rely on in court. Anything you do say may be given in evidence. Do you understand?'

It's come out so quickly and unexpectedly that nobody, least of all Owen, seems to know what to say.

'I haven't done anything,' Owen eventually manages.

The female officer turns to Beth: 'Are you over eighteen?' she asks.

'Seventeen.'

The officers exchange a glance and then the man speaks again, talking to Owen this time. 'It's best if there's an adult to accompany you to the station,' he says. 'Are your parents around?'

'Mum's at the hospital. There's my stepdad, but I don't know where he is.'

He starts to look around, trying to perform a real-life Where's Wally in order to find Neil – and then, finally, he and Beth notice me.

'Neil's been arrested,' I say.

This surprises everyone. The two officers turn to one another again, while Beth and Owen do the same.

'Arrested?' Owen replies.

'He punched someone in the marquee,' I say, jabbing a thumb in the general direction of the tent.

'He *punched* someone?'

'I think it was a manager from Hendo's.'

The scene turns somewhat surreal as both officers, Beth, Owen and Petey all turn to one another, unsure what happens next.

The male officer speaks next, talking to me. 'Who are you?' he asks.

'Abi,' I reply. 'A friend of Owen's mum.'

'Can you accompany him to the station?'

'What do I have to do?' I ask.

'Be an adult.'

I almost reply that I've never been comfortable with whatever 'being an adult' entails but, instead, I nod towards Owen.

'Is this all right with you?' I ask.

'I didn't do it,' he replies.

The officer seemingly takes this as a yes, offering a quick 'let's go' before turning towards the road and guiding Owen away by his elbow.

THIRTY-TWO

I'm beginning to wonder whether police officers around here have a different definition of the phrase 'right back'. My phone says it's been twelve minutes since the uniformed officer led me here, then disappeared, claiming he'd be 'right back'.

The walls are a dull grey, which matches the floor and ceiling. I was expecting a mirrored wall, plus a video camera – something like what's on television – but there's none of that. This feels like a forgotten room in a forgotten corner. There are a pair of office chairs, one of which has the foam spilling from the back. Aside from a handful of posters on the wall warning of things like not leaving valuables on show, there's nothing else here.

I'm about to poke my head into the corridor when there's a loud clank from the distance. Moments later, there are footsteps – and then the door opens.

Owen's face is drained of colour. He's taller than the uniformed police officer, but his stick-thin arms and legs make him by far the least intimidating of the two.

'You can wait here,' the officer says, nudging Owen towards the spare seat.

I wondered if Owen might be cuffed – but I've probably been watching too much television. The only indication he can't leave is when the officer says he'll be outside the door. Moments later, he heads out, leaving us alone.

There's a long pause as Owen stares at the ground.

'Are you okay?' I ask.

'They took my shoes,' Owen replies, holding his boat-like foot up for me to see.

'Why?'

'Dunno. They've got my phone and wallet, too.'

'I'm sure you'll get everything back…'

Owen doesn't acknowledge this. He shuffles in the seat and I wonder if he might have been more comfortable had I left him the chair that wasn't falling apart. You snooze, you lose and all that.

Perhaps, on reflection, I'm not the best 'adult' for this job.

Owen glances to the door and, more likely, the unseen officer beyond. He lowers his voice to something that's a little above a whisper. 'Mum's on her way,' he says.

He sits with his head low, almost between his knees. His angled elbows jut wide.

I don't know what to say – and don't want to go with anything like 'it'll be all right' – because I'm not sure that it will. Owen might have been arrested for some sort of driving offence, but I very much doubt that's the only reason he's here. They'll be wanting to question him about where he was when his brother was hit. Perhaps someone got around to checking statements and apparent whereabouts? Owen certainly wasn't where he told his mum he was.

'I didn't do it,' Owen says out of nothing. He's still staring at the floor.

'Why do you think they arrested you?' I ask.

'I don't know.'

'They said something about a licence and no insurance. Does that mean they think you've been driving without a licence?'

He doesn't answer and, though I don't know the terms they used, I suspect it's precisely this. Owen's driving test is supposed to be next week, but perhaps he couldn't resist the urge.

'Mum says don't trust the police,' Owen says. 'They fitted up Granddad.'

I think of Holly's anger over me talking to her son – yet here I am alone with Jo's. Do I tell him the truth and risk Jo's wrath, or go along with it? There's not much choice.

'I don't know about that,' I say.

'They're gonna do the same to me, aren't they?'

'I don't think your granddad was fitted up.' I suppose I'm hoping for some big revelation. That Owen will look up and thank me for freeing him from this lie. He doesn't – he barely moves. 'I don't know what to say to you, Owen. I don't think lying will get you too far today.'

He squeezes his ears, then pushes back into the chair and stares towards the door. 'They want me to talk to a solicitor. I said I couldn't afford it and neither could Mum – but they reckon it's free.'

'That sounds right. You should talk to whoever it is.'

'Tell them what?'

'Only you can answer that.'

'What if someone tries to fit me up?'

I wait, somehow knowing he's going to look to me. When he does, and I realise he's craving assurance, it's suddenly the most adult I've ever felt.

'I don't think it's like that any more,' I say. 'If it ever was. All those TV shows of blokes in terrible brown suits throwing people down the stairs don't feel real.'

'But Granddad—'

'I knew him,' I say. 'Everyone in town did. The day before he was arrested for selling stolen goods, he knocked on our door and tried to sell my dad a TV.'

Owen's eyebrows dip into a frown. 'Did he?'

'My dad would've had one if he had the money. Elwood was that sort of place then. If someone wanted a new TV or a video player, something like that, we wouldn't head off to the nearest Argos.'

Owen cracks the slimmest of smiles but doesn't say anything.

'What?' I ask.

'I was going to ask you what a video player is.'

He grins a little wider and then it shrinks away.

I let out a genuine laugh and then continue. 'People would ask around to find out if a neighbour or a friend had a cheap telly they didn't want. Stuff like that would do the rounds. Everything felt so expensive. I don't know what happened. Either way, Jo's dad – your granddad – came knocking with televisions to sell. He went up and down, knocking on everyone's door. The next day, the police found a load of stolen TVs in a garage registered to him. Does that sound like he was stitched up?'

Owen tilts his head to the side. His bemusement makes it look like I've just told him Santa isn't real.

'There would have been other evidence as well,' I say. 'They'd have traced the TVs back to wherever they were stolen. They'd have found out where your granddad was on the night of the theft. They'd have checked his bank account, or looked for cash. People don't get sent to prison *just* for having TVs in a garage.'

He nods and I wonder if, deep down, he already knew.

'All I'm saying is that you shouldn't automatically assume people are out to get you. If there's a solicitor to talk to, I'd be certain they're there to help you.'

He presses back into the chair, apparently considering this.

I want to ask about Beth, Petey and Chris – plus how they're all connected to Ethan. If not everything, I get the sense that Owen knows *something*. It's probably not the moment and, even if it was, I don't get the chance because the door flies open without warning.

'Get your hands off me.'

Owen and I stand as Jo blusters into the room while shrugging off the police officer who'd led in Owen. He tries to block her way, but she's having none of it.

'I knew this would happen,' she adds. 'Just what happened to Dad. You lot are all the same. I'm gonna go to the papers. Someone will get fired over this.'

The officer tries a 'Mrs Ashworth' – but she talks over him, focusing in on Owen.

'What have you told them?'

'Nothing, Mum. I'm waiting for the solicitor.'

'I've told you before not to trust anyone.' She turns back to the officer. 'I'm not having this. I want to speak to your supervisor.'

'He's—'

'Don't give me any of that. I'm not having you fitting up another member of my family. It's—'

'Mum!'

Everyone stops and turns to Owen, who has finally cracked.

'What?' Jo says, slightly quieter than before.

'I'm going to talk to the solicitor.'

'But—'

'I want to do it now – by myself.'

Jo stops and rests against the door frame, as if not able to hold up her own weight. 'What are you saying?' she asks – and it's like she's a different person. The insistence of innocence from moments ago has gone.

'I'm saying I want to talk to a solicitor.'

That's not all he's saying, of course. If nothing else, he's making it as clear as can be that he doesn't want his mother present for whatever it is he has to say to the solicitor.

The officer's not stupid and gets right on it.

'I'll sort it,' he says, offering a hand towards Owen that's eagerly used for him to shuffle past his mum.

'I'll see you later,' Owen says as he disappears out of the room with the officer.

The door slips closed, leaving Jo and me in the room. Jo turns between the door and me, watching disbelievingly.

'What's going on?' she asks.

'They arrested him at the fete. Something to do with driving with no licence or insurance.'

Jo looks at me quizzically, as if wondering if there's a punchline to come. 'What…?'

'I don't know any more than that. They asked me to come along because he's under eighteen.'

'Why didn't they get Neil?'

I stare at her for a moment, wondering if she's having me on. 'Hasn't anyone told you…?'

'Told me what?'

I glance across to the chairs. 'You should probably sit down.'

THIRTY-THREE

The fete is starting to wind down as I get back into the centre of town and the park beyond. Many of the families have drifted away, eager to get off home and have something to eat, or possibly to catch whatever talent show is currently polluting the major TV channels. The main bulk left are groups of young people, who have claimed their own corners of the park. A large mass of fifteen- or sixteen-year-olds are grouped underneath the trees where the cricket game was happening earlier. There's no sport now, unless passing around a two-litre bottle of cider and a joint somehow counts. Twenty years on and the more things change, the more they stay the same.

At the turn for Beverly Close, I stop and take in Ethan's tribute. Some of the flowers towards the back are already starting to brown and, though I can't be sure, I think a few of the newer bunches closer to the road have been stolen. A couple of the footballs have definitely gone. I suppose it was always going to happen sooner or later.

I continue along towards the house but can't face going in quite yet. There's something else I should do anyway. I make my way through the streets until I get to Holly's road. It's quiet, but the smell of barbecue lingers. It's the type of warm, dry Saturday evening that lures Britons out to their back gardens en masse.

The first thing I notice is that the graffiti on Stephen's door is still there, although it has faded slightly. His window has been repaired, which is one thing, I suppose. There are lights on inside his house, though nobody in sight. I move past his towards Holly's. The car she got into outside the pub yesterday is parked on the road by her house. I'd paid no attention to it before, but it's a nearly new dark blue Audi. Perhaps her oils and other boxes of tat aren't tat at all. Maybe she really does make money from it all?

When I knock on her front door, it swings open within a few seconds. There's nobody in the hallway but, as I step inside, Holly's voice sounds from behind the door.

'I thought we said back door.'

It sounds like she's joking but as she starts to close it she realises it's me and she's left in blinking disbelief.

'Oh…' she says.

'Sorry,' I say. 'Were you expecting someone else…?'

Holly stands with her arm outstretched, holding onto the half-closed door. She looks between me and the back of the house but doesn't answer.

'I wanted to apologise about yesterday,' I say. 'You're right. I shouldn't have been so dismissive over your business and I'm really sorry. It's not an excuse, but it's been a really weird week for me. It's partly being back here – but then there's everything with Jo and Ethan – plus with Dad, and the house. My head's all over the place.'

Holly seems frozen, unable to either close the door, ask me to leave, or say anything at all.

'I'm sorry for anything else I said,' I add. 'Mum turned up on my doorstep the other day and—'

'Your *mum* showed up?'

'Right.'

Holly pauses for a moment, considering her options, and then finally makes a move by closing the door behind me.

'When did you last see her?' she asks.

'She walked out a short time before I did, so twenty years.'

'Wow… didn't she ever contact you?'

'No. I didn't know anything about her. I didn't know why she left, or where she went. She never contacted me and then, out of nothing, she was on my doorstep.'

Holly frowns wordlessly, though it's hard to blame her for not knowing what to say. It still feels like something I might have dreamt.

'Why did she come back?'

I turn backwards, towards the kitchen. 'Can we sit down? I've done a lot of walking today, with the fete and everything.'

Holly stares past me and screws up her face. I can tell she wants to say no – but she also wants to hear what I have to say.

Curiosity wins.

'I've not got long,' she says.

'I guess we could talk another time…?'

She breathes out loudly, but then makes her decision, passing me and scooching around the boxes towards the kitchen. 'Come on,' she says.

I follow her, wondering why she never seems to sit in the living room – and hoping it isn't because it's full of boxes.

Holly continues standing, resting on the counter at the rear of the kitchen, in front of the back door. I sit, because I was the one who'd brought it up. Holly doesn't offer a drink, or anything else. She's drumming her fingers.

'I don't really know why Mum came back,' I say. 'Perhaps to see if Dad was really dead. We ended up arguing. I guess that's what I do. I didn't mean to argue with you either. I didn't come back for any of this.'

Holly dips her head slightly. There's a second or two in which it feels like things could go either way, but then: 'Maybe I over-reacted, too. It's not like I want Rob to live in Elwood forever – I just want him to think about going to a uni around here.'

The sound of a television drifts through from the adjacent room. It's hard to make out anything specific, but somebody on screen is getting incredibly excited. I wait for a moment, remembering how much my younger life revolved around the small TV my dad got me for my bedroom when I was seven or eight. For whatever reason, it's only today's conversation with Owen that makes me realise it was probably stolen. It was shiny and new – and there's no way Dad would have been able to afford something like that if it was in a shop.

'I'm leaving Elwood,' I say, blinking back to Holly's kitchen.

She stares at me for a moment and then: 'Because of our argument?'

'No. Because of me. Someone's coming in to clear Dad's house on Monday, then I'll get some cleaners to do the rest. I'm going to put it on the market after that and take whatever someone will offer. I'll use that to get started somewhere else.'

'You're not going back to London?'

'It doesn't feel like home any more.' A pause. 'Nowhere does.'

There's a sound from somewhere towards the back of the house and Holly spins quickly, before looking back to me.

'I'd love to talk more,' she says, 'but I've got to—'

Holly doesn't finish because the back door clunks and then swings into her back, where she's trying to block it. She's forced to move further into the kitchen – and then a familiar man blusters his way inside. He spots me before he sees Holly, frowns, and then takes a step back outside before he realises it's too late.

The last time I saw Jo's ex-husband, Mark, was when he was arguing with Jo and Neil in the car park at the back of the hospital. He's in smarter trousers and a fitted shirt now, looking like he's ready for an evening out. He shares a sideways look with Holly and then turns back to me and forces a smile.

'Hi, Abi,' he says. 'I didn't recognise you outside the hospital the other night. Nice to see you again. How have you been keeping?'

'I've been away for twenty years, so there'd be a lot to cover.'

He forces a smile. 'Good point.' Another glance to Holly. 'I was just coming over to help with the plumbing. Boiler's been playing up, hasn't it?'

Holly nods along. 'Yeah, um… the hot water keeps running out.'

'You're a bit overdressed,' I say.

Mark looks down at his outfit. 'I'm just checking it over tonight. I'll be back with the tools and everything another time. Got to make sure I've got what I need and all that.'

It's suddenly clear as to why Holly was so defensive of Mark and so down on Neil. It feels like all our conversations have been dancing around precisely this. Mark's the father of Jo's two children – and Holly is Jo's best friend.

'I'll leave you to it,' I say, pushing myself up and taking a step towards the door back to the hallway. 'We can do this another time.'

I'm already in the hall when Holly calls me back. When I turn, she's standing right in front of me and we're wedged in by the boxes.

'You won't tell Jo, will you?' she asks.

I weigh it up for a second, but only because there's a part of me buried deep that would embrace the drama. 'I think she's got enough on her plate.'

THIRTY-FOUR

Kylie is playing over the speaker system as I run and throw myself into the inflated wall of the bouncy castle. The springy material pings me away and I land on my back, laughing as someone jumps over the top of me. I push myself up, but, as my hand goes down, the platform underneath starts to feel squishy. There's a loud squealing of air and the walls of the castle start to collapse inwards. Everyone else who was bouncing has disappeared and I'm by myself as everything starts to get darker. I'm fighting to get out, but everything's so heavy. I call for Dad, then Mum, but nobody comes. Kylie is no longer singing about doing a brand-new dance; instead, there's a jingly, buzzing that sounds like it's getting louder and closer and…

My phone is ringing. I roll over in my bed and pluck it from under the pillow. The bright light burns, with the word 'Jo' seeping into my mind.

'Hello,' I say. My voice sounds groggy but, for the first morning in a long time, my throat isn't gravel.

'Abi?'

'Are you all right?'

She lets out a noise that's something between a gasp and a sob. I'm not awake enough to know, though I push myself up into a sitting position.

'Can you come over?' Jo says.

'What's happened?'

'Just… please come. I need you.'

'Are you at the house?'

There's no reply because she's already gone. There are so many things that might have happened – whether to Ethan at the hospital, or Owen, Neil, or both, at the police station. Then there's her ex-husband with her best friend. Any of those things on their own would be enough to bring a person to their knees – but all together…

I heave myself out of bed and am on the way to the bathroom when I realise I went the entire day yesterday without my bottle. It's been almost an extension of myself recently. A third arm or leg. Something with which I rarely part. I try to remember the last time I was without it. I definitely had it at Christmas last year and for a few months before that. It could even be a whole year. It's not only that I was without it yesterday – but that I didn't *think* about it.

The bathroom still turns my stomach, but I force myself to get on with things – and then put on some clothes and leave the house.

Ethan's tribute seems to have shrunk even further from when I last saw it. At one stage, there had been four or five footballs – but only one remains. I continue past that onto the park, which is like a festival campsite on a Monday morning. Empty bottles and food wrappers have been dropped intermittently across the lawn, while on the far side there's a van parked next to the marquee and a small group of people are in the process of taking it down. The sight of the deflated bouncy castle has me blinking back to a dream I'd forgotten, wondering if I actually had been on one once, calling for my dad.

The rest of the town is deserted. The blue sky and early-morning heat only make it eerier. As I head along the High Street, it feels like I'm walking through a horror movie set. Other than the workers on the park, the first person I see is a man mowing his grass a street or two over from Jo's. It's a Sunday morning, so I suppose it's a rule that there's always one person who has to annoy the entire neighbourhood.

There's no answer when I knock on Jo's door. I tap on the glass, but that gets no response either, so I try calling her. I'm beginning to wonder whether she wanted me to find her somewhere else, but then the front door pops open and she offers a weary wave towards the inside.

There are dark rings under her eyes, her hair's greasy and unwashed and she's bare-footed in a towel robe.

'Have you slept?' I ask, as we head inside.

'Not really.'

I follow her into the living room and Jo flops into the armchair. There's a mug of coffee on the table next to her, with a small, dark puddle on the floor underneath. I sit on the sofa and wait.

Jo yawns and then tugs her hair into a ponytail, securing it with the tie around her wrist. 'The police have CCTV,' she says.

'Of what?'

'Owen.'

She yawns again.

'Doing what?' I ask.

'Filling up Neil's car at a petrol station just off the ring road.'

It takes a second for me to figure out what she means. 'Owen drove Neil's car there…?'

She nods – and I suppose that explains why Neil was complaining about the mirrors on his car being out of place. I can predict where this is going. Owen wouldn't have been arrested in the way he was if it was a straightforward case of driving on a provisional licence.

'Was he on his own?'

She nods again. That's definitely illegal – and the police apparently have a recording of it. What a silly thing to do.

Jo puffs out a long breath and then has a large mouthful of her coffee. When she returns it, more sloshes over the top, onto the table and the floor. She doesn't seem to notice.

'It was fifteen minutes before Ethan was hit,' she adds.

I almost don't want to ask the question – but I get the sense Jo wants to talk. She invited me here, after all.

'Do they think he was driving the car that hit Ethan?'

Jo doesn't reply. Her throat bobs and she bites her lip, before she takes a large breath. 'I don't know. Probably.'

'What does Owen say?'

'I don't know that, either. They kept him in overnight.'

'Beth said he was nervous about his test. Maybe he was trying to get in a bit more practice…?'

Jo shrugs. 'There's no way he hit his brother. He wouldn't do that.'

I almost say that I doubt anyone set out to hit Ethan and that it was almost certainly an accident. I suppose that isn't the point. Whoever it was still chose to drive off – and has kept quiet ever since.

'Did you get to see Owen last night?'

'For a couple of minutes. He didn't say much. I think he was worried they were listening in. He knows what they're like. He knows what they did to Dad. He shouldn't have talked to them in the first place.' She stops for more coffee and then adds, 'I'm hoping he'll be out later today. The solicitor woman said they can only hold him for twenty-four hours anyway.'

'How's Ethan?'

'Same as before. I'm going to see him at ten.'

Jo offers her mug towards me and bats away a yawn. 'I don't suppose you could…?'

I take her mug and head into the kitchen. After filling and turning on the kettle, I hunt through the cupboards looking for more coffee. I'm not sure if Jo's the type who usually has a bit of everything in – and then replaces whatever runs out. If she is, then she hasn't been shopping for a long time because the cupboards are generally bare, other than a few cans of fruit, some cup-a-soup packets and the usual random oddities that tend to come with a house. One cupboard holds a mishmash of spices and a small jar of Bovril.

I finally find a jar of instant coffee behind the bread bin, which reminds me of the pills I found in Jo's toilet cistern. Before that, she'd taken something from Petey at the back door and left it in the bread bin. It seems like such a long time ago, yet it was only four days.

The loose slices of Warburton's inside the bread bin are growing a nice beard of fluffy green mould and it's such a grim sight that I wince away after opening the lid. I use a wooden spoon to nudge them to one side and then crouch to peer inside, where, sure enough, a small white tub has been pushed to the back. There's no label on the lid and – after a fight with the child-proof cap that proves somewhat adult-proof – I find the same small orange pills inside as I first saw upstairs.

I'm about to return the tub to the bin when there's a noise from the doorway. Jo's leaning wearily against the frame and fights away another yawn as she holds out her hand. There seems little point in resisting, so I give her the tub and then watch as she tips a pair of tablets onto the counter and then swallows them down with a mouthful of water.

'What are they?' I ask.

Jo returns the tub to the bread bin and then, as the kettle clicks off, she dumps three spoonfuls of instant coffee granules into her mug as before. She fills it with steaming water and then steps away.

'I wasn't sure you'd find the coffee,' she says.

'What are the pills?' I repeat.

'Percocet.'

'I don't know what that is.'

Jo turns her back on me and returns to the living room. I follow and she retakes her seat, while I sit on the sofa and wait. A good minute passes without either of us speaking until I can't leave it any longer.

'You asked me to come here,' I say.

'They calm me down,' Jo replies. She sounds more tired than annoyed. 'They help me sleep… well, usually. It didn't help much last night.'

'Isn't stuff like that on prescription only?'

'I know someone that can get them.'

'Chris…?'

She looks up for the first time, although it's hard to say whether she's actually watching me because her eyes are barely open.

'How'd you know that?'

'Does it matter?'

'Guess not.'

'How long has it been going on?'

Jo makes a *pfft* sound. 'Does it matter?'

'Guess not.'

We sit quietly for a moment. No wonder Beth was so annoyed with Chris if he's got her eight-year-old brother making deliveries for him. I can't believe it's an accident – Chris will know that the legal age of criminal responsibility is ten. Chris would be in serious trouble, but Petey's untouchable.

Jo has more of her coffee. 'I've got to go soon,' she says.

'To see Ethan?'

She nods but doesn't move.

'What about Neil?'

Jo rolls her eyes and lets out a disgusted gasp. It's the most animated she's been since I got here. 'He's still at the police station. The idiot. I wasn't allowed to visit him yesterday – not that I wanted to anyway. I was there in this little room and had this woman over me, talking about how they had Neil in one cell and Owen in another.'

'What's going to happen to Neil?'

'I don't know. He got drunk and punched the guy who's been brought in to run the factory. I heard management is trying to play it down and pretend it didn't happen. The shop guys found it hilarious, apparently. As of last night, the boss said he didn't want to give a statement. They kept Neil in overnight for D&D, but I guess I might end up having to pick up the pair of them.' She sighs and reaches for her mug again before adding: 'How are things with you?'

'I'm getting the house cleared tomorrow,' I reply.

'That's good.'

Jo gives the impression that she's not listening, though I don't blame her for the self-centredness. It doesn't feel the right time to add that I'm going to be leaving once the house is sorted.

She pushes herself up from the seat and repeats that she has to go. I get up, too, ready to follow her into the hall, but she stops in the doorway and turns.

'Can you do something for me?'

'What?'

'Go to the petrol station.' I wonder if she's asking me to fill up her car, but then she adds: 'The one that caught Owen on camera.'

'Why?'

She already has her phone in her hand and is tapping something onto the screen. 'I'll send you the details in case you don't know it.'

'But what do you want me to do?'

She blinks, as if I'm stupid for not knowing. 'Ask around,' she says, like this is normal. 'See what they know.'

'Know about what? Wasn't Owen caught on camera?'

'Exactly. Just ask around. Find out what really happened.'

She turns and moves towards the stairs. She has so much going on that I don't think I can turn down a request – and yet this seems like madness.

'We'll catch up later,' Jo says.

'Okay,' I reply – although I'm still unsure what I've agreed to do.

THIRTY-FIVE

Not that I blame her for being distracted, but when Jo asked me to visit the petrol station I'm not sure she realised that I don't have a car. I walk along the edge of the main road out of Elwood and then traipse along the overgrown grass at the side of the narrow country lane that leads towards what everyone calls 'the ring road'. It's not a ring road in any sense, because it doesn't form a ring and it doesn't go all the way around the town. Instead, it's a link route that connects Elwood to the nearest motorway junction. Another of those local quirks, I suppose. I'm old enough to remember when the road was being built.

The lane gets narrower as the hedges that line the side become more overgrown. I'm forced onto the side of the road itself, while trying to remember if people are supposed to walk with traffic, or against it. Either way, I don't fancy my chances if someone roars around a blind bend at ridiculous speed.

It takes me over an hour to walk to the petrol station. Having lived in a city for so long, I'm so used to seeing petrol stations operated by supermarkets or the large oil companies that it feels odd to see anything else. This one is a throwback to the times when any trip into the countryside would be accompanied by a stop-off at a random place in the middle of nowhere. Those were often operated by the type of person who'd be near the top of any list for likely serial killers.

This one has no major company logos, just a sign that reads 'Stapletons' across the top of four pumps. There's a market towards the back of the forecourt, plus the price board – and then four CCTV cameras very obviously pinned to poles in each corner.

There must have been a serious lack of judgement for Owen to stop here while driving illegally. The likelihood is that, if he drove alone while on a provisional licence this time, he probably did it before without being caught. If it wasn't for the collision, the police would have had no reason to find the camera footage out here. I can only think he stopped here because he was so short on fuel that he feared breaking down.

It's taken me a long time to walk from Elwood – but it's certainly true that Owen could have driven from here to where Ethan was hit in a relatively short amount of time.

That doesn't mean it was him – even if the police kept him in for questioning. It's hard to imagine one brother doing that to another and then driving off – but then Cain and Abel is a story that's been around since the time when people started writing things down.

The forecourt is empty, so I walk across the centre and head into the minimart. The air conditioning blows cool against the warmth of outside and I shiver as I pass through the door. The place seems empty at first but, as I move along the nearest aisle that's loaded on both sides with chocolate and sweets, a head pops out from a room beyond the counter. It's a woman with glasses and a phone in her hand. She squints out towards the forecourt, probably expecting a car considering the distance from town, and then looks back to me.

'Can I help you?'

I close in on the counter and clock her name tag 'Linda'.

'I'm Abi,' I say, stumbling over the words. 'I've got a bit of a weird question. I'm friends with Jo Ashworth and—'

'Is this about her lad?'

'Owen,' I reply.

Linda backs away from the counter a little. She sounds part defensive, part panicked – as if I'm some sort of slightly sweaty henchwoman sent here to smash things up.

'It wasn't me that told the police. I ain't no grass.'

'That's not why I'm here,' I say.

'Oh… so why are you here?'

I start to say something and then realise I'm tripping over the words. I wonder if Jo actually did send me here to get a name for whoever could've contacted the police. Snitches get stitches and all that.

I'm interrupted by a car pulling onto the forecourt. We both turn and watch as a guy gets out of his shiny BMW and then tries to stretch the hose from one side of the car to the other. When it doesn't reach, he stomps his feet, gets back into the car and repositions it on the other side of the pump.

'How often does that happen?' I ask.

'At least three or four times a day. You'd think people would know which side of the car everything's on.'

We watch as he wrestles with the hose, spills petrol on his shoes, and then finally sets it going.

'How much d'you reckon?' I ask.

Linda blinks at me. 'Huh?'

'How much do you think he'll put in?' I dig into my bag and place a pound coin on the counter. 'Winner takes all.'

She stares curiously for a moment and then digs into a back pocket of her jeans, before placing another pound on the counter. 'You first.'

'Sixty quid,' I say.

'No chance. BMW owners are terrible drivers and stingy gits. I'm going fifty-nine, ninety-nine.'

'That's cheating.'

Linda smiles but doesn't reply and it's a surreal scene as we both watch a man filling up his car through the window.

He stops after all too short a time, then clanks the nozzle onto the edge of the tank – which only makes him spill even more on his shoes. He doesn't seem to notice, and wrenches the hose back into place, before setting off towards the minimart.

'How much?' I ask.

Linda smiles wider but doesn't reply.

The man doesn't remove his sunglasses as he comes inside and barely looks up from his phone.

I move out of the way, letting him get to the counter as he pulls out a platinum AMEX and hands it across.

'That's thirty pounds and two pence,' Linda says.

'On that,' the man replies.

Linda sorts his payment and hands him back the receipt and the card – although she might as well be passing him a donor card for all the attention he pays. He mooches out of the shop as Linda slides the two pound coins into her hand.

'Easy money,' she says. She waits until the man is back in his car and then turns to me once more. 'I still don't know why you're here.'

She sounds more relaxed now.

'I'm not sure either,' I reply. 'Jo wanted me to come and ask about what happened with Owen. She heard there was footage, but I don't think she's seen it and I know Owen hasn't talked to her. I think she just wants to know what's going on.' I pause and then add: 'She's got a lot on her plate.'

'I'll say. That poor kid.'

'Ethan,' I say.

'Yeah, Ethan. I hope he makes it. It's terrible what happened to him. I was at the fete yesterday morning and everyone was talking about it.'

'What actually happened with Owen?' I ask.

She nods towards the back room. 'Police came in on Friday and asked if we had CCTV. I asked if they had eyes, then pointed at the cameras outside. The bloke wanted to see footage from last Tuesday. I told him it's lucky he came in because we only keep everything for a week. It's all on a hard drive, then it starts recording over the old stuff.'

'What *was* on it?'

'Cars. Loads of them. It was busy on Tuesday, for whatever reason. I left them with the footage and the computer while I was serving out here. They called me in and asked about the timestamps. They seemed really excited.'

'Because of the time?'

She shakes her head. 'I didn't recognise him at the time but they were pointing at that Owen kid when he was heading into here to pay for the petrol. They wanted to double-check that the time on the screen was matched up with the actual time.'

'Was it?'

'Definitely. The time doesn't come from us. It's synced from an external server and can't be wrong. When I told them that, they said they needed to take the footage.'

'You said you didn't recognise Owen at the time…?'

'I don't know him, not really. I didn't know the police were here for anything to do with what happened to his brother. When they were pointing to him on the screen, I vaguely knew him but couldn't remember from where. It was the next day when I realised he'd been on telly with his mum. That's when I figured it all out.'

'Figured what out?'

Linda looks at me curiously, as if thinking I already know the reasons. 'He did it, didn't he? He was driving the car that hit his brother – and then he ran for it. That's why they were checking the times. He filled up the car here and then he was driving home.'

She likely doesn't know that Owen was driving by himself on a provisional licence and I wonder how many people she's told of her theory. The rumour is probably already on its way around Elwood.

'What was Owen doing?' I ask.

'Not much. He put some petrol in the car and I think he bought a Double Decker. I wasn't paying proper attention.'

'Was he definitely by himself?'

'The police asked me that. He came in here on his own, but I didn't know if there was anyone else in the car. I had to show them how to look at the other camera angles. They were zooming in and out – and then they took that footage, too.' She waits and then adds: 'I don't think there was anyone else in his car.'

I'm not sure what else to ask. It's looking bad for Owen if only in the sense that he's been caught doing something he definitely shouldn't.

'I should head back,' I say, angling towards the door.

'Hang on,' Linda says, with urgency. 'Do you think he did it?'

'Owen?'

'Can you imagine hitting your own brother with a car and then driving off?'

I think about how best to answer. I suspect Linda's made up her mind anyway. It's no wonder she was happy to talk about this. Since she realised the identity of the person in whom the police were interested, I'd bet she's been bursting to talk to anyone and everyone.

'I don't know him very well,' I say.

'I don't think I could live with myself.'

'It's amazing what some people can live with.'

My phone starts to ring and Jo's name flashes on the screen. Linda watches as I apologise and say I have to take the call. I press to answer and head outside, where I'm hit by the wall of heat.

'Where are you?' Jo asks. She's short of breath.

'At the petrol station.'

'Can you come?'

'Where are you?'

'The hospital. It's Ethan.'

'What about him?'

I feel my own heart thumping at the frantic tone of her voice.

Jo doesn't answer, so I repeat myself. There's still no reply and, when I look at the screen, she's hung up.

THIRTY-SIX

The woman who answers the phone at the taxi company tells me a car will be at the petrol station in five minutes. That inevitably means that it takes fifteen for the guy to turn up. By the time I get to the hospital, it's half an hour since Jo called. I pay the driver with the cash I found at the house and then dash across the car park towards the main building.

I'm about to head through the sliding doors at the front when I spot Jo sitting on the kerb a little way along the pavement, close to a row of hedges. She finishes smoking a cigarette, mashes it into the ground and then takes another from her bag and sparks it with a lighter. She holds it to her mouth and breathes deeply, before closing her eyes and pressing backwards, stretching her legs into the road, holding the smoke in her mouth.

I approach slowly, not wanting to jolt her.

Jo holds the smoke for longer than I've ever seen anyone manage, before she huffs it out with the merest of coughs. She opens her eyes and spots me, giving the slimmest of smiles.

I sit on the kerb next to her and match her by extending my legs into the empty road.

'Everything okay?' I ask.

She reaches into her bag and removes another cigarette, before passing it to me.

I shake my head. 'I've not had one in years.'

'Do you remember when we started? There were those trees at the end of the back field at school and we'd go down there every break time. What were we? Thirteen? Fourteen?'

'Something like that.'

'We thought we were sneaking around, but we had to cross the field every time we went there. Everyone must've known what we were doing. I didn't figure that out until about a year ago.'

'Rite of passage,' I say. 'Everyone in the years above us used to creep down to those trees. We were only copying them. Then the ones in the years below used to follow us. The kids probably still do it.'

'Not now. The school sold part of the field a few years ago. There's a row of houses where those trees used to be and they built a fence to separate it from the school.'

She takes a wistful breath and continues smoking the cigarette.

'Do you remember when Holly got grounded because her mum saw her smoking by the memorial that time?'

'Her mum told mine – but all that did was let mine know that I looked old enough to buy cigarettes for her.'

Jo nods along. I watch her, not knowing what to say, or what any of this means.

Jo has almost finished the second cigarette when she speaks again. 'Do you sometimes wonder if we are who we are because of our parents?'

'All the time. I don't think I've ever stopped.'

'My mum was always into something when I was growing up. She had those exercise videos, Jane Fonda or something like that. She'd get up and do the routine every day for a month or two, then she'd lose interest and move on to something else. She was always on some sort of new diet. She got a juicer one time and bought loads of fruit. Then she had us drinking these horrible green things every day for a week. She moved onto weight-loss pills, then creams to get rid of her wrinkles, even though she spent half her time on sunbeds.'

Jo sighs again and finishes the second cigarette by squishing it into the road on top of the first one. I think she's going to reach for a third, but she doesn't.

'It killed her in the end,' Jo adds.

'Sunbeds?'

'No… well, sort of. Everything went a bit mad when she discovered the internet. Obviously that happened a few years after everyone else figured it out. She'd keep saying, "I don't know why you spend so much time on the computer when there are real people out there," and then, one day, I went round and she'd had broadband installed. She barely left the house after that. She kept finding these groups and forums where people would be talking about the latest diet pills – then that led to people posting these articles about how doctors were deliberately keeping people fat. After that, she refused to ever go to the doctor, no matter how ill she was.'

'How long ago did she…?'

'Just over a year. She was all in by then. She'd got into the anti-vaxxer stuff and kept saying how I'd wrecked Ethan because he had the MMR jab. We argued about it almost every time I saw her. We didn't speak for six months – and I didn't know she had cancer until it was too late. She wouldn't go to the doctor and I found out afterwards that she'd got into all this faith healing stuff. There were so many pills. By the time I realised what was going on, there was no going back.'

She reaches into her bag and removes a third cigarette. This time, she simply holds it between her fingers.

'I've not smoked in years,' she adds, holding up the cigarette. 'I bummed three off one of the orderlies. I think he recognised me.'

'Why did you start again?'

She shivers. 'Ethan woke up.'

It's hard to hide my surprise. 'Oh… that's good, isn't it?'

'They had to put him back to sleep again.'

'Why?'

'He couldn't feel his legs and he started to panic. He was crying and shouting and they couldn't calm him down. I was there, but I couldn't help, either.'

We sit silently for a while, watching as an ambulance emerges from the other end of the road. It pulls away from the hospital and then the lights spin and the siren blares as it disappears off into the distance.

'Is it paralysis?'

'They don't know. They said something about blood flow, but I didn't really take it in. I couldn't stop seeing Ethan's little face when he realised he couldn't move his legs.'

Jo returns the cigarette to her bag, unsmoked.

'It's such a mess,' she adds. 'I've got one son who's paralysed, another who's locked up, a boyfriend who's also in jail – and then an ex who always wants an argument and whose sons won't see him.'

There's little I can say to negate that, so I rest what I hope is a comforting hand on her knee instead.

'It's me, isn't it?' Jo says.

'Of course it isn't.'

I reply instantly and instinctively, but the truth is that I don't know. The people who say they hate drama and don't want it in their lives are often the ones who attract it. That's not to say any of this is Jo's fault, but I haven't been around her for long enough to know.

Jo pushes herself up and cricks her back. I stand too and she does another mini stretch, pushing her arms high above her head and letting out a low moan.

'I should probably go back in,' she says. 'Thank you for coming.'

'Do you want me to stay with you?'

'I—'

She doesn't finish the sentence because her phone starts to ring. She digs into her bag and then holds it to her ear.

'Oh' – 'I could've told you that' – 'Right' – 'Why didn't you say that yesterday?' – 'Okay' – 'Right' – 'Okay'.

She presses the screen to hang up and then drops the phone back in her bag.

'Owen's being released,' she says, although she sounds more weary than happy.

'That's good.'

'Can you go to the police station and meet him? They didn't want to properly let him go without an adult.' She nods at the station. 'I can't really leave yet and Neil's still in custody.'

The fact she doesn't consider contacting Mark, Owen's dad, says plenty.

'I don't have a car, but I can get a taxi over. Or walk.'

'That'd be great.'

She leans in and hugs me, with our arms sticking together from the sweat and the heat. When she pulls away, she bats off a yawn and then dabs the corners of her eyes with her fingers.

'I'm so glad you're back,' she says, leaving me with no idea of how to reply.

THIRTY-SEVEN

When I get to the police station, Beth is already waiting in the reception area at the front. She looks up to me curiously, wondering what I'm doing here.

'Are you here for Owen?' she asks.

'Jo's at the hospital with Ethan. She asked me to come.'

The man at the counter checks who I am and then tells me to wait a couple of minutes. He disappears through a back door, leaving me alone with Beth. That only lasts a moment because a tall, thin young man sweeps in through the front door. He turns in a semicircle and then spots Beth.

'Is he still…?'

Beth nods to me. 'Should be out any minute.'

The young man eyes me suspiciously. He has incredible blond hair, with everything swooshed expertly to the side. It's the type of look that might be on the front of a magazine.

'This is Lewis,' Beth says.

'Abi,' I say.

Lewis offers his hand and I shake it, although there's no indication of who he is, other than – presumably – a friend.

We wait in silence, although I sense a lot of non-verbal communication between Beth and Lewis. They seem to be having a lengthy conversation with little more than eyebrow twitches and nods.

It's not long before there's a banging of doors and then Owen emerges from the side, with the officer a little behind.

When he spots me, I can see in the way his eyes widen that Owen has some idea of what's going on.

'Is Ethan—?'

'He woke up,' I say. 'Your mum's with him at the hospital.'

'Awake…?' He blinks his way towards me. 'That's great.'

I figure I'll let him have the moment, if only until we get outside.

Owen seems unsurprised to see either Beth or Lewis and the four of us head through the doors and down the steps into the sunshine. When we get to the bottom, Beth rubs Owen's arm and asks if he's okay. He says he is and then turns to me, lifting his feet.

'They gave me back my shoes.'

I laugh, although it's short-lived. I've not told him the full story about Ethan yet.

'Do you want to go to the hospital?' Beth asks, talking to Owen.

He groans a little. 'Yes. Let's walk. I've been sitting down for ages.'

The three of them set off, leaving me at the bottom of the stairs. They've only gone a few steps when Owen stops and turns.

'Are you coming?' he asks.

'Sure.'

It's a strange feeling – and no doubt an odd sight – as three teenagers amble along with me at their side. Nobody's saying much, certainly not anything about what Owen might have told the police. It's a good few miles from the police station to the hospital and we're almost twenty minutes into the walk before Beth says anything of note. We are in the back alleys when she slows almost to a stop. Little chance of anyone overhearing. Owen mirrors her and then Lewis follows. It's only me who ends up a few paces ahead.

When I turn to see what's going on, Beth nods towards me. 'Is she all right?'

I have no idea what's happening, but Owen nods towards me. 'Yeah.'

'Did you tell the police?' she asks.

'What else could I do?'

'What did they say?'

'Nothing really. They went away for a bit and then returned and told me they'd have to check a few things. When they came back next, they said I could go. I've still been charged for no licence or insurance – but that's it.'

'They know you didn't hit Ethan…?'

'They said I'm not under suspicion for that any more.'

Beth lets out a long breath and looks towards Lewis. 'I'm so sorry,' she says.

'It's not your fault,' Owen replies. 'I should've told people before. Especially after Ethan got hit.'

The end of the alley is barely steps away and I have no idea what's going on, but Owen catches my eye and then takes Lewis's hand.

'We've been going out for about four months,' he says.

'Oh…'

I have no idea what to say. It's one of those things that feels like a surprise, even though it doesn't matter. I suppose I have no gaydar.

'Mum doesn't know,' Owen adds.

He looks to Lewis and they smile to one another in a way that makes me ache for my own youth. There's such purity there, which is something I'm not sure I'm capable of any longer. Every passing year brings more and more cynicism to the point that it's now the norm.

'I suppose she might know about *me*,' Owen says, 'but I've never told her – and she doesn't know about Lewis. I don't know how she'll take it…' He tails off and watches me, as if my approval will somehow mean it's fine with his mum, too.

'I don't know her well enough any more,' I say. 'I don't see why she'd have a problem.'

Owen exchanges a look with Beth that makes it seem like I've read things wrong. 'We once saw two women kissing at the seaside,' he says. 'Mum called them dykes. Not to their faces, just to me. It was a long time ago but…'

I wish I could say something comforting, but it would surely make things worse if I assure him everything is okay and then it turns out that Jo does have a problem.

'I'm not saying she's right to say that, but we used to use that word a lot when we were young. We called lots of the boys "gay" or "homo" and plenty more girls "dyke". At first, when we were much younger than you, we were copying what we heard other kids saying. We had no idea what any of it meant. Then it ended up being just a thing we'd say as an insult. Instead of saying something was rubbish, we'd say it was gay. If we didn't like some girl, we'd call her a dyke. That doesn't excuse whatever Jo said – but maybe it's an explanation…?'

Owen looks at me and I don't get the sense he's convinced. It's not that I blame him. There were so many things we used to do and say as teenagers of which I'd be thoroughly ashamed now.

'I took Neil's car and drove out to see Lewis,' Owen says. 'On Tuesday, when Ethan was hit. He doesn't live in Elwood and neither of us has a licence. It's why I've been wanting to pass my test so much.'

He glances to Lewis, who seemingly reads his mind. 'I've failed twice,' he says. 'Mounted the kerb first time and too many minors the second – though I still say it was because that examiner didn't like me.'

Owen rolls his eyes and it's hard not to laugh. Even without words, I can tell they've been bickering about this ever since it happened.

Lewis slips into another smile and, just for a moment, everything's perfect. It falls from his face barely seconds later and he squeezes Owen's hand tighter before releasing him.

Beth is the one who says it. 'It's not like coming out in a city, is it? There's no gay village here. No parade, or rainbow flags on buildings.'

She lets it hang and then Lewis chips in: 'It's barely the twenty-first century in Elwood.'

He sounds angry, but Owen scolds him with a look that's light-heartedly stern. 'It's not that bad,' he says.

Beth looks to me again. 'You get it, don't you? You left.'

'I get it,' I say quietly.

She turns to Owen now. 'We've gotta get out of this place,' she says.

'I like it here.'

'Do you? *Really?*'

He doesn't reply.

The four of us are left looking at one another until Lewis speaks. 'Now you've told the police, do you think it'll get out about us?' He's talking to Owen, who is looking to the floor.

'I don't know. Maybe.'

'Maybe it should…?'

Owen doesn't reply and it's clear this is a conversation for another time.

Beth nods towards the end of the alley. 'Shall we get going?' she says.

We do, although much of what had to be said already has.

Beth asks Owen how he slept at the police station and he talks about an uncomfortable bed with only a blanket. He didn't hear anything of Neil being kept in a nearby cell and seems uninterested in whatever is happening with him. It's not hard to see that they have little connection and I wonder whether Neil yet knows, or suspects, that Owen 'borrowed' his car. He'd have had to tell the police he took it with permission, else Owen could be charged with theft.

When we get within sight of the hospital, Lewis takes Owen's hand. 'I've got to go,' he says. 'I came in on the bus and they only go every two hours on a Sunday. If I don't catch the next one, I'll miss lunch and then Dad will want to know where I've been and why…'

After hearing this, Beth keeps walking, so I follow her lead and give Owen and Lewis some space. She slows to let me catch up and we continue towards the hospital.

'How long have you been covering for him?' I ask.

'Since we were about thirteen.' She laughs to herself. 'I have no idea how he's kept it quiet this long.'

'Not just Lewis, then.'

Another little laugh. 'I keep telling him that he's going to have to cover for me one day. As it is, Mum couldn't care less what Petey or I get up to.'

There's a bitter tinge to her tone.

'I didn't actually mean to lie to you,' she adds. 'Afterwards, I told Owen you knew something was wrong because he'd told you one thing and I'd said another. We only realised when he told me he could be in trouble if anyone found out he'd been in a car when Ethan was hit. He sent me round to tell you I'd been mistaken about the days, but I said you'd already known something was up.'

'I didn't know what to think.'

'You knew we were lying, though.'

'Yes…'

'And you didn't say anything…'

'Who would I tell? And why? You're not the only ones lying in this town.'

Beth doesn't reply to that and it's only a moment until Owen rejoins us. He starts toward the main hospital doors, but I call after him.

'I need to tell you something,' I say.

He and Beth stop and turn back towards me.

'I'm not sure if I'm supposed to be telling you this, or if it's your mum – but I don't think it's fair for you to go inside without knowing.'

'What happened?' he asks.

'Ethan woke up, but they had to put him back to sleep again. He couldn't feel his legs and was starting to panic. The last I heard, they don't know what's happening with him.'

There's a pause and then: 'He's out of the coma, though?'

'Right. They don't know if the paralysis is temporary, or…' I tail off and then add: 'I should've said before, but you'd just been released and—'

'It's okay.' He looks towards the hospital and then back to me. 'Are you coming in?'

'I've already been here once today. I think I'll leave you to it.'

He nods along. 'Thank you for coming to get me.'

'You're very welcome.'

'Mum's happy that you're back. When she's not talking about Ethan, she's talking about you.'

I offer a slim smile because this only makes it harder for me to tell Jo that I'm leaving again.

'I'll catch up with everyone later,' I say.

Owen and Beth offer small waves and then they turn and head towards the hospital. I watch them go and, for all the world, they could be a couple. Owen rests his head momentarily on Beth's shoulder and she briefly takes his hand before letting him go. It makes me ache for those friendships of youth. The ones that feel like they'll last forever before things like marriage, kids, houses and everything else gets in the way. As an adult, there's nothing quite like it.

I watch them disappear through the doors at the front of the hospital and then turn to leave. My legs are tired from all the walking and errands. It feels like it's been a long day already and it's barely midday.

It's as I turn that I feel a peculiar prickling at the back of my neck. I don't believe in clairvoyance or anything like that – so it's hard to explain quite how I know I'm being watched. There's a car on the other side of the road that, at first glance, is parked in between two others. It's only when I stare across that I realise it's Holly's vehicle. I almost wave – we left on reasonable terms, after all – except it's not her in the driver's seat.

Mark is sitting there, slightly slumped in the seat, peering across the road to where I'm standing. I wonder how long he's been watching – and why. I don't get a chance to ask because, as soon as he realises he's been seen, Mark revs the engine – and then pulls away. Holly's dark blue Audi sputters fumes into the air and, for the first time since I saw that vehicle waiting in the middle of the road by Ethan's shattered body, the memory flares.

Maybe, just maybe, I've seen this happen before.

THIRTY-EIGHT

I wish I could stop thinking of the property as Dad's house – but it's burned into me. There are many reasons to sell, but this might be the most important of all. It's mine – but it will never *be* mine.

When I'm on the corner next to the house, I spot Chris's car parked on Helena's drive next door. I head along the path to Dad's house but can't stop myself from staring across to the car and the replaced bumper. If finding out the truth about Owen has taught me anything, it's that assumptions are dangerous. There could be a perfectly reasonable explanation for why the previous bumper was scuffed – and why Chris had it changed. Perhaps his wife, Kirsty, really did hit a post?

I only realise I've been staring too long when Helena's front door opens. It's not her who emerges, it's Chris. He's in three-quarter shorts and a T-shirt that's a size too small. He heads straight for me, hands in pockets, more resigned than angry.

'You're not gonna let it go, are you?' he says.

'What?' I reply.

'You think I did it, don't you? You think I hit that kid and drove off.'

I look from Chris to the car and back again. I can't get over how some things in this town feel so familiar that it's as if I never left.

'Did you?' I ask.

He boggles at me, probably amazed I've asked the question outright.

'Kirsty hit a post,' he replies. 'I told you.'

'You've got a new bumper.'

'I realised how bad it looked when you were checking out the car by the bookies. I had to do something in case someone else noticed.'

'If it was only Kirsty hitting a post, then what would it matter if someone else noticed?'

He huffs loudly and glances back towards his mum's house. 'Did you see the graffiti on that guy's house when they pulled his car out of the quarry? He had his car nicked and that's what they did to him. What do you think they'd do to me?'

My eyes drift back to the car again.

'I know you've been away,' he adds. 'But what kind of person do you think I am?'

'I don't know you.'

'But you knew me once. I'm not *that* different.'

It's hard not to sigh. I look towards Dad's house, then Helena's, then the car. Anywhere except Chris. If I had any thoughts of staying, I'd shut my mouth. That's what people do when they're invested in a community. The power lies in saying nothing.

'You're a drug dealer,' I say.

It sounds worse out loud than it did in my head – and it sounded bad enough in there. It's such an emotive pair of words. 'Drug dealer' can be anything from someone passing a joint onto a teenager, to someone lacing a wrap of heroin with fentanyl. It's not all the same, and yet, with those two words, it is.

Chris cranes his neck backwards, his eyes narrowing. 'Why do you say that?'

'Because I'm not an idiot. I know what you're up to with Petey and the pills—'

'*Shush!*'

Chris spins to check his mother's house and only turns back when he's certain there's nobody to overhear.

'How'd you know that?' he asks.

'I told you: I'm not stupid. It's hardly a complex web of companies based in the Caymans, is it?'

He stares at me, not knowing what I'm on about.

'Petey's eight years old,' I add. 'You're getting him to make drug deliveries for you – so, yes, you *have* changed a lot since I knew you.'

Chris checks over his shoulder once more and then waits for a car to pass. It's barely louder than a whisper when he replies.

'You wouldn't understand. It's not like some big city here.'

'I know what it's like here.'

'You don't though. You've never worked at Hendo's. You've never been laid off. Do you know how many people are worried they're going to lose their house? Or not be able to pay rent? Or have to move?'

I want to answer, except that he's right. I *don't* know what any of that's like.

'Exactly,' he adds, seeing the uncertainty in me. 'There aren't loads of jobs here, or ways to make money. You've got to look after your own, haven't you? I've got a family to feed.'

The cycle seems obvious to me. There's Chris who, however misguided, has a point. He wants to look after his family and Elwood feels like a town that's dying. I have no idea where his pills come from – but they get sold on to people like Jo, who's stuck with an addiction she either can't, or doesn't want to, control. She even knows it's happening – *Do you sometimes wonder if we are who we are because of our parents?* The only person who's winning is whoever's at the top, sending those tablets downwards. Like Holly and her pyramid.

'What if you get caught?' I say. 'How's that for looking after your family?'

'That's ifs. What's definite is that, if I don't do this, there's no food for my girls. No school uniform. No one to pay the mortgage.'

He checks over his shoulder again and then steps close enough that I can see the patch underneath his chin that he missed shaving. He gulps and his voice is barely a whisper.

'Do you think I'm a bad person?' he asks.

I take a breath and look to the floor, not knowing how to answer. Drug dealers are bad, aren't they? It's an easy yes-no, black-white issue. He was using an eight-year-old as a mule. But here, whether it's Chris or whether it's me, I simply don't know.

'I think about it sometimes,' Chris adds. 'When I see Kirsty and the girls. I wonder if I'm the bad guy. Have you ever thought that? Like when you watch a movie and there's a villain and you wonder if they ever stop to think about whether they're the bad guy. Is that me?'

'I don't know,' I say.

'I don't either.'

We stand silently for a moment until he takes half a step backwards.

'Were you at the back of the house?' I ask.

The change of subject catches him by surprise and he blinks rapidly. 'Huh?'

'A couple of nights ago, there was someone at the back window in the house. Was it you?'

'Of course not. Why would it be?'

'I don't know. I thought I saw someone out there.'

He turns to look at Dad's house, then his mum's, then he looks across the road towards the other properties.

'Someone was burgled on this street about a year ago,' he says. 'I can't remember which house, but Mum was really worried. Your dad used to go over and sit with her some evenings because she was scared about it happening to her. She's lived here all her life – and now this.'

There's anger in his voice, but it sounds forced and I wonder if, deep down, he's scared, too. If it wasn't for that, I might point out the irony that a decent amount of burglaries are carried out by people trying to fund drug habits. The precise type of habit he himself is helping to create. A day ago and I probably would've done.

I don't get a chance anyway because Helena's front door opens and Kirsty appears. She walks towards us slowly as Chris steps away from me.

'What's going on?' she asks, the anger brimming in her tone.

'We're just talking,' Chris replies, although the edge to his voice probably won't help.

'What about?' she demands, looking to me.

'Things,' Chris says.

If she was a dragon, Kirsty would be breathing fire at this moment. I don't necessarily blame her. Chris hasn't helped.

'Stay away from him,' she says, wagging a finger in my direction.

'Do you really think I'm chasing him?'

'You keep running into him, don't you? If you're so happy wherever it is you've been living, then where's *your* man?'

She pushes forward, angling around Chris's outstretched arm with her chest out. There would have been a time, long ago, where I'd have taken the challenge. I'd have had Jo and Holly cheering me on as I threw myself into battle. I suppose that's another thing I left behind.

'Do you think I need someone to be happy?' I reply. 'Do you think I need *a man*?'

She sneers and then it turns into a laugh. 'You don't look very happy.'

There's a terrible feeling when somebody makes a point so perfectly sincere and correct that there's no answer. Like trying to argue a square is a circle until someone points out that it's unquestionably round. There's nowhere to go. I feel sick.

'Thought so,' Kirsty says, as she brims of satisfaction. 'Leave him alone. Leave *us* alone.' She turns to Chris, on a roll: 'Let's go.'

Chris looks to me for a moment, but he can hardly tell his wife that we were having a cosy chat about his drug dealing. He mooches towards the car and gets into the driver's seat as Kirsty crouches into the passenger side. It feels as if she never stops watching me as the car shoots off the drive with a spray of small stones.

I feel fixed to the spot for a moment, but then, with them gone, I let myself into the house. It's cool in the shadows of the hallway, though the sun spills down the stairs, casting a spotlight onto the ground in front of me.

I drift across to Dad's dusty trophies, knowing that, unless the house clearer decides to keep them for some reason, they will be landfill within a day. I wonder if he took any pleasure from these at the end; whether they gave happy memories of better times, or if they were simply decoration. Something that had become part of the fittings to the point that they might as well have been a cupboard handle, or a curtain.

I'm tired and wonder if I could sleep, or if I want to, and then there's a solid thump from upstairs. It stops me still at the bottom of the stairs, haloed by the light coming through the upstairs window. It has always been a noisy house of creaks and squeaks – but the noise was too solid to be something like the plumbing.

I wait, listening, and then a few seconds later, there's another bump. It's louder this time, like someone stamping on the floor, or dropping something solid. The tightness in my chest makes me realise I've been holding my breath and, as I breathe out, there's a third bang. I rest a foot on the bottom step, looking upwards, knowing with certainty that's there's someone in the house.

THIRTY-NINE

I've seen horror movies. I've been that eye-rolling viewer cursing the lead character for opening doors or going upstairs when the only thing they should be doing is getting the hell out of wherever they are. I've shouted at screens as each lazy character looks to a phone that's conveniently out of battery. I get all that. I should leave and probably call the police. The reason I do none of that is something that's harder to define. Curiosity is part of it – there's someone in the house and I'd like to know who it is. It's also outrage at the bare-faced cheek that someone's in this house in the middle of the day when they have no right to be.

That's the stuff that feels reasonable in the moment – but there's irrationality, too. A single, dangerous thought that tickles the back of my mind.

It's Dad.

He's dead, I know that. There was a funeral that he paid for and planned. But I never saw the body. The only proof of any sort is the solicitor's letter and the death certificate. They can be faked, can't they? Perhaps this was all some big plot to get me back to Elwood?

If not him, then Mum. She got in somehow and…?

I creep towards the kitchen and open the door as quietly as I can. The window hasn't been broken, the back door is closed, and the dirty dishes are still in the sink. There's no sign anyone but me has been here – although an obvious thought occurs that a potential burglar is unlikely to stop and do the washing-up.

I take a knife from the rack and, even though it's blunt and couldn't cut a sausage in half, I figure it'll do for show.

As I return to the hall, there's another bump from above, although it's more muffled this time.

I creep up the stairs, moving from light to shadow and back again until I reach the landing with a steady, low creak. I stop still and wait. There's no bumping now, but there's definitely some sort of rustling coming from the spare bedroom.

Since getting back to the house, I've ignored the two bedrooms that aren't mine. I've avoided Dad's largely because I don't want to know what's inside. It's morbid enough having to see the way he was living through the contents of the living room and the kitchen. The idea of having to sort through his clothes, his *underwear*, makes me feel slightly sick.

There was no particular reason to avoid the spare room, other than that I've never spent any time in there. When I lived here two decades ago, it was full of junk that Dad didn't want to throw away. I think it might have been a generational thing of not wanting things to go to waste, or believing things can always be fixed. The large fake Christmas tree would always be jammed in here, back when we celebrated things like that as a family. There's no reason to assume the contents of the room has changed in any way since I left. It's not like the rest of the house has.

I wonder if I should call out and perhaps give whoever it is a chance to leave the house. The knife feels heavy in my hand and I know I couldn't use it in any meaningful way. It's a prop. Tina from the police gave me her number and I could call her, instead of 999 – except it would still take time for someone to arrive.

There's a scratching, scrabbling coming from the room that doesn't feel like it's dangerous. Chris mentioned there had been a burglary a while back and, if it *is* a burglar, then what could they possibly be ransacking from this room?

I step across the landing, to where the door to the spare room is open a sliver. I know it was closed this morning, the same way that the door to Dad's room is still clamped in its frame.

If there was any doubt before, then it's gone now. Someone is here.

I hold the knife to my side with one hand and nudge the door open with the other. It's impossible to miss the whining, screech of the rusting hinges as the door swings inwards. I take a breath and step inside.

I don't know what I expect – Dad, Mum, some big, overpowering burglar – but it's none of those things. Instead, there's a girl sitting cross-legged in the middle of the room. She's maybe fifteen or sixteen and wearing jeans with a bright T-shirt that has a duck on the front. She peers up to me over thick-rimmed glasses, flicking her dark ponytail back over her shoulder.

We stare at one another, though her gaze slips to the knife in my hand. I suddenly feel embarrassed to be carrying it, even though she's an intruder.

'You were at the funeral,' I say, recognising the girl in the black dress.

She twitches, as if about to speak, but nothing comes out.

'Who are you?' I ask.

'Um…'

'How did you get in?'

Words seem caught in her throat, like she's forgotten how to talk. Instead, she reaches into the pocket of her jeans and pulls out a key, which she holds up in the air.

I squint towards it, then lean forward and take it from her. I can't be certain, but it looks identical to the one I received in the mail from the solicitor.

'Where'd you get this?' I ask.

'Mum.'

The word comes out as a croak and only leaves me more confused.

'What do you mean?'

'I got it from Mum.'

'Who's your mum?'

She shuffles a little and there's something about the way the light catches the angles of her cheeks that makes me know the answer before it comes.

'*Our* mum,' she says.

There's a pause in which I can't speak – but the girl fills it anyway.

'I'm Megan – and we're sisters.'

FORTY

'Well, half-sisters,' Megan adds. 'Same mother, different dads.'

'How old are you?'

'Nearly seventeen.'

She smiles slimly and I know she's telling the truth from the way the crinkles form around her mouth. She has Mum's smile. She has *my* smile. She would've been born four years after Mum walked out. Four years after I left.

'Megan…' I say, apparently unable to come up with a cohesive statement other than repeating her name.

'You're Abi,' she replies – and it's not a question. She already knows.

'I, well… yes.' I tie myself into a knot with the words. It's all too much and a few seconds pass before I realise she's still let herself into the house.

'Why are you here?' I ask.

Megan points down to a dusty album that's flat on the floor. The pages have browned over time and a few are hanging loose. A couple of grainy, washed-out photographs are stuck to the top page, though I can't make out what they're supposed to be showing.

'I did knock,' Megan says when she looks back up.

I've still got her key in my hand and slip it into my own pocket. 'I tried the bell, too. And I went round the back.'

There's a familiarity in what she's saying.

'Were you around the back the other night?' I ask. 'After dark.'

She looks away, which is answer enough. 'I didn't know if I should knock. It was late and I wasn't sure why I was here. I thought I'd go around to see if I could spot you through a window. I don't know what I was thinking. I just wanted to say hello to you.'

'That doesn't explain why you let yourself in today.'

'I suppose I, um, got a bit bored of waiting. It's really hot outside. I had the key, so thought it would maybe be okay…'

Megan sounds so unsure of herself that there's no way this is convincing her, let alone me.

'How could it ever be okay? It's breaking and entering.'

'I didn't break anything.'

'Entering, then.'

'I'm sorry.'

She looks down to the album and then turns away, though it's too late for me to miss the gentle upturn in her lips.

I bite my lip, but then let out a little snort. 'I guess it's not just me who gives apologies I don't mean.'

Megan twists back and smiles wider. 'We have that in common.'

I suddenly realise I'm still holding the knife, and so place it on the nearest box. Megan watches but says nothing.

'What are you looking at?' I ask.

'Photos of Mum. I sort of found them.'

'You let yourself in, came upstairs, went into the spare room, and "sort of found them"…?'

Megan gives that get-out-of-jail-free smile once more. 'Mum said one time that the only photos of her from when she was young were at the old house where she used to live. She said everything was packed away in a spare room where nobody went. When I got inside and had a look around, I kind of guessed it was here.'

I pat the key in my pocket. 'Did Mum really give you this?'

'Sort of.'

'Is that a yes, or a no?'

'It's more of a… *borrowed*.'

'I think I get the picture.'

'The key had a tag that said "old house" on it. I found it years ago when I was looking through Mum's jewellery box.'

'Why were you going through her jewellery box?'

The smile is back and I can imagine Megan using it to bluff her way through anything. I certainly can't believe she's ever been in serious trouble.

'I was home alone and got a bit bored.'

'Is her jewellery box the one with the red lining that plays Beethoven when you open it?'

'I don't know if it's Beethoven, but it definitely plays something.' She stops and then adds: 'How do you know it does that?'

My turn to grin: 'I was home alone and got a bit bored.'

'So it's not just me!'

'I didn't *borrow* a key and let myself into someone else's house.'

'I didn't set out to do that… it just—'

'Sort of happened. I know. That doesn't answer much, though. Did Mum tell you about me? About this house? I don't understand.'

Megan slides around the floor and presses her back against the unmade spare bed. I feel weird standing over her, so slip down to the floor myself. The carpet is scratchy and old, with holes through to the floorboards. I press myself up against a stack of boxes opposite her and we sit with the photo album between us. It's not comfortable, but it feels right for the moment.

'Mum's terrible on the internet,' Megan says. 'We've got a laptop and she opens loads of windows and never closes them. She doesn't know anything about browser histories, or firewalls, or anything like that. Not only that, she believes *everything* that's on there. I'd picked up the laptop after her and it was running *so* slowly. I keep telling her she's got to close things, or it stops working.'

Megan sighs and shakes her head.

'I was closing the windows and then I saw that she'd opened this article about a man who'd been found dead in his home. There were hardly any details – with no name and no address. It just listed the road and said that an ambulance had gone out. I didn't know why she was looking at it, but then she'd gone off googling "Dennis Coyle".'

'Did she ever tell you my dad's name?'

'No – but it wasn't hard to figure out after that. She was looking for things like "Dennis Coyle dead", trying to figure out if it was definitely him in the article.'

'What did she find?'

'Nothing. I don't think there was anything that named him at the time.'

It sounds about right. There might well have been a small article in the paper, and online, about a man being found dead in his house. There were probably more after that, in which he might have been named. It's not like the official funeral notice was the first time his death would've been noted. Besides, Mum already told me she still knows people around here. She could have quite easily phoned someone to ask what they knew.

'Once I had the name "Dennis Coyle", I got searching,' Megan says. 'I found out he lived here and about the house. Then I used one of those family tree apps and found out about you – and Mum.'

She sounds happy with herself – and I suppose she has every right to be so.

'Mum never told you about me…?'

'All she ever said was that she was married before. But once, when I was young and playing up, she told me off and called me "Abigail". I asked her who that was and she said "no one". It was too quick, though, and she got angry when I asked again. I used to write down the name in the back of my old schoolbooks, so I wouldn't forget it.'

I should probably be offended at being called 'no one' but it fits with who my mother is.

'How long ago was that?' I ask.

'Seven or eight years.'

I press back against the box and think about the little girl who spent seven or eight years searching for a long-lost sister who might not exist.

It feels like Megan can read my mind as she offers a sad-sounding 'I knew you were out there somewhere…'

'Do you have any other brothers or sisters?' I ask.

'Just you… unless *you* have other brothers or sisters?'

I shake my head. 'Just you.'

We look to one another and I wonder if she sees in me what I see in her. She's me as I could have been when I was sixteen. There's a feisty exterior, but I'd bet there's more to her than that. I'm almost forty now and the idea of someone being so ancient would have repulsed me at that age. Looking at me might be a grim glimpse into the future for her.

'How long have you been checking Mum's internet history, hoping you'd stumble across someone named Abigail?'

'Years. She never said that she used to live in Elwood, but she'd mentioned it here and there. This one time, we were trying to get home from the seaside. There was loads of traffic backed up, but she knew a shortcut through Elwood. When I saw that story about the dead man and Elwood, I think I knew what it was.'

'Where do you live?'

'Stoneridge.'

I know it by name. It's a small town, or maybe a village, that's around twenty miles from here. I'm not sure I've ever stopped there, or if there's anything to see, but I'd have definitely been in a car with my dad when he was driving through it. Whenever I thought of my mother leaving, I imagined she'd gone to the opposite end of the country. She'd be in Scotland, or Wales – but she was only a short distance away. No wonder she said she still knows people in the town. They probably still meet up.

'How did you get here?' I ask.

'Bus – but my friend, Carla, has passed her test and she's dropped me off a couple of times. I knocked on the door, but you're never home. I found out your name on the family tree app, but I didn't know where you lived. They named the street where your dad died in the paper – but not the exact house. When I came here, it didn't take much to figure out this was the right place.'

'How?'

'Because it looks like a dump and nobody ever seemed to be in.'

She has a point.

'I didn't know if you lived here,' she adds. 'I thought you might be back because of your dad – then I saw the notice about the funeral and figured I'd finally be able to meet you. I almost did. I saw you there, but you rushed away and I had a bus to catch back. Then I remembered the old key I found. I thought I could let myself in and see if there was anything with an address for you, or a phone number…'

I almost ask her if she saw the note on the fridge.

'You should get the locks changed,' Megan adds.

I don't understand what she means at first – but then I realise Mum kept her key from twenty years ago and that it still works. It's hardly surprising how little has changed in all this time. If the lock ever got a bit stiff, Dad would've emptied a quarter-can of WD40 into it and carried on as if it was fine.

I don't answer her, mainly because it won't be my concern for much longer. I don't want to tell her I'm leaving again yet.

'I'm guessing Mum doesn't know you're here,' I say.

'No.'

'She has no idea that we've met?'

'None.'

'Nor that you went to the funeral?'

'No. After I saw that notice and decided to come, I waited outside the funeral place, hiding behind a car in case Mum showed up for some reason. I didn't think she would but didn't want to risk it. When it went past the start time and she wasn't there, I went in. I was going to say something to you after the ceremony but, um…'

It's probably tact that she doesn't finish the sentence, given that I ran off to the pub.

'Thank you for coming,' I say. 'Sorry I didn't hang around.'

She shrugs in the carefree way that teenagers do when they don't think anything's wrong.

'Does that mean you forgive me for letting myself in?'

'For the breaking and entering…?'

'Just entering.'

She laughs and then looks down towards the photo album, which she nudges across the floor towards me.

'Look at Mum there,' she says.

I spin the book around, which helps to dislodge another loose page. I slot it back inside. On the open page is a pair of photographs that have browned and faded.

'Didn't anyone ever take photos in focus back then?' Megan laughs as she says it.

'It's a lot easier with phones,' I reply. 'You're too young to know about sending films off to be processed, or going into Boots and paying a fortune for them to do it in an hour.'

'Sounds like a lot of faff.'

'It was.'

Megan's right that the photo is barely in focus. Even with that, the main figure is unquestionably Mum. She has an eighties perm and is wearing an itchy-looking pink top with shoulder pads. At her feet is a short girl with curly blonde hair that, for a reason that seems inexplicable now, is cut into a point at the top, before getting wide at the bottom to create a weird triangle.

'Is that you?' Megan asks.

'Yes.'

'Nice hair.'

She laughs, but there's nothing mean there.

'I always wanted a sister,' she adds.

I'd love to say the same – and maybe I should anyway – but it never occurred to me that I'd want a sibling to put up with Dad on his bad days.

'Who's your father?' I ask.

Megan's face falls slightly. She takes off her glasses and starts to clean the lenses on her top.

'He died two years ago of heart disease.'

'I'm sorry…'

'It's okay. It was after that when Mum started talking about her old life. Not you – not even Elwood – but she'd let things slip. She'd get drunk and say things like she didn't want to start over for a third time.'

We sit and stare across the album towards one another. I'm thinking it – but it's Megan who says it first.

'What now?'

FORTY-ONE

It's been six days since I arrived and when I get up and go downstairs, I finally do the dishes. Megan's presence has almost willed me to do it, in order to stop myself from seeming like such a slob. There is wire wool under the sink and I get through two of them in attempting to get rid of the welded-on grime.

I'm drinking water from a clean glass when Megan edges into the kitchen with a curious smile on her face. 'Morning…' she says.

'How was the spare bed?'

'Couple of dodgy springs and it smelled a bit – but it could be worse.' She looks towards the fridge expectantly. 'What's for breakfast?'

'You have a choice. There are some tomatoes in the fridge that are a tiny bit mouldy. There's some tinned fruit or half a box of out-of-date Weetabix – but no milk.'

'That's not a choice.'

'Shall we go out?'

'Hell, yes.'

We get a taxi out to the rest stop a little past the petrol station where I ended up interrogating Linda. Megan spends the whole journey pressed to the window, seemingly enchanted by Elwood. She watches the town, while I watch her. When I met her last night, I saw myself in her – but she's more than that. She's quieter than I ever was and, when she speaks, it's far more thoughtful than I was at her age. She's determined, kind and funny. I wonder if I was any of those things when I was sixteen.

Jo's question rattles endlessly around my mind – *Do you sometimes wonder if we are who we are because of our parents?* – and it's hard not to see the differences between Megan and me. We come from the same mother, but that's only half the story. I never met him, and know nothing about who he was, but I would gamble a lot on the fact that Megan's father was a great guy. I can see it in her – but that might mean she can see my father in me.

I'm lost in my thoughts as the taxi rolls to a halt. The rest stop is a giant car park – but that's not why we're here. Nestled at the back end is The Cosmic Café, which is perhaps the thing I miss most about living around here. It's mainly for lorry drivers, but, because it's in the middle of a few towns, it turned into a hangout for young people with cars. I've not been here in two decades but the moment I push through the doors, I'm transported back in time.

The walls are covered with the faded record sleeves of bygone eras. Vinyl records might be making a twenty-first century comeback, but the cardboard covers here are the originals. The café smells of baked beans, frying eggs and sausages. People don't come here for salad or soup.

All of a sudden, I feel hungry. It's the first time I've craved food since I got back to town.

Megan follows me in and we head to an empty booth off to the side. At one point, the bench would've been covered with red leather, but it's long since faded to a mucky pink. Megan looks around the walls and nods approvingly.

'I never knew this place was here,' she says.

'I used to come when I was about your age. We'd have six of us piled into a booth and would waste a whole night spending as little money as we could get away with until Rahul kicked us out.'

'Who's Rahul?'

'The owner… or it was. I have no idea if he's still around.'

I slide a menu across the table and Megan starts to scan it when her phone rings. She glances at the screen and then holds it up for me to see.

MUM

She doesn't answer and the call rings off. Moments later, there's a double beep and Megan picks up the phone again.

'Text from Mum,' she says. 'She wants to know when I'm going to be home. What should I tell her?'

I consider whether to be diplomatic.

'You could tell her that refusing to tell her two children that they each have a sister is a pretty terrible thing to do.'

Megan offers up her phone and, for a moment, I think she might reply with just that.

'We kinda had that conversation on the phone last night,' she says.

'I heard the shouting…'

Megan's smile isn't genuine this time. It's a mix of embarrassment, annoyance and, perhaps, fear.

'If you're sixteen, then you're still legally a child,' I say.

'People can get married at sixteen.'

'Only with a parent's permission – and I'm assuming you're not about to head down the aisle…'

She dips her head. 'I'm not a child,' she says.

'I know you're not, but Mum is still legally responsible for you. As much as *I'd* love to tell her to do one, *you* can't.'

'So what do we do?'

'At the moment… I don't know. Tell Mum you'll be back later.'

Megan taps something into her phone and then places it on the table. She picks up the menu and then, without looking at it, asks me what I'm having.

'I'm on the all-dayer,' I say.

'The all-day breakfast?'

'When I was your age, my friends and I would try to get lifts out here from anyone with a car. We'd order a milkshake each and then try to make it last for as long as we could. I once had a strawberry milkshake last for almost three hours until we got kicked out. When I had a bit of money left over – and when my friend, Holly, wasn't around – I'd order the all-day breakfast.'

'Why wouldn't you order if Holly was around?'

'Because she was the slimmest person I knew and I wanted to be like her.'

'Not now?'

'Definitely not now.'

Megan glances back to the menu and then looks up. 'I guess it's two all-dayers.'

I leave her in the booth and cross to the counter, where I order two all-day breakfasts, plus a coffee and a Coke. I pay with the cash I found at Dad's house and know he would approve of the food, if not the company.

Back at the booth and Megan is busy thumbing her phone.

I place the can of Coke in front of her. 'Everything okay?' I ask.

'I had to Snap a pic of the walls,' she says, nodding towards the record sleeves.

'I have no idea what you're talking about.'

She laughs and then puts her phone down on the counter.

'If you're sixteen,' I say, 'does that mean you've just done your GCSEs?'

'A month or two ago.'

'When do you get the results?'

'Just over a week.'

'Are you confident?'

She lets out a *pfft*. 'I'd say I was quietly confident – but if I do say that, then it's not very quiet.'

I want to ask her about what's next: A-levels, GNVQs, or whatever else it is that kids do now. Does she want to go to university?
Is she a budding entrepreneur? Is she desperate to get into work?
It's almost like those early days of a relationship where you can't
get enough of the other person and want to know everything
about them. I hold back. It would be a lot for anyone, let alone
a sixteen-year-old.

Megan sips from her can and then places it back on the table.
'I told you I always wanted a sister, didn't I?' she says.

I remember her saying this – and I get the sense she wants me to
reciprocate and tell her I wanted a sister, too. I wish I could – and it's
not as if this would be the only lie I've told – but something stops me.

'You did,' I say.

'I thought it would be easier to find things out from an older
sister than from Mum.'

'Things like what?'

Megan tilts her head a little and that's all it takes. We explode
into giggles at the same time and I laugh so much that I need to
use the napkin on the table to blow my nose. Megan can't stop,
either, and the only thing that finally calms us is when the waitress
arrives with our food. She puts a plate in front of each of us and
then heads back to the counter. All the while, Megan and I struggle
to stop ourselves from sniggering.

One thing Megan and I certainly have in common is the way
we rip into food when we're hungry. We barely speak for the next
ten minutes or so as we each demolish our plates of beans, bacon,
sausages, hash browns, tomatoes, mushrooms, fried egg and fried
bread. It's been a long time, but the quality of the food at The
Cosmic has remained.

Megan still has a few mushrooms remaining as I mop up the
remainder of the bean juice with some fried bread. I finish my
coffee and then sit back and watch her polish off her food and then

slurp down the rest of the Coke. Watching her drink makes me think of the bottle that I abandoned. It's the first time I've thought of it in a day or so. Whatever urge I once had seems to have gone.

'That was amazing,' she says.

'I know.'

'We should do this regularly. Once a week or so. Maybe twice?'

She's happy and excited, and I have to look away from her, out towards the car park, in order to get the words out.

'I'm leaving Elwood,' I say.

She slumps a little and is silent at first before she lets out a quiet: 'Oh…'

I force myself to look at Megan, who's fixed on me.

'Why?' she asks.

'Because Elwood hasn't been my home in a long time. Being back has proven that it still isn't. I'm not sure it ever was. It's just where I grew up. The house is getting cleared later today and then I'm going to find an estate agent to sell it for me.'

Megan doesn't speak for a while. She shakes her can and, even though there's no sound and it's empty, she holds it to her mouth.

'Where are you going to go?' she asks.

'Maybe back to London? I don't know.'

'Do you have a job there?'

I catch the server's eye and do the universal sign of tilting an invisible mug towards my mouth, asking for more coffee.

'You're the first person to ask me that,' I say. 'People keep asking if I'm married, or have a boyfriend. They want to know if I have kids, but those would all involve other people. Nobody seems fussed about me.'

'I am.'

I gulp away something that could easily escalate into an embarrassing breakdown. 'I took redundancy,' I say. 'I worked for the planning department at a borough council.'

Megan stares but says nothing.

'It's not as boring as it sounds.'

I realise I'm not even convincing myself, let alone her.

'You're not going back to that, are you?'

'No. With the sale of the house and the redundancy money, I was thinking about maybe going back to college, or perhaps even looking at a university.'

Megan raises a sceptical eyebrow and looks at me as if I've just announced I'd like to grow an extra head.

'I can't wait to leave school and you want to go back.'

'I guess…'

We go quiet as the waitress comes across with a pot of coffee and refills my mug. She takes our plates and balances them expertly along with more dishes from the adjacent table. If it was me, everything would be on the floor before I'd turned – but she heads off towards the kitchen as if nothing is untoward.

'We just found each other,' Megan says. 'Now you're leaving.'

'I made that decision before I knew anything about you.'

She sits up straighter: 'So you could stay…?'

I can't meet her eye. 'Not here. Not Elwood. I'm done with this place.'

'But somewhere near…?'

'I don't know.'

It's an impasse and I find myself looking up to the television at our side. The local news has come on and there's a picture of Ethan. The sound is muted, but the subtitles are on and the newsreader is saying that he's out of his coma.

When I look back down, I realise Megan has been watching, too. 'Do you know him?' she asks.

'His mum was my best friend at school.'

She turns to look up at the screen once more. 'It's been every-where this week. Mum's had the news channel on all day, waiting for an update.'

'I found him.'

'Oh…' She watches the screen for a little longer and then adds: 'Did you see the car that did it?'

'Yes… but not really. It was in the distance. I saw it stop and drive off – but that was all. I couldn't identify the car and don't know who was driving.'

'Mum says it has to be someone local. She reckons nobody drives through Elwood unless they live there.'

'That's what everyone says.'

Megan reaches for her empty can once more and then glances towards the fridge full of soft drinks that's over near the counter. As subtle as a brick.

'We need to get you home,' I say.

'I want to stay with you.'

'She's still your mum. We don't want her to report you missing, or kidnapped.'

'She wouldn't do that.'

'I wouldn't want to try her.'

Megan squeezes the centre of her can and then uses her palm to mash the top down, so that it's nearly flat. She picks up her phone and glances to the screen, before putting it down again.

'Can I stay with you today? At yours?'

'The clearance people are coming.'

'I can help.'

'You're sixteen – you don't want to spend the day clearing junk out of a house. *I* don't want to spend a day clearing junk out of a house.'

'I do.'

I know she doesn't, not really. She wants to spend the day as sisters.

'I'll get you a taxi back to Mum's house,' I say. 'But we'll catch up soon. I promise.'

'How soon?'

'Really soon. There's something I need to check first.'

FORTY-TWO

The taxi takes me back to the house and I ask it to wait momentarily as I give Gav a key, so he can start the house clearance. After that, I say goodbye to Megan and tell the taxi driver to take her back to her address in Stoneridge. I give him the cash upfront – and then I set off walking in the opposite direction.

The dark blue Audi is parked outside Holly's house when I get there. The street is empty and the graffiti has finally been cleared from Stephen's house. Her car is unassuming, one of a handful parked on the road, and I try to remember the feeling I had when I saw it pull away close to the hospital. It was like the déjà vu of walking down a street and sensing that it's not the first time it's happened. I recognised the vehicle but wasn't completely sure from where.

The last few days have given me too much experience in looking at cars for little discernible reason. I suppose that's now something I have in common with my father. He was never any kind of mechanic – and yet he would begrudge a single penny he had to spend to get a car fixed. He'd rather stand on the roadside with a spanner and a hammer, cursing under his breath and banging various parts of the engine. That was preferable to paying the AA or RAC to come and tow him home.

When I reach Holly's car, I crouch and look at the bumper on the driver's side. At first, I can't see anything untoward. It's only when I start to stand and the angle of the light changes slightly that I spot the blemish in the paint close to the headlight. It's *almost* the same shade of dark blue, but not quite. Like comparing a faded patch on a wall where the sun shines every day with an adjacent spot that's always in shade. It's the same but not. Only visible to anyone standing close enough and looking at a certain angle.

I push myself up until I'm fully standing and, when I turn, Holly is at her front door, leaning on the frame and watching.

She walks down the path slowly, her gaze never leaving me. She continues until she's barely a step away.

'What are you doing?' she asks calmly.

I think about walking away, about doing nothing. I'm leaving Elwood anyway and it would be the easiest thing to do.

'It was right in front of me all the time,' I say quietly.

Holly leans in. 'My car?'

I glance down to the patch of discolouration, even though it looks no different to the rest of the paintwork from my current angle.

'Not the car,' I say. 'Everything else.'

'I don't know what you're on about.'

I angle across towards Stephen's house, trying to remember the scene. 'After that argument on the street with Jo and Stephen, you came over and then I went back to your house. We were in your kitchen and there was something dark on your face. I thought it was a scab and wouldn't have even mentioned it – but *you* said you'd been redecorating. You were thinking about it more than me. Then I went upstairs looking for your toilet – but none of the rooms are being painted.' I nod down to the car. 'I'm pretty sure the stuff on your face was dark paint.'

There's such a long gap before anything happens that it's as if someone's pressed pause on a TV show. We stand a short distance apart, staring at each other as the strangers we are.

Friendship can be the most random thing in a person's life. We live in these villages, towns and cities and the person we sit next to when we're five years old is somehow the person we remain closest to twenty years later. *Forty* years later. Those tiny, insignificant choices, such as which desk to use, change everything.

'What are you saying?' Holly asks. Her tone is husky and quiet.

'You kept wanting to know what I'd seen. Every time we spoke, you were either asking about that, or whether the police had spoken to me.'

'Because Ethan is Jo's son. Of course I'm concerned.' She sounds annoyed.

'Then you were the person who was trying to push that it was Neil. I'd never met him, but you were already telling me how he'd been driving while banned.'

'He has!'

I break the stare. The sun continues to singe from above and I can feel the sweat pooling at the bottom of my back.

'You didn't answer the question,' Holly says.

'Which one?'

'What are you trying to say?'

I turn back to her again and she stares with defiance. Or, perhaps, fear.

'Do you know who was driving the car that hit Ethan?' I ask.

'Of course not.'

'Ethan's paralysed from the waist down.'

Holly squints, taking me in, wondering if this is some sort of strange lie.

'He's out of the coma,' I add, 'but they had to send him to sleep again because he was panicking about not being able to move.'

'I didn't know that…' She tails off and then adds: 'I should call Jo.'

I don't say anything to that.

Holly has zoned out, but then she straightens and seems to click back into the moment. I suspect she's wondering why I already know but she doesn't. She and Jo are supposed to be best friends… or perhaps that's a lie, too.

'Was it you?' I ask.

'Was *what* me?'

'Were you driving?'

Holly's look of disgust is either a piece of incredible acting, or she is genuinely outraged by the suggestion.

'I'm not even going to answer that,' she says. 'You've got some nerve.'

'Was it Mark?'

The difference in reaction would be noticeable even to someone who wasn't looking for it. It's not the same indignation as before, it's surprise.

'Why would you say that?'

'I saw him driving your car near the hospital.'

'So what? You know he's Ethan's father, right?'

'Of course.'

She puts her hands on her hips, as if that settles it. 'You think a father would drive a car into his own son and then disappear? You don't know him at all. What kind of sicko are you?'

'That's a different question…'

There's a flicker of movement from the front window of Holly's house. I watch over her shoulder, but nobody appears. It could be just the breeze. She turns and follows my gaze, but then twists back without saying anything.

'I don't know Mark any more,' I say.

'No, you don't. He's a good bloke. He loves me and he's been brilliant for Rob. We've only been keeping things quiet to spare Jo. That was *his* call. That's the type of guy he is – thinking of his ex, even though she broke it off.'

'Jo told me that he hit her.'

'That's a lie.' The reply is spat back instantly. 'Mark's not like that and, even if something did happen, you've seen what Jo's like when she went knocking on Stephen's door. She was out of control.'

It's always a strange argument that something didn't happen…
oh, but if it did then there was a reason anyway, so it was fine.

'Jo said Ethan doesn't want to see his dad because he's been let
down so many times.'

'That's only one side of it. You don't know how much Jo
obstructs and makes it difficult.' She gulps and glances back to
the house once more. 'You don't know…'

We stand at an impasse. Holly knows something about what
happened, but she's hardly going to tell me.

'You should go,' she says earnestly. 'Go for good this time. I
don't know why you came back.'

'My dad died.'

'*Really?* That's the reason? You *left* because of him. If it was
just about the house, you could have got anyone to sort it out
and sell it.'

She's right. I've thought it myself in the quieter moments. I
suppose I came back because I wanted to. Elwood's a part of me
and I'm a part of it.

'I should tell the police,' I say.

'Tell them what? I had paint on my face?' She laughs at me. 'Do
you think that, if this was something to do with Mark or me, it
wouldn't have been sorted by now? A new bumper. Matching paint.
Off the books. No sign it ever happened. If it *was* something to
do with me, do you think I'd be taking chances if I didn't already
know everything was cleaned up? If there weren't perfect alibis? Do
you think I'd have parked my car right here, where anyone can see,
if I had any reason to think it would be traced back to a crime?'

It's a lot to take in. She's spoken so quickly, and with such
clarity, that it's almost impressive. It's nearly a confession – why
else use the word 'alibis'? – but not quite. There's nothing to tell
the police, even if it wasn't only my word against hers.

She's not finished anyway.

'You know you brought it all on yourself, don't you?'

'Brought what on?'

'I never got beaten up by my dad. Neither did Jo. Just you. My dad didn't slam my head into a wall. Jo's dad didn't kick her down the stairs. Our mums didn't walk out on us. Just yours. Just you.' Her top lip curls into an amused snarl. 'You know I'm right,' she adds.

I can't speak. It feels like Holly has punched me in the stomach and taken my breath. She might as well have done. I blink away tears that feel close but don't come. It's taken all these years, but someone has finally said out loud the thing that's been my first thought almost every morning of my adult life: *Is it me?*

Holly's on a roll now. 'Just go, Abi. Go. There's nothing for you here. Do everyone a favour. You left Elwood once, so do it again – and, this time, don't come back.'

FORTY-THREE

I've been walking for anything between five minutes and an hour when I realise I don't know where I am. For all my thoughts of things never changing and homing instincts and the like, I find myself staring at a row of new-looking red-brick houses – which is when I realise I'm lost.

After Holly was done, I turned and walked away – then kept walking. I remember almost none of it. There were houses and countryside, but it's a blur. I have to use my phone to figure out that I've walked from one side of Elwood to the other. I must have passed the park at some point but have no memory of it.

My arms are tingling and, when I look at them closer, they've turned a gentle pink in the sun. I have nothing with which to cover them, so cross the road and stand in the shade of a tree as I figure out a route back to the house.

As I'm doing that, a text pings through from Jo.

Neil's been released. Affray charge. Idiot.

I hold onto the phone, wondering if there will be any more, perhaps with news of Ethan. When nothing comes, I put it in my bag and then set off back towards the house. I try to stick to the shade as much as I can, although part of that is an attempt to avoid people as well.

When I get back to the house, the clearance is in full effect. The large white van with 'Trash, Bang, Wallop' across the side is parked at the front, with the back doors open. A teenager is carrying out one end of the sofa, while Gav has the back. They lug it to the rear of the truck and then put it on the ground when Gav notices me. He waves me across and wipes his brow with his arm.

'Hot out here,' he says.

'It *is* August.'

'Good point.'

He reaches onto the van's lowered tailgate and grabs a bottle of water, from which he downs half, before passing it across to his helper.

'He's my lad,' he says, flexing his arm to make his muscles bulge. 'Needs to get a bit of meat on his bones.'

Gav's son offers a sheepish smile and I suspect he's been told this roughly two dozen times today already.

Gav nods across to Megan, who is watching us from the front door. I do a double take, unsure why she's here – especially as I packed her into a taxi earlier. 'Your, er, daughter was asking about a few things,' Gav says. 'I said it was up to you.'

Megan's wearing that smile again. 'I hung around,' she calls across.

I turn back to Gav. 'She's my sister,' I say.

He looks me up and down. 'Sorry, I thought…'

'Give me a minute.'

I cross to Megan, who's still in the doorway.

'Why didn't you go home?' I ask. I want to be annoyed but somehow can't.

'I didn't want to.'

'You'll have to at some point.'

'I know.'

'What did Mum say?'

'Not happy – but she'll live. She says you're a bad influence, but I told her I'll be back tonight.'

'How am *I* a bad influence?'

Megan shrugs and breaks into a smile. 'Leaving me alone here with strange men, I guess.'

'I didn't leave you! I put you in a taxi. And what happened to the cash I gave the driver?'

Megan digs into a pocket and holds up some notes. 'He kept some of it,' she says.

I take the money and drop it into my bag. 'What did you want from the house?'

'The photo albums.'

'Fine.'

'How about the TV?'

'I don't know how you're going to get that on a bus.'

'I was thinking about another taxi…?'

'You paying?'

She doesn't say anything, but she bites her lip in a clear indication that this wasn't in her plans.

I reach into my bag and then hand her back the cash. There's so much of me in her that it's almost overwhelming.

'Thanks,' she says, still cradling that smirk. 'There was one other thing, too.'

'What?'

'There's a bunch of vinyl in one of the boxes upstairs.'

'Dad's old records,' I say.

'Can I have them?'

I sigh and turn between her and the van. 'I'll check with Gav because I already told him he could take what he wanted. I'll ask about your TV too.'

'You're my favourite sister.'

I snort at that. The cheeky so-and-so.

When I cross back to Gav, he's sharing a sandwich with his son. He nods across to Megan. 'She's got some good arms on her, that one. Been lumping all sorts into the van.'

'She asked if she could have the TV and some records. I know I told you that you could keep whatever, but—'

'Fine by me. If you'd said on the phone how much stuff there was, I'd have come yesterday.' He stops for a mouthful of water and then adds: 'There's some personal stuff in the front bedroom up there. Figured you should have a look before we cart it away.'

Gav nods up to Dad's bedroom above us and I almost tell him he can take whatever it is. I'm not sure what stops me, but I thank him for the tip and then head inside, away from the sun, and go upstairs.

There's a scrabbling from the spare room, where Megan is boxing up the items she wants. I leave her to it and, for the first time since arriving back in Elwood, nudge through the door to my father's bedroom.

Gav must've opened the windows because, instead of the musty Old Spice I'd have expected, there's a calm breeze bristling through. The doors are open to the built-in wardrobe at the back of the room, and it's been cleared of the clothes and shoes that would've been inside. Much of the room is empty, although the bed remains. It's been stripped, though I don't know if this was done by Gav. The mattress has gone and there's a box sitting on the bare slats. I sit on the floor and pull it down so that it's next to me.

The card on top is my father's birth certificate and, directly underneath that, is his marriage certificate. The sight of Mum's maiden name is striking and I almost call through to Megan, wondering if she'll get a kick from it. I stop myself because I can't predict how she'll react. We share a mother, but we don't. Her life is chopped into two – before and after the day she walked away from this house. I have no idea what last name she was using before she married a second time and had Megan.

Underneath the certificates are a stack of loose photographs. It's more time travel. There are pictures of Dad that I've never seen before. Perhaps even proof that his tall tales of sporting dominance as a young man weren't that tall at all. There are black and white pictures of him playing football, in which he looks fit and fast. His hair is slicked back and he's such a good-looking young man that it's only the shape of his face that tells me it's definitely my father.

There's a photo of him in hospital, with his leg in a cast, then another of him in a wheelchair next to a row of trees. Then there's a small, dog-eared picture of his wedding day. It's sunny and he's in a horrendous, flared brown suit. Mum's in white, but her dress looks scratchy and uncomfortable. I don't recognise either of the two witnesses they're standing awkwardly alongside outside the register office.

I'm a squat little blob in the early photos of me. A bloated head on paunchy legs. I suppose it's good fortune that I wasn't like that for too long. In the next photo, I'm in a caravan somewhere, climbing on the table. I'm probably five or six and have no memory of this apparent holiday. There's food around my mouth and a series of mucky fingerprints on the table. I'm also wearing a ballerina dress I don't ever remember having. The thing that's most apparent is how blissful I am. I'm beaming with joy at whoever's taking the photograph.

I was happy once.

The final photo leaves me dizzy with déjà vu and melancholy. I'm a little girl in front of the bouncy castle at Elwood Summer Fete. Mum must have taken the picture because Dad's at my side, resting his elbow on the top of my head as if he's using me to hold himself up.

It's my dream, or part of it, and it definitely happened.

I consider returning it to the pile, but then drop it into my bag instead.

Underneath the photos is an envelope crammed with cash. I don't count it fully, but I do flip through the notes. There's a mixture of paper and plastic and, if I can trade in the old ones at the bank, there's around five hundred pounds. It'll help pay for a hotel somewhere, so that I don't have to sleep here any longer.

I take that, too, and then quickly flick through the rest of the stack. There are football programmes, some old receipts, and a few industry certificates Dad earned through his work. I return all of those to the box and use the bed frame to push myself up. I'm about to go and find Megan when there's a bang from outside. I go to the window and watch as Gav and his son lug one of the armchairs into the back of the van. His lad seems strong enough to me.

It's as I turn away that I notice a black, plasticky tube in the very corner of the window. At first I'm not sure what it is but as I pick it up, I realise it's a camera. A red light blinks at me and I suddenly remember returning here after the funeral. I was drunk and trying to get inside when I saw something flare from above. I'd put it down to my intoxication – but it must have been this flashing red light from Dad's window.

I follow the wire at the back of the camera down towards a small, black metal box that's slotted into a metal bracket which is screwed to the wall. There is a row of seven SD cards inserted into the box.

One card for each day of the week…

Helena told me that Dad was worried about security and Chris said there'd been a break-in on the street. I didn't know that Dad had any idea about cameras and security systems – but then I didn't know him.

I take the metal box through to my room, which is the only one I told Gav to avoid for now. My suitcase is still open on the floor, with my clothes forming a perfect floordrobe. For the first time since getting here, I open the lid to my laptop. I try the second SD card from the box but, as soon as I start playing the MP4 file, I can see that the date is from Sunday. I watch the footage for a little while anyway. The camera was angled towards the corner, giving a wide view of the road at both the front and the side of the house. I skip through it but almost nothing seems to happen.

The odd person walks by, or a car darts past – but that's about it. Hours and hours of nothing.

With Saturday apparently counting as day one, I take the fourth card from the box and slot it into my laptop. Linda at the petrol station told me that their CCTV system recorded over the old footage – and I feel a jolt as I spot last Tuesday's date in the top corner of this material. After midnight tonight, it would have likely started to override what I have in front of me.

The footage starts at midnight and I scroll forward quickly, watching the night vision grey turn into the brightness of daylight. It jolts ahead in bulky increments, stopping at quarter past four in the afternoon.

My heart is racing as I click backwards a minute at a time. I found Ethan at ten past four – and I push back five times. Then two more. Then I click go and watch.

It's so simple. So ridiculous that, every time I went to sleep in this house, the answer was sitting a few metres from me. Beverly Close is a short road that runs from where I found Ethan to a junction, where it intersects with this house on the corner.

I watch the video twice as Holly's car slows for the corner and then jolts away. It happens seconds after Ethan was hit.

I don't need to watch it a third time, nor zoom in, because the driver who hit Ethan looks both ways and, in doing so, offers a perfect profile shot for my father's camera.

I know who it is.

FORTY-FOUR

There's no need to knock on Holly's front door. I simply lean against her car and wait. It only takes two or three minutes until she emerges from the house. She's more curious than angry, looking both ways towards her neighbours, before slowly moving along the path towards me.

She doesn't say anything, but I suspect she sees something different in me this time.

I wait until she's close enough, and then: 'I know who was driving.'

Her eyes narrow. 'What do you mean?'

'I know.'

It might have been twenty years since we were friends, but there's still that part of us that knows one another as well as anyone.

Holly nods towards the house and takes a deep breath. 'Are you coming in?' She moves onto her path and looks back to where I haven't moved. 'Will you give me a chance to explain?'

'Should I?'

'We were friends once, weren't we?'

Holly keeps moving and, when she gets to her house, she holds the door open and waits. I think about walking away, but if I do that, there'd have been no point in coming here in the first place. I realise that the reason I came was precisely to hear the reasoning.

I head up the path and into the house, waiting in the hall as Holly closes the door behind me. She leads the way past the boxes into the kitchen and we sit as if everything is perfectly normal.

A minute passes, maybe more. Holly glances up to the clock and then down at me.

'What are you going to do?' she asks.

'I don't know.'

'How do you know?'

'My dad had a camera pointing at the street. I think he was worried about being burgled.'

She takes a breath and then glances towards the window. She must know it's over. 'Who's seen it?'

'Just me.'

Holly slides down into her chair and lets her head flop backwards, so that she's staring at the ceiling. She stays there for a short while and then pushes herself up, angling forward with her elbows on her knees.

'He's got his whole life ahead of him…'

She could be talking about Ethan, but she isn't. There's a quiver to her voice and she sounds heartbroken. No, not just *sounds* heartbroken. She is.

I can see why. When he turned side-on in the video, just moments after hitting Ethan with the car, as his knuckles seared white through gripping the steering wheel, there was complete terror in Rob's face.

Holly's son is supposed to be a young adult on his way to university, but, in that moment, he was a terrified child.

'Rob's always been a nervous driver,' Holly says. 'If anything, it might have been a bit worse after he passed his test. He always had someone in the car with him when he was learning, but then he had to make decisions by himself. He'd get home after driving somewhere and he'd be shaking. We were supposed to be sorting him out with his own car this summer, but he didn't want it. I was trying to encourage him to use mine to get him used to driving. I went out with him a few times, but I can't be with him all the time.' She sighs and then adds: 'He's not one of those kids who gets a ridiculous car with a bass you can feel thumping through you. He doesn't drive fast. He's a quiet kid and he's smart.'

'But he didn't stop…'

The only sound comes from some kids in a back garden nearby. They're running around, screaming and having fun.

Holly tugs at her hair and then, from nowhere, aims a kick at the nearest box. It tumbles onto its side, spilling a small mound of vials onto the floor. She doesn't move to pick it up.

'Ethan was dead,' she says, not looking at me. 'That's what Rob thought. If he stopped and waited for the police, or the ambulance, or whatever, then it wouldn't make any difference. If you're dead, you're dead. None of that would have brought Ethan back. Why would Rob give up his own life for someone he thought was already gone?'

'He wasn't dead, though.'

'No…'

Holly stands and crosses to the fridge. She removes a can of supermarket-brand lemonade, crunches the tab, and then drinks. When she's had a large mouthful, she offers me the can, though I shake my head. She doesn't sit, instead pacing back and forth until she eventually stops next to the back door. It seems like a lifetime ago that she did this when trying to stop Mark from blustering inside and giving the game away that they were seeing one another.

'Rob can't go back in time,' she says. 'None of us can. This can't be undone. I know that one life might have been wrecked – but if you tell people, it'll wreck two.'

'You can't put that on me.'

'But it *is* on you. You have the power here.'

'Ethan can't feel his legs. He might never walk.'

Holly stops and stares at the ceiling for a moment. 'They always say that,' she says. 'Then there's a story a couple of years later that some kid's walking again. It's on Comic Relief every year. You must've seen it.'

I stare at her, wondering if this is the real person she is.

'What have you done with the video?' Holly asks.

'Nothing yet.'

'Are you going to tell the police?'

'I should.'

'You don't have to, though.'

She looks to me, *implores* me.

'Can I talk to Rob?' I say.

Holly pauses for a moment and there's a second or two where I think she might say yes.

'He's gone,' she says instead. 'He couldn't stand being here and was talking about going to the police. I told him to get out of Elwood, so he's gone to stay with his cousin for a while.'

'You stopped him telling anyone?'

'I *saved* him from himself.'

'He was going to do the right thing.'

'The right thing for who? Not him.'

'When's he coming back?'

Holly looks up to the clock once more and then, as if on cue, there's a bump and bang from the back door. It swings open with a creak and then Mark ambles in. He's sweaty and red-faced, as if he's been out running or exercising.

He closes the door behind him and then turns to take in Holly and myself with a confused expression. 'I thought—'

'She knows.'

It's only when she speaks that I realise Holly has shifted so that she's standing in the doorway to the hall. I turn between her blocking one door and Mark the other. It's only two words, but there's such knowing there that I realise she's been stalling. Not only that – but Mark already knows who left his son for dead.

Mark exchanges a glance with Holly and a shiver surges through me. 'Who else knows?' he says.

I'm about to answer when Holly talks over me: 'Just her.'

I look up as his face clouds and his eyes darken. 'What do you want me to do?'

FORTY-FIVE

I turn from Mark to Holly but realise that she's now frozen. She's staring at the wall, then the floor. Anywhere but me.

Staring into the abyss.

There's a sharp scurrying sound and then Mark's suddenly over me. In a flash, he's pulling me up by the straps of my top. I try to flail or shout, but it's already too late. He has the crook of his elbow under my chin and is pressing hard enough on my throat that I can hear myself wheezing for breath.

I have no idea what happens next. It feels like there's a flash of movement and then, in a blink, I'm on the floor. My head throbs as pink stars swim across the kitchen floor in front of me. I'm staring at a scuffed pair of tennis shoes on the bottom of some tanned, hairy legs. Did he punch me, or…? What?

I push myself up, using the legs of the kitchen table for support. There's a clear path to the back door but as soon as I try to move, my legs become jelly. It's no use anyway, because Mark steps across so that he's in front of the door once more. I'm left on the ground, on my knees.

'Hol,' he says sternly. 'What do you want to do?'

Holly's still in the kitchen doorway, or a fuzzy version of her is. I can't focus properly. She doesn't reply and then there's another sharp movement from the side. The next thing I know, Mark's fingers are digging hard into my scalp as he grabs me by the hair. I scream – or think I do. I'm not sure, but I definitely hear, or possibly see, Holly say a clear '*Don't.*'

The pain instantly disappears from my head.

'What's the alternative?' Mark says, talking across me. 'Are you going to let Rob go to prison?'

I crawl a couple of steps away from Mark but am still between the two blocked doors, with nowhere to go.

'He's your son,' I say, twisting back to Mark. It comes out as something of a croak '*Ethan's* your son. Not Rob.'

I use the names on purpose, making it personal, but when Mark looks down towards me, it's achieved the opposite. His features are screwed into a mix of despair and disgust. 'What good is a son that won't see his father?

'There has to be a reason for that.'

A brief shake of the head. '*This* is my family now.' Mark flicks his head towards Holly, who's behind me. 'You have to choose between her and Rob.'

There's no answer and I spin around on the floor, looking up towards Holly who is still standing in the doorway. She's blank, staring towards the fridge instead of anything that's happening in front of her.

'Hol,' Mark says firmly. 'Tell me what you want.'

'Let me go, Holly,' I say.

'I'll do whatever you want me to do,' Mark continues. 'I'll do anything for you. *Anything*.'

I start to shiver and it feels as if the fridge is open and I'm directly in front of it.

'No one will miss her,' he says. 'You said it yourself last night. She has no family.'

Jo's words flash back to me – *there was this look in his eye that I'd never seen before* – and, as I look up to him, I wonder if I'm seeing the same. There's steel there. Danger.

'Hol!' He barks at her and I twist between them.

Holly glances down to me and then flickers away again. Then, very slowly and deliberately, she turns her back to face into the hall.

FORTY-SIX

'You don't have to do this,' I say.

Mark stands over me, shoulders hunched. 'I *didn't* – but you couldn't keep your nose out. Everything would've died down. Things would have gone back to normal, but you wouldn't have that.'

He's calm and measured, which is so much worse than a manic scream or shout. He and Holly have obviously been talking about me and I wonder how much Mark has already prepared for this. Then I think of what Holly told me. No one else had their head slammed into a wall by their fathers; no one else was kicked down the stairs.

Is it me?

Do I attract this?

Mark grabs a handful of hair and pulls me up. I can feel his meaty fingers on top of my head. The pain sears down through my neck and shoulders. I scream Holly's name, but she's still facing the hall, with her back to the kitchen.

'Shush…' Mark coos.

I feel myself being swung to the side and then a crunching *thunk* blasts through me before I hear the bump.

I've moved again and am now slumped against the wall by the fridge, out of Mark's grasp. Time must have passed, but I don't know how long. Probably seconds.

Mark's speaking, but it's like I'm underwater. The words are there but not quite clear.

'Hol!'

He's trying to get her attention and, though she's now facing the kitchen once more, she doesn't seem to be paying him any attention. Mark claps his hands loudly and she jolts.

'Where's that big roll of plastic wrap?' he asks. 'The stuff we used for painting.'

'Basement,' she says.

'Go and get it.'

I watch her look to me, pause for a second, and then make her decision. She turns and disappears into the hall. A moment later and there's the sound of a door opening. I'm sitting with my legs outstretched and my head resting against the side of the fridge. There's a smear of red crested across the white of the surface.

When I was young and Dad had drunk too much, I would cower, cover my head, and cry. I'd plead with him to stop, but he never did. Mum would conveniently be in the other room, or upstairs. Then she left anyway. I'd end up letting him punch and kick because what else was there to do? It's two decades on and I'm there again. Nothing's changed…

…Except it has. I'm not a teenager any longer and Dad is in a box, in the ground.

With Holly gone, Mark turns back to me and takes a step forward. It's when his other foot is off the floor that I lash forward with my foot, crunching it into his standing leg a little bit under the knee. It doesn't matter how strong a person might be, they still need legs to stand on – and Mark's no different. He crumples sideways like a broken ironing board, his head cannoning into the counter as he folds to the floor.

I push myself up, but my legs are unsteady, too, and my head's still spinning. I dart to the back door and slam down the handle, ready to throw myself through.

It doesn't move.

I shove it again, only to realise it's locked. Mark must have done it during one of the moments in which I found myself on the floor. When I turn, he's using the counter to groggily pull himself up. He's red in the face, with a gush of blood pooling from a slice across the top of his eye. There's fury in his face as he growls like a cornered dog. I slide sideways, shoving the boxes to the floor and putting the kitchen table between us.

'Hol!'

Mark calls for her and, though there's no sign or sound of Holly, there's little hope I'll be able to hold him off for long. I'm hoping that, if I can get him to head around one side of the table, I'll be able to dash towards the hall and the front door beyond. He sees straight through the plan, not bothering to chase me and instead standing in the hall door. With the back door locked, there's no other way out.

'Hol!'

I grab a mug from the table and hurl it in Mark's direction. I'm not sure if I expected it to hit him, but he's too quick anyway, ducking his head out of the way as the cup smashes into the wall. A sludge of browny-black coffee has sprayed across the floor, with shards of ceramic crashing to the ground. He's watching me properly now as I pick up a handful of Holly's oil vials and throw them too. There's no need to avoid these because they're so flimsy that they bounce off him.

'Holly!'

There's a bump from the hall and Mark moves from the door as she appears with a large roll of thick, clear plastic wrap. She frowns towards the shattered pieces of mug and then drops the plastic on the ground.

I really am cornered now.

It might be that the woolliness has cleared, but Holly now seems more decided than she was before. She focuses on me and I can see the sad determination.

'He's my son, Abi. What do you want me to do? I told you to go, but you had to come back. I didn't want this.'

I finally spot the knives, but they're on a rack on the other side of the kitchen. I was close to them when next to the fridge, but Mark is in the way now. He takes a step towards me. There's still the table between us but, with Holly on one end and him at the other, I'm trapped.

'You don't have to do this,' I say.

Holly kicks the roll of plastic wrap and it unspools across the floor.

'I'm sorry,' she replies. 'I love my son.'

She gives a small, barely perceptible nod towards Mark – and then he steps across the kitchen towards me.

FORTY-SEVEN

The knock on the door echoes through the house like a gunshot. Mark freezes and then turns slowly to look at Holly, who has turned towards the hall. It's only a moment – but that's all I need.

'HELP!'

Mark lunges across the table towards me, trying to get his hand across my mouth. I wriggle and battle against him, hurling an elbow in his direction and connecting with his shoulder. He's so much stronger, but I manage to scream another three or four cries before he clamps his palm across my face.

That's all it takes. After the knock on the door, there is a series of loud thumps, and then a mighty bang. An enormous bloke in a police uniform bursts into the kitchen, almost barrelling through Holly in the process. A step behind him is Sergeant Davidson.

Mark releases my mouth but keeps his arm around my neck. My first impressions of Davidson are long gone because I've never been more grateful to see a person.

The uniformed officer waits next to a resigned-looking Holly, while Davidson is on the other side of the table from Mark and me. He is so tall that his head is almost touching the light fitting above.

'Let's not make it any worse than it is,' Davidson says, sounding so calm that, even with Mark's arm across my neck, I start to relax.

'I just…' Mark's grip loosens a tiny amount. 'I want to protect my family.'

'That's what we all want,' Davidson replies.

Mark's grip slips even further. He still has the crook of his elbow under my throat but there's no pressure. 'I only wanted my boy to enjoy seeing me, but...'

He tails off, but Davidson has used the moment to move forward a step. He grips the table and slides it off to the side with a loud screech. Some of the junk drops onto the floor with a tinkling splat. There's now nothing between him and us.

'We can talk about that,' Davidson says.

He reaches ahead, but Mark's grip tightens and I gasp as he presses harder against my windpipe. Davidson spots it and edges backwards. The kitchen feels very cramped with five people, not to mention the boxes, the table, the roll of plastic wrap, and everything else that has spilled onto the floor.

'Mark...'

It's Holly who speaks. She sounds defeated.

I can't see Mark, but I can see her and her gaze is fixed on him. There is puffiness around her eyes and it looks like she's going to cry.

Mark's grip loosens again.

'It's over,' she says.

Mark's arm drops to his side and, from nowhere, I'm free. I step away from him, though there's still a grey smog around the corners of my vision. I continue moving, treading around Davidson and then stepping over the plastic wrap that has unspooled. Nobody stops me, nobody speaks, so I keep moving into the hall. I slip around the side of the boxes, spotting the open door to the basement in between them, and continuing on to the front door.

It feels like I'm floating, on some sort of magic carpet where I'm moving even though it doesn't seem as if my legs are working.

Outside, and I spot Megan before anyone. She's at the end of the path, arms behind her back. I have to move around three uniformed officers, all of whom I'd somehow missed until I almost walk into them. One of them motions towards me, but I shake my head and keep going until Megan's in front of me.

'You're bleeding,' she says.

I touch a hand to my forehead and come away with reddened fingers. There's a stab of pain that I hadn't felt until now.

'Both sides,' she adds.

'Are you all right?' I ask.

'You're the one who's bleeding. How are you?'

'I think I'm okay.'

She angles closer, eyeing whatever marks are on my face. 'Did I do it right?' she asks. 'You said to give it fifteen minutes and then call the police.'

I continue on towards her, pressing an arm around her shoulders and pulling her in until her head is wedged into my shoulder. It's partly to hold me up but more so because I need to feel something; to feel someone.

'You did great,' I say.

FORTY-EIGHT

Jo stares down at the quilt of wilting flowers and then turns and heads to the bench. She grips my hand and squeezes, before letting it go.

'I don't know if I'm supposed to clear it all up,' she says. 'I'm not even sure why they left things. People must've thought he was, well… y'know – and then, when one person left stuff, more followed.'

'I think the council will sort everything.'

'It's all for Ethan, though. Maybe I should take it back to the house?'

'Maybe take the football stuff and leave the flowers…?'

Jo doesn't reply. She leans into the backrest and lets her head rock back as she peers up to the blue sky. I can't remember a stretch of good weather that's lasted this long before.

'I can't believe you have a sister,' Jo says.

'It's not what I expected, either.'

'What happens now?'

'How do you mean?'

'With your mum and your sister.'

A woman is striding along the pavement on the other side of the road. She slows and almost stops as she looks sideways towards Jo and me. When she realises we're watching her, she turns back the way she's heading and keeps moving. I've had a fair few of those glances over the past couple of days and I'd bet Jo's had it far worse.

'I don't think I want to see my mum again,' I say.

'What about your sister?'

'Megan,' I say, liking the way her name sounds in my voice. It feels like she's mine. 'I think we're going to be great friends.'

'Does she think that too?'

'I think so.' I pause, picturing her youthful face; knowing she's a better version of me. 'I hope so.'

There's another game of football going on across the park, with all the sound of joy and competition that goes with it.

'I already knew about Mark and Holly,' Jo says. 'I didn't care. I was waiting for Holly to say something, but she never did. We were supposed to be best friends.'

'How did you know?'

'I'm not sure. It was more of a feeling. She said his name once and it was all there. Sometimes it only takes one word.'

'Sometimes not even that.'

Jo doesn't reply to that.

We sit and we listen to Elwood doing what it does. It's so quiet compared to a city and yet that's a soundtrack on its own. I hate it – but, wherever I go next, this will always be home.

'You've not told me what Mark did to you in front of her…?'

It's a question that's not a question. Jo saw the darkness in her ex-husband long before I got to.

'Not much,' I say – although the scrapes above my eyes and around the back of my head tell a different story. I don't think I ever accepted how dangerous things were in Holly's kitchen. I was scared – but I've been scared before. I've been at the feet of worse men in the past – and I'm still here.

'It sounds like the police got there just in time…?'

'That's true.'

'Megan…?'

Just the sound of her name makes my heart quicken a little. Being alone is a state of mind that's impossible to explain to people who are in relationships or who have had brothers or sisters their whole lives. It's something that runs deep into a person's soul, far beyond any sort of conscious thought. I've felt like that forever and now, suddenly, that darkness has gone.

'Megan,' I confirm. 'When I set off to Holly's, I told her to give it fifteen minutes and then call Sergeant Davidson directly to tell him what was on the SD card.'

'Why didn't you call him yourself?'

'I think I wanted to hear what she had to say. I wanted to give Rob a chance to hand himself in. I don't think it would have been covered up if he'd been by himself. You didn't see his face in the video. He was terrified. He was going to hand himself in until Holly stopped him. She made him leave town.'

It's only saying it out loud that I realise how it sounds.

'Sorry,' I add. 'I should've thought of Ethan and gone to the police.'

Jo rests a hand on my knee for a moment and then removes it. 'I think you did the right thing,' she says. 'If it was Owen, I'd have wanted the chance for him to go to the police himself.'

I push back into the bench and stare up towards the blue until stars start to swarm. There's a part of me that could live in this town and never want to leave. I love it and I hate it.

'What do you think will happen to him?' Jo says.

'Who?'

'Rob. He's… I don't know. I was going to say he's a good kid, but…'

She shifts her weight and, though I keep looking at the sky, I can tell she's looking towards the flowers at our side.

'Did you see the news this morning?' I ask.

'No. I was at the hospital.'

'He's already been charged with driving without due care, plus failing to stop at the scene. I don't know after that. People are pretty angry.'

'What about Mark?'

'Kidnapping charges, which Davidson said might change into something more relating to assault. He said they go with the most serious thing they can realistically charge at the beginning because it's easier to revise down than revise up.'

'*Kidnapping…*' Jo repeats the word and I know what she means. The very sound of it creates images of children being bundled into a van by a stranger. It literally has 'kid' at the beginning. Mark did stop me leaving Holly's kitchen, but I don't know if that means anything. I find myself running a finger across the scratch that's embedded along my hairline. It might well turn into another scar for the collection.

'What do you think should happen to him?' I ask.

'I don't know…' There's a pause and then, 'He's Ethan and Owen's dad, but they'll lock him up, I guess. They probably should.'

'What about Rob?'

Jo sighs and then reaches across and takes my hand. I look down from the sky and close my eyes as the stars continue to swarm on the back of my eyelids.

'I don't want to say.'

She lets me go and we sit for a while, listening to the sounds of summer. There's still a game of football going on, but there's also a low hum in the air from someone using a lawnmower a street or three over. What is there to say? Rob is eighteen years old and he made a terrible mistake. One moment of inattention and that's it. None of us are perfect and who's to say that flight instinct wouldn't have beaten out fight in the moment.

'Owen's on his driving test,' Jo says.

'Now?'

'Right. They said he could postpone, but he wanted to go for it. What with Ethan and everything, he seemed determined to get it done.'

She stops, waits, and then adds: 'We've converted the living room, so Ethan can sleep in there. We're going to put his posters on the wall and bring down the PlayStation. He'll be happy about being able to play on the big telly, rather than using the little one in his room.'

'Is there any chance…?' I don't know how to finish the sentence.

'Nobody knows,' Jo says after a pause. 'He still doesn't have any feeling in his legs. He might be in a wheelchair for life.'

She gulps and then takes a huge breath.

'This has been a nice detour,' she adds. 'But I've got to get to the hospital. There's a new specialist coming in this afternoon to see Ethan and then he might be able to go home by the end of the week.'

The fact she's by herself probably says more than it needs to about whatever's going on with Neil. I don't ask.

She stands and then waits as I do the same. We hug and her skin's clammy and warm. Mine is probably the same. We move apart, looking to each other as we are now. No longer those teenagers who thought we ran this town.

'Are you still leaving?' she asks.

'Yes.'

'For good?'

I nod and Jo reciprocates. She gets it. Sometimes it's not just people that need to be cleansed from a person's life; it's places.

'It's been nice seeing you this week,' Jo says. 'I wish it was different. All of it. That we could've seen each other without this.'

'I know.'

'You can't choose your family, but you *can* choose your friends, right?'

I nod in agreement, but she's only telling half the story. Life isn't only defined by a collection of family and friends. Sometimes, just sometimes, it's the wretched patch of land on which you take your first breath.

AUTHOR'S NOTE

In July 2017, I was riding my bike on a straight road under beautiful blue skies. I'd cycled for 101 miles and was so close to home that I could actually see the building. And then, for seemingly no reason, a taxi coming the other way drove straight into me. He was turning and, for whatever reason, didn't wait; instead smashing into my bike.

There's lots of things I could write about the driver and what happened, but the one thing for which I will give him some credit is that he didn't drive off. When I fell, I separated my shoulder and damaged my right knee. It was a long road back to anything approaching normality after that. I was supposed to be training for a marathon at the time.

The only positive to come from what happened is that, at some point in the days afterwards, when I was still in a sling, I wrote the words 'What if he drove off?' on my great big pad of ideas. It's because of that note that *The Child Across the Street* exists – so I suppose I should thank that driver for one thing.

If you think that Stoneridge or The Cosmic Café sound familiar, then it might be because you've read one of my other books – *Last Night*. Both are in that. If you recognise Diane Young, then she's in *The Wife's Secret*. I like leaving these little Easter eggs throughout my work. Those are the obvious two in this, but if you spot anything else like that, email me. If you're the first, I'll send you something.

Thanks for reading. More from me soon.
- Kerry Wilkinson

The Child Across the Street publishing team

Editorial
Claire Bord
Ellen Gleeson

Line edits and copyeditor
Jade Craddock

Proofreader
Liz Hatherell

Production
Alexandra Holmes
Caolinn Douglas
Ramesh Kumar

Design
Lisa Horton

Marketing
Alex Crow
Hannah Deuce

Publicity
Kim Nash

Distribution
Chris Lucraft
Marina Valles

Audio
Leodora Darlington
Arran Dutton & Dave Perry –
    Audio Factory
Alison Campbell

Rights and contracts
Peta Nightingale
Martina Arzu

Lightning Source UK Ltd.
Milton Keynes UK
UKHW010628040222
398207UK00002B/173

9 781838 887490